DENIZENS
OF EARTHDAWN VOLUME ONE

FASA CORPORATION

CONTENTS

DENIZENS OF EARTHDAWN
Volume I

Writing
Louis J. Prosperi, Tom Dowd, Marc Gasgione, Shane Lacy Hensley, Sean R. Rhoades, Carl Sargent, John J. Terra

Additional Writing
Robert C. Charrette, Diane Piron-Gelman

Development
Louis J. Prosperi

Editorial Staff
Editorial Director
Donna Ippolito
Managing Editor
Sharon Turner Mulvihill
Associate Editors
Diane Piron-Gelman, Robert "Snorky" Cruz

Production Staff
Art Director/Project Manager
HRH Jim Nelson
Project Midwife
Steve Bryant
Cover Art
Janet Aulisio Dannheiser
Cover Design/Color Section Design
Mark Ernst, Jim Nelson
Black & White Illustrations
Tom Baxa, Joel Biske, Steve Bryant,
Liz Danforth, Janet Aulisio Dannheiser,
Earl Geier, Jeff Laubenstein, Darrell Midgette,
Jim Nelson, Mike Nielsen, Tony "Suds" Szczudlo
Color Plates
Joel Biske, Jeff Laubenstein,
Jim Nelson, Tony "Suds" Szczudlo
Layout
Steve Bryant
Production Assistant
Ernesto Hernandez

EARTHDAWN™, DENIZENS OF EARTHDAWN™, and BARSAIVE™
are trademarks of FASA Corporation.
© 1994 FASA Corporation.
All Rights Reserved.
Printed in the U.S.A.

Published by
FASA Corporation
1100 W. Cermak, Suite B305
Chicago, IL 60608

ON THE WRITING OF THE DENIZENS OF BARSAIVE

How many of us can claim friends or acquaintances of every Name-giver race other than our own? Indeed, in the aftermath of the Scourge that isolated many of us in our own racial enclaves, how many of us have any knowledge of another race other than the superficial? Who but the t'skrang understand the true meaning of *haropas*? Do any folk but the elves truly feel the tragedy of Blood Wood's dreadful transformation? Do any but humans see the human race's worth? Who but a windling knows what it feels like to fly? Few Barsaivians can answer these questions, but all of us should have such knowledge. In order to give us a truer understanding of each other, I and my assistants have created this remarkable work, entitled *Denizens of Barsaive*.

During the compilation of *An Explorer's Guide to Barsaive*, my colleague Jerriv Forrim and I traveled extensively throughout the land and met many Name-givers of whose ways we knew little or nothing. It came to Jerriv and I that our ignorance of our fellow Name-givers was no less inexcusable than our former ignorance of the wonders and dangers of Barsaive, and so we determined to somehow correct that fault. Together, we conceived the idea of writing several volumes on the nature and ways of Barsaive's Name-giver races, each volume devoted to a particular people.

We presented our idea to Merrox, Master of the Hall of Records, who swiftly saw the wisdom of our proposal and graciously acceded to it. Undaunted by the magnitude of the task before us, we fell to with a will. To my great sorrow, poor Jerriv soon found the long hours and hard work too much for his frail constitution. Though he went to great lengths to deny the seriousness of his condition, often insisting on working almost as late as I did in an effort to prove his fitness, it became clear to me after only a few weeks that his health could not bear the strain. Indeed, it was not long after the last meal we shared that he collapsed—his health had become so precarious that even a simple meal of baked t'skrang fish did not agree with him. I took him at once to the healers, with whom he yet remains. He was so weak he could barely talk, but could not be induced to lie down quietly and take his medicine until he had extracted a promise from me that I would take on the burden of completing our great work.

Finding myself solely responsible for this great project, I spent many months sifting through countless historical records, travelers' journals, treatises, scholarly essays, and firsthand accounts, attempting to distill these diverse sources into accurate, interesting, and complete portrayals of each Name-giver race. I have labored to decipher and read a veritable mountain of documents, both in the Library of Throal and outside it. Though King Varulus III once again refused permission to visit the Eternal Library at Thera, I have managed to obtain one document from a Theran source that mysteriously found its way to our Great Library. Such a find is miraculous indeed and only serves to prove that the Passions truly love the work of the scholar above the petty considerations of politics. Though the task has been grueling, I can say with confidence that the information in these volumes constitutes an informative, complete, and fascinating record of the nature and ways of the Name-givers of our world. If anyone in Barsaive cares to know something of a race other than his own, I bid him come to the Great Library and peruse this great work—he will find no better source in all the land.

The eight volumes of *Denizens of Barsaive* describe the races of our land in alphabetical order: from Volumes 1 to 8, their subjects are dwarfs, elves, humans, obisidmen, orks, trolls, t'skrang, and windlings. I remind all readers of this work that every individual sees the world through his own eyes. Though I have tried to pass on only verifiable facts, the nature of the material is such that facts cannot be separated from the attitudes of the writers.

During the final stages of the compilation of this work, I was most ably assisted by many of the archivists and scribes who were my colleagues in the creation of *An Explorer's Guide to Barsaive*. It is with great gratitude that I acknowledge their contributions. As with the aforementioned work, myself and my colleagues—and occasionally other readers—have added marginal notes where appropriate to clarify points made in the text.

The greatest measure of my gratitude, of course, goes to my poor friend Jerriv Forrim, whom sad circumstance has relegated to a relatively minor role in the very work he helped bring to fruition. I believe that he will be more than happy with the final form of this work, and I wish him the good health in which to read it for many years to come.

—Thom Edrull, Archivist and Scribe of the Hall of Records, 1506 TH

THE REMARKABLE
HISTORY OF THE ELVEN PEOPLE

The following excerpt from Volume II of Denizens of Barsaive comes from the writings of Liandra, an elven troubadour now dwelling in the city of Urupa, on the coast of the Aras Sea. This particular essay is unique in that its author is one of the few living Barsaivians born before the Scourge. Liandra was but a young child when he and his family took shelter from the coming of the Horrors in an underground kaer. Though many have wondered which kaer was Liandra's home for so many centuries, the troubadour himself has said no more of it than to ask why it matters. He far more often speaks of the time before the Scourge, attempting to give people an understanding of the scope of the tragedy that the Scourge has wrought on the elves of Barsaive.
—Presented for the edification of the reader by Thom Edrull, Archivist and Scribe of the Hall of Records, 1506 TH

As a traveler who has seen many sights and shared many stories with all manner of people, I have discovered among the Name-giver races a vast number of different and often conflicting beliefs regarding the elven people. As an elven scholar and troubadour, I feel it my duty to share the truth of the life of an elf in Barsaive.

TO LIVE AS AN ELF
SINCE THE CORRUPTION

In the wake of the Scourge, to be elven is wonder and tragedy at the same time. In wonder we behold once more the beauties of nature so long denied us, as we help the world heal itself and restore our land to its former splendor. Our tragedy lies in what we have lost, for we have become a people without a soul. The Scourge-born Corruption of the Elven Court at Wyrm Wood has destroyed the very heart of the elven race, and not an elf in Barsaive truly feels whole. The Elven Court bound us together, and its loss has left us blinded children crying in the dark. For centuries, all elves knew undying faith and trust in the guidance and wisdom of the Elven Court. Now we have lost our way and must find anew our place in the world among our fellow Name-givers.

OF THE ELVEN COURT
AND ITS POWER

To fully understand the elven people, the reader must know of the Elven Court and the vital place it once held in elven lives and hearts. Unlike a kingdom such as Throal or the city-state that became the Theran Empire, the Elven Court held no temporal power.

It commanded no armies, though the warriors who swore fealty to it defended it well from all perils. The Queen and her courtiers did not govern, at least not in the Throalic sense of the word. Indeed, the Elven Court cared little for the doings of the lesser elven courts throughout the world, unless the actions of those courts came into conflict with the elven way. Only then did the Elven Court dabble in political matters, if the reigning Queen deemed it wise. The Court passed no laws, enforced no peace and certainly collected no taxes. Instead, the Elven Court served as the standard by which all the world's elven kingdoms judged how truly elven they were. From the Elven Court, the elves of the world learned how best to live.

All things good in elven life and culture took seed and grew from the Elven Court. It gave us our arts, our language, our mode of dress, our most sacred rituals, and all things that give life meaning. Even changes in our ways first began within the Court, just as the change of season that turns a green leaf golden begins within the heart of a tree. We looked to the Elven Court to understand who and what our people were. It was our model, our example, the pinnacle of elven accomplishment that all strove to reach.

ON THE CHOOSING AND REIGN OF THE QUEEN

As the Elven Court was once the heart of elven culture, so the Elven Queen was the heart of the Court. Upon the death of the previous queen, the courtiers chose a new queen from those elves within and outside the Court who best embodied the ideals and ways of the elven race. For all the centuries of her reign, each queen led her people not through temporal might or the power of coin, but by example. Her words and deeds guided and inspired the elves of all the world. From her seat upon the Rose Throne, in the Chamber of Voices in her magnificent palace where she held audience, the queen proclaimed true elven ways, and all elves followed her.

Upon her accession, each queen had a new Rose Throne crafted especially for her. No two Rose Thrones looked alike. From each to each, only the name endured. In the years since discovering the Corruption of Wyrm Wood, I have wondered if the Rose Throne might not have some connection with the terrible Ritual of Thorns. It is my devout hope that this is not so; the thought of our former beauty and grandeur having anything to do with the present, twisted mockery of it chills my heart. Still, the image is there, for every rose has a thorn, does it not?

As the avatar of all that is truly elven, the Elven Queen wields potent magics surpassed by none other in her realm. Many are ceremonial magics, used at the Festal Days of the Court calendar. Others protect and preserve the person of the Queen. In one of the few examples of which I may freely speak, magic enables the Queen of the Elven Court to outlive her fellow rulers of the lesser courts by many years. Queen Alachia of Blood Wood was born before the Scourge, as was I. Yet the five centuries between the sealing of the kaers and this day weigh but lightly upon her.

THE CALAMITOUS PASSING OF QUEEN DALLIA

For hundreds upon hundreds of years, the rule of the Elven Court passed unbroken from queen to queen. And as I have said, the queen ruled over not only the elves of the land that we now Name Barsaive, but over all the elves of the world. But time and distance make strangers of us all, and so it was between the Elven Court and the faraway realm of Shosara. In the reign of Queen Dallia, the elves of Shosara began to stray from the ways of the Court, choosing to obey the queen's edicts only when convenient. They remained loyal to her, in their way, and honored her in their hearts as a grown child honors her mother; but like such a child, they desired independence. How, they asked, could the queen fully understand life in the northern lands, when she had never seen those places?

When Queen Dallia heard that the elves of Shosara had begun to create traditions and customs not sanctioned by the Elven Court, she made preparations to visit Shosara in order to better understand the minds and hearts of her northern

subjects. But alas, her compassion was to have an ill reward. No sooner had the royal caravan departed Wyrm Wood, than they were set upon by the dragon Alamaise. The dragon railed at Queen Dallia and her retinue, demanding restitution for the supposed crimes of the Elven Court. The queen tried to assuage the dragon's anger, but could not convince him of her people's innocence. In his rage, Alamaise slew Queen Dallia, leaving the Court bereft of its leader.

THE COMING OF QUEEN FAILLA

For two years, the Elven Court remained leaderless, for none among the courtiers was worthy to serve as queen. Some among the Elven Court even began to whisper that Alamaise was right, that the Court must have committed some dreadful crime for the Universe to allow such a calamity as the slaying of the queen. The faint-hearted whisperers were silenced, however, when Queen Failla of the Western Kingdoms came to Wyrm Wood to claim the throne. No other claimant could prove herself worthy to lead the Elven Court, and so Queen Failla ascended the Rose Throne amid much rejoicing.

But where Queen Dallia had shown patience toward Shosara, Queen Failla chose another course. During her reign over the Western Kingdoms, Queen Failla had kept unbroken faith with the Elven Court, obeying the Elven Queen's every whim as though the existence of the elven people depended on it. She found even the smallest glimmer of disobedience shocking, even insulting. Mere weeks after her accession, Queen Failla sent word to the leaders of Shosara that to continue with their unsanctioned ways risked retribution—perhaps even the dreaded, formal sundering known to all elves as Separation.

Of the Separation of Shosara and the First Splintering

Shosara's queen pleaded with Queen Failla for patience and compassion, and her pleas were echoed by Queen Failla's favored advisor, Elianar Messias. Messias argued that the queen would serve her Shosaran subjects best by allowing the northern kingdom to loosen the cultural shackles that bound it to the Elven Court, but Queen Failla refused to hear him. Blindly convinced of her own rightness, Queen Failla declared Shosara Separated from the Elven Court. When Messias openly opposed her action, the queen banished him from the Court for a hundred years. Messias traveled to a monastery in the Delaris Mountains, to the southwest of Wyrm Wood, where he discovered the Books of Harrow. The rest of Messias' tale—the dawn of the Theran Empire and the coming of the Scourge—is one that every child of Barsaive knows, and so I will not repeat it in this text.

The Separation of Shosara and the banishment of Messias, meant to safeguard the unity of elven culture, instead marked the beginning of its splintering. Contrasting Queen Dallia's compassion with Queen Failla's hard heart, many elven kingdoms in the land that would become Barsaive began to question Failla's edicts. Though none dared defy her openly, they questioned and wondered in secret. For the first time, a great many of the world's elves began to doubt the rightness of their queen.

THE TUMULTUOUS REIGN OF ALACHIA

Queen Liara succeeded Queen Failla and ruled the Court with the iron hand of her predecessor. Still none rebelled, for none dared risk Separation, but more and more questioned the edicts of the Elven Queen. Upon the death of Queen Liara, Queen Alachia ascended the Rose Throne, and for a time it seemed that Queen Dallia had come again. Alachia had seen the signs of dissent among the elven people, and though she would not allow independence, she clothed the iron hand of Queens Failla and Liara in a glove of velvet. Soon after her accession, Queen Alachia took steps to make the Elven Court a shade or two more open to the desires of elves in other, faraway lands. By so doing, she made the Court's ways even more desirable to the elven people than they had been before and soothed the troubled hearts of the dissidents. Her efforts were rewarded when all the world's elven kingdoms, save for Shosara, swore new oaths of devotion to Alachia and her court.

Though Liandra reports the dragon's murder of Queen Dallia as fact, it is only a tale that may not be true. I have heard another story of Dallia's death, much told among dwarfs, that the queen and her retinue died in a sudden storm sent by the Passions to punish them. Punish them for what, the tale does not tell.
—Karon Foll

To readers interested in pursuing the story of Elianar Messias, the Books of Harrow, and the terrors they foretold, we recommend "An Explorer's Guide to Barsaive" and the writings of Jallo Redbeard. Both works are in the Great Library of Throal.
—Merrox, Master of the Hall of Records

With the passing of time, the praise that Alachia had won and the influence she wielded kindled in her great vanity, a vainglory that would have momentous and calamitous consequences for the elven people. As the Elven Court's influence over the world's elves grew stronger and its culture grew richer, Alachia came to believe that the elven people surpassed all other Name-givers. She even began to wonder if the Elven Court should rule over the lands of other races.

Fifty years or so after the beginning of Alachia's reign, the nascent Theran Empire began to trade with many realms, including Wyrm Wood, for the precious magical metal orichalcum. As the profit to be had from orichalcum grew, so did the lust to possess it, and in time a troll raid on Shosaran orichalcum stores sparked the terrible battles of the Orichalcum Wars. The dwarf kingdom of Scytha and countless other nations made war against the Elven Court, which prevailed against its enemies only after great struggle. Queen Alachia, furious that any would dare attack her court, determined that her people would never submit to the rule of any other. When the Therans used the ongoing fighting as an excuse to close their iron grip over most of the peoples of Barsaive, Alachia resolved to hold her people's sovereignty no matter what the cost. This resolve set the stage for the momentous events that scholars of history call the Elven Schism.

Of the Schism and the Scourge

Having translated the Books of Harrow and learned of the coming Scourge, the Therans devised the Rites of Protection and Passage to guard against its ravages. The Therans then sent envoys across all the lands of Barsaive, offering to share their defenses against the coming Horrors in exchange for loyalty and subservience to the Theran Empire. Most of Barsaive's kingdoms and city-states accepted the Therans' bargain, fearing the Horrors more than they feared enslavement. Queen Alachia alone steadfastly refused to accede to Theran demands. Proudly, she spurned their aid, declaring that the elven people needed no Theran magics to protect them.

When news of Alachia's action reached the other elven realms, elves outside the Elven Court faced a terrible choice: to support their Queen and risk destruction, or to accept Theran protection and break with the Elven Court. In her vanity Queen Alachia believed her subjects would follow her; but most forsook her and bargained with the Therans out of sheer terror. Bereft of the loyalty of so many of her subjects, Queen Alachia was left to rule over an Elven Court much diminished in power. Her refusal to accept Theran protection from the Horrors splintered the elven people into countless separate kingdoms and provinces, each left to find its own path through the ravages of the Scourge.

Queen Alachia also chose a path, one which destroyed the Elven Court in all but name. She chose to build a wooden kaer, hedged about with elven magics, and placed all her faith in it, despite warnings from elven scholars outside the Court that such a kaer would fail. It did, and the Court's next step along the path of survival has deprived all the elven people of their very soul. I will speak no more of the Corruption of the Elven Court itself, for all know that tale and it pains me to tell it. Instead, I shall speak of the effects of the Corruption on the elves of present-day Barsaive.

The Corruption of Wyrm Wood Revealed

During the long centuries of the Scourge, many elves outside Wyrm Wood sustained themselves with the hope of rejoining the Elven Court at the Scourge's end. Knowing that such a traumatic event as the ravaging of the world by the Horrors would do much harm to the elven people and their ways, the world's elves hoped to aid the Elven Court in restoring the beauty and grace of elven culture. Naively, the elves believed that Queen Alachia would forget her anger against her rebellious subjects, forgiving them for a transgression born only of the need for survival. Even the most skeptical of the elves outside Wyrm Wood believed that Alachia's offended pride would be soothed by the opportunity to reclaim the role of the elven people's cultural heart. Alas for the vain hopes of my people! The rejoining and restoration of which they dreamed has not yet, and may never, come to pass. The Horrors had left the world a scarred, twisted mockery of its former beauty, and Queen Alachia's vanity had wreaked far worse harm on herself and the Elven Court. In a misguided effort to stave off the Horrors, Alachia and her courtiers made virtual Horrors of themselves. They caused thorns to grow from within their flesh, which inflicted never-ending agony upon them. Once-beautiful Wyrm Wood became Blood Wood, a place of tainted loveliness and seductive corruption.

News of Wyrm Wood's dreadful transformation did not reach the world outside the wood for some time. Travel through Barsaive in the first years after the Scourge often proved both difficult and dangerous, and those few who reached Blood Wood often died at the hands of blood elves protecting their domain. The blood elves themselves had little interest in making contact with the outside world, and so the rest of Barsaive knew little of the awful change that the Scourge had wrought. At length, those travelers who reached Blood Wood and escaped alive (or persuaded the blood elves that they meant no harm) brought word of the changed Elven Court to the dwarf kingdom of Throal. As word spread from Throal throughout Barsaive, the elves outside Blood Wood learned the bitter truth that their heart and soul was lost to them. The hopes of a reunified elven people that lie in every elf's heart and mind became yet another victim claimed by the Scourge.

WHAT THE CORRUPTION WROUGHT UPON THE ELVEN COURT

The Scourge and Queen Alachia's terrible choice have changed the role of the Elven Court drastically and perhaps permanently. Before the Scourge, the heart of the elven people and culture beat strongly and soundly. The Court gave a home to elven artists, musicians, craftsmen, and troubadours from all over the world. From every elven realm, the greatest practitioners of every elven art made pilgrimage to Wyrm Wood to display their prowess, exchange tales of their endeavors, and to offer their wisdom and experience to others. And it was not only the elves who came, in those far-off glory days. The Court opened its heart and hearths to travelers of all the Name-giver races, eager to share the wonders of elven ways with all who sought to know of them.

The Court also gave birth to all rituals observed to this day by the elven people, and those who lived there practiced them with the full regality and beauty that other elves elsewhere had often laid aside. Elven families from many realms asked that the rites of birth, pronouncement, and passage take place in the Elven Court. To have this favor granted was considered among the greatest honors that an elf could receive. And, as befits the soul of a people, the Elven Court served as guardian and recorder of elven history, keeping records of significant events that occurred within every elven realm. The lesser courts and kingdoms knew only their own history and perhaps that of their nearest neighbors, but the Elven Court knew all that had befallen both the greatest and least of its subjects.

Of the Court in the Years After the Scourge

The most pronounced of the changes wrought by the Scourge lies in the physical corruption of the elves of Blood Wood. The thorns that pierce the flesh of the blood elves make the skin crawl to look upon them, marring the true elven beauty that they once possessed. My people are truly beautiful, in spirit and in flesh. The blood elves are repugnant, twisted images of true elves. Perhaps even more horrible, their bleeding thorns and constant anguish have not robbed them of their loveliness, but instead changed it from a wholesome beauty to the seductive appeal of pain. That agony can attract the heart is perhaps the most terrible truth that the blood elves' existence has revealed to the elven soul.

Just as the Ritual of Thorns marred the faces and bodies of the blood elves, so has their neverending pain blighted the arts practiced among them. They continue to paint, sculpt, make music, dance, and use magic as elves always have, but their creations are tainted by the terrible harm they have wrought upon their inmost souls. If a blood elf paints a flowering tree, a close look at his painting shows that the trunk is decaying from the inside and the blossoms are tainted by blight, worms, or the brown stain of rot. If a blood elf sings or plays, his sweet, unearthly notes soon begin to subtly grate upon the ear. Though the sound he creates is still beautiful, it is unnatural. So it is with all the elven arts as practiced by our unwholesome brethren; they retain the outward beauty of all things elven, but at the heart of them lies rottenness. The blood elves can no longer see the loveliness of the world untainted by agony, and their twisted vision infects everything they touch.

Most of the elves of Barsaive and of elven realms throughout the world have forever forsaken the Elven Court. They no longer consider Alachia's blighted realm part of elven culture, let alone its heart. But this belief holds within it a sad paradox, for all elves secretly wish that the Court was yet whole. Though it pains any true elf to admit it, we all long for the restoration of the Elven Court. From our earliest childhood, we are raised to revere our ways and uphold our traditions. Our history tells us that the Elven Court decides what is truly elven—but since the Corruption, no elven nation, city, or kingdom has yet taken up the Elven Court's fallen mantle. Without the Elven Court we have no heart, and yet we cannot accept its evil ways.

Ever since the Scourge, of course, Queen Alachia has insisted that her Court remains the true heart of elven culture and that she remains Queen of all the world's elven folk. Most elves outside Blood Wood reject these pronouncements—we believe that Alachia forsook her right to the Rose Throne the instant that the first thorn pierced her skin. Yet without our Queen and Court we are lost, each elf forced to seek his own light in the darkness. I and many others rightly fear such a fate and long for the day when we can once again pledge our loyalty and love to the Elven Court. Toward that end, many among us actively work toward the Court's restoration.

A DISCOURSE ON ELVEN SPIRITUAL BELIEFS

Elves are a deeply spiritual people whose beliefs, traditions, and culture embody their truest selves. Our solemn joy in our existence in the world makes us quiet and contemplative, and because so few other races share our depth of understanding, we find it easiest to keep our thoughts and feelings close to our hearts. Sadly, our silence and need for privacy fosters the illusion of the

dispassionate, analytical, even cold-hearted and indifferent elf. In truth, we are much different than we seem. Elves bring deep feeling to all that they do, but where other races demonstrate their feelings with action, elves do so through devotion and discipline.

It is difficult to express our beliefs in a few, simple paragraphs, and so I have devoted considerable space to this all-important subject. An elf begins to learn of the spiritual Paths in infancy, and his journey along them never ends.

OF THE JOURNEY AND THE WHEEL

An elf sees all life as a journey of discovery, change, growth, and ascendancy. Throughout his life, the elf treads a metaphysical pathway represented by the *Draesis ti'Morel*, the Wheel of Life. The Wheel contains five Paths, each corresponding to a different stage of life. As an elf ages, his journey along the Wheel leads him through each Path until he reaches the Wheel's heart. At this still center of being, he prepares for ascension into the metaplanes, to the mystical place known as *Tesrae ke'Mellakabal*, the Citadel of the Shining Ones.

Each Path represents ever-greater spiritual maturity. Though a few elves disagree, most accept the following five Paths: *Mes ti'Meraerthsa*, the Path of Warriors; *Mes ti'Telenetishsa*, the Path of Scholars; *Mes ti'Cirolletishsa*, the Path of Travelers; *Mes ti'Perritaesa*, the Path of Sages; and *Mes ti'Raeghsa*, the Path of Lords. Each Path has certain regalia and rituals associated with it that mark its Followers. I discuss these below, within the text dedicated to each Path.

ON THE FOLLOWING OF A PATH

As an elf walks along the Wheel of Life, he is said to be Following one of its Paths. He Follows each Path in order, from *Mes ti'Meraerthsa* to *Mes ti'Raeghsa*. Though each Follower is meant to tread the Path of Lords before he dies, any elf who dies untimely can still find a place in the Citadel of the Shining Ones.

Elven *Eoerin*, scholars of the Paths, continue to dispute the point at which an elf ceases to Follow one Path and takes his first steps on another. Some believe that an elf steps onto the next Path upon achievement of the Eighth Circle in the Discipline that elf has chosen to represent his or her journey along that Path. Among holders of this view, known as *Sa'mistishsa*, or "strict Followers," an elf embarking on a new Path must take a new Discipline to represent the next stage of his journey. At this time, known as the *Chaele ti'Désach*, the Days of Change, the elf may change not only his Discipline but also his mate if he chooses. I will speak more of this latter custom in the text devoted to marriage rituals, further on in this work.

Other *Eoerin* take a less literal view of the change in Paths. They believe that because the Paths represent a journey of the spirit, the change from one to another need not have any physical manifestation. An elf may therefore Follow all the Paths within the same Discipline, remaining with the same mate (if he has one). According to holders of this view, known as *Dae'mistishsa* or free Followers, the Follower alone knows when he has stepped onto the next Path, though the transition is often marked by a significant event.

For myself, I cannot say which view is right. Each elf must choose his own belief in this matter, and all Followers respect each other's choice. One way or another, we all walk along the Wheel.

OF THE DIFFERENT PATHS

For each of the five Paths that lead to the transformation and ascension of the elven spirit into *Tesrae ke'Mellakabal*, at least five specific associations (and sometimes six or seven) are sacred to Followers. These associations are colors, regalia, elements, hours, age, and—among different sects of Followers—Passions and Disciplines. I will endeavor to explain each of these associations below.

On the Meaning of Colors

A Follower displays his Path in the colors of his clothes, so that others may know his Path and show him the respect due him.

On the Meaning of Regalia

Sigils, symbols, designs, jewelry, and sacred objects also show a Follower's Path. The specific regalia chosen can vary greatly from Follower to Follower.

LIANDRA IS EITHER TERRIBLY NAIVE OR DELUDING HIMSELF. SOME ELVEN COMMUNITIES ARE SO STRONGLY SA'MISTISHSA OR DAE'MISTISHSA THAT THEY DRIVE OUT ANY ELF WHO THINKS OTHERWISE. PARTICULARLY FANATICAL PEOPLE ON EITHER SIDE, MANY OF WHOM ARE QUESTORS, SEE THE OTHER VIEW AS OUTRIGHT HERESY AND REACT ACCORDINGLY.
—MERROX, MASTER OF THE HALL OF RECORDS

On the Meaning of Elements

Each Path has a certain element associated with it: Earth, Air, Fire, Water, or Wood. These elements and anything made of them are of great significance to the Follower of that element's Path.

On the Meaning of Hours

Certain times of day have meaning for Followers of a given Path. During these sacred hours he must perform a special Path ritual, similar to an adept's karma ritual but focused on the Follower's Path. The brief ritual, a mere ten minutes in length, reinforces the Follower's dedication to his Path.

On the Meaning of Age

The age associated with each Path serves as a guideline to the time of life at which each elf should reach a certain Path. Many reach a given Path earlier than the given age, some reach it later. Many Dae'mistishsa see the birthday that marks the given year as the point of transition from one Path to the next.

On the Meaning of the Passions

Some *Eoerin* and Followers, but not all, believe that a particular Passion guides the Follower in his journey along each Path. Others believe that all the Passions watch over a Follower as he journeys. Most elves believe the latter; those who hold to the former belief are called *Beletre*, the Passionate.

On the Meaning of Disciplines

At the heart of the debate between the Sa'mistishsa and the Dae'mistishsa is the question of which Discipline a Follower takes during his walk along a given Path. The Sa'mistishsa believe that a Follower may adhere to only one, specific Discipline for each Path, while the Dae'mistishsa believe that a Follower may espouse any Discipline at any time during his journey as long as that Discipline allows him to adhere to his Path's philosophical precepts.

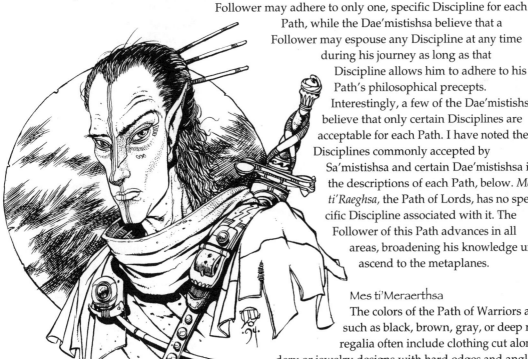

Interestingly, a few of the Dae'mistishsa believe that only certain Disciplines are acceptable for each Path. I have noted the Disciplines commonly accepted by Sa'mistishsa and certain Dae'mistishsa in the descriptions of each Path, below. *Mes ti'Raeghsa*, the Path of Lords, has no specific Discipline associated with it. The Follower of this Path advances in all areas, broadening his knowledge until he is ready to ascend to the metaplanes.

Mes ti'Meraerthsa

The colors of the Path of Warriors are dark earth shades such as black, brown, gray, or deep red. Such a Follower's regalia often include clothing cut along sharp lines, embroidery or jewelry designs with hard edges and angles, and swords or other weapons. The element of this Path is Earth, and its hour is Midnight. Each Follower begins with this Path, and may walk it at any time between his coming of age and his sixtieth year. Some elves believe that the Path of Warriors belongs to Thystonius, Passion of Valor and Conflict. The Sa'mistishsa associate the warrior Discipline with this Path, and many Dae'mistishsa also recognize the Disciplines of the beastmaster and the thief.

FOR AN ELF AS WELL ACQUAINTED WITH THE WAYS OF OTHER RACES AS LIANDRA SEEMS TO BE, I FIND IT INTERESTING THAT HE TAKES EVERY DETAIL OF ELVEN SPIRITUALITY AS OBJECTIVE FACT RATHER THAN A SUBJECTIVE WAY OF EXPLAINING THE ELVES' PLACE IN THE WORLD. HE WRITES AS THOUGH ELVEN SPIRITUAL BELIEFS ARE "TRUE," AND EVERYONE ELSE'S ARE BY IMPLICATION LESS TRUE. HAVE LIANDRA'S WRITINGS ABOUT THIS SUBJECT HAD ANOTHER HAND IN THEM, PERHAPS?
—JERRIV FORRIM

The Warrior's Path tests an elf's physical strength and abilities. While following this Path, each elf discovers the limits of his body. Emotions rule over reason, and instinct reigns over intellect. As the Follower walks this Path, he learns of the wonders and dangers of the world. He has little time for philosophy and debate, acting and reacting too swiftly for thought.

Mes ti'Telenetishsa

The colors of the Path of Scholars are bright, rich shades of red and yellow. Favored regalia includes rich embroidery, textured artworks, and symbols of fire, the sun, and the like. The element of this Path is Fire, and its hour is Midday. An elf begins to Follow this Path between the ages of 60 and 120. Some elves believe that Floranuus, Passion of Revelry, Energy, Victory, and Motion, guides their steps on this Path. Its Disciplines include the elementalist (according to the Sa'mistishsa) and the archer, cavalryman, and swordmaster (according to certain Dae'mistishsa).

The Follower who walks this Path begins to explore his inner nature. The Scholar's Path is not a call to introspection, but rather an exploration of the reasons behind action. The Follower of this Path examines purposes, defines motives, and reveals intent. Though he still acts in the physical world, he acts with deliberation and purpose. Along this Path, the Follower begins to perceive much of the inner workings of the world and of his own, inner self.

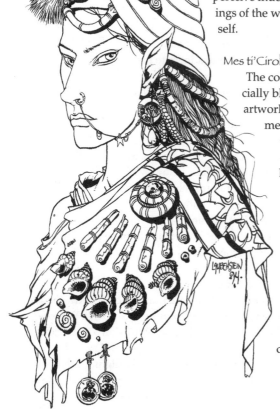

Mes ti'Cirolletishsa

The colors of the Path of Travelers are light shades of the sky and seas, especially blues, whites, and greens. Favored regalia include dramatic, flamboyant artworks and designs, musical and writing instruments, and the like. The element of this Path is Air, and its hour is Mid-day. An elf commonly walks this Path between the ages of 120 and 180. Many elves believe that Astendar, Passion of Love, Art, and Music, watches over this Path. Its Disciplines include the troubadour (accepted by the Sa'mistishsa) and the illusionist and weaponsmith (accepted by certain Dae'mistishsa).

The Follower who walks this Path moves from the inward soul to the outward world. Where in the *Mes ti'Telenetishsa* the Follower explored the inner relationship between thought and action, along the Traveler's Path the Follower discovers the relationships between actions or between expression and inspiration. As he walks this Path, he begins to touch upon the deeper patterns that link all things in the Universe. Many Followers of the *Mes ti'Cirolletishsa* find themselves near centers of power or deeply involved in adventure. In places of power and peril, the Follower can see many connections in the physical world through tales, song, and legends.

Mes ti'Perritaesa

The colors of the Path of Sages are rich and deep, such as dark blues and reds, gold, and black. Favored regalia include symbolic, abstract works of art, especially those that incorporate detailed designs and mystical symbols. The element of this Path is Water, and its hour is Sunset. An elf commonly Follows this Path between the ages of 180 to 240. Some elves believe that Jaspree, Passion of Growth, Care of the Land, and Love of the Wilderness, guides Followers of this Path. The accepted Discipline among the Sa'mistisha is the wizard; some Dae'mistishsa also accept the Discipline of the nethermancer.

The Follower of the Sage's Path turns inward once more, finding the inner world far more complex than the outer one. The Follower begins to explore the inner connections between all things, seeing patterns and defining truths once hidden from him. The cycles of nature become clear, and he begins to understand the true workings of the world. Revelations abound as the Follower perceives the hidden causes behind seemingly unconnected events. Along this Path, the elven spirit emerges and begins to move toward the Center.

Mes ti'Raeghsa

The colors of the Path of Lords are silver, gold, and bronze. Favored regalia include embroidery and artwork of simple designs that include deeply significant personal symbols. The element of this Path is Wood, and all hours are sacred to it. An elf commonly treads this Path between the ages of 240 and 300. Some elves believe that this Path belongs to Mynbruje, Passion of Justice, Compassion, Empathy, and Truth. All elves, whether Sa'mistishsa or Dae'mistishsa, accept all Disciplines as associated with this Path.

The Follower of the Path of Lords achieves true harmony, bringing the body into balance with the mind. Having achieved mastery of himself and the world he inhabits, all the world's mysteries are the Follower's to ponder and control as he seeks the final balance of self and spirit. Once he has achieved this balance, the gates to the metaplanes will open, so that he may make the final journey to *Tesrae ke'Mellakabal*.

Mes ti'Raeghsa is a Path of great calm, but also of great power. The Follower uses all that he has learned to prepare himself for entrance to the Citadel of the Shining Ones. No one knows when the gates to *Tesrae ke'Mellakabal* will open for him, so the Follower must always be ready.

OF ELVEN RITUALS

Rituals mean much to the spiritual life of an elf. Performed at such pivotal moments in life's journey as birth, Naming, coming of age, marriage, death, and many other occasions, most of these rituals involve magic. Because most elves prefer to share their deepest mysteries and most sacred traditions only with their racial kindred, few rituals are performed in racially mixed villages and towns. Instead, the participants often travel to an elven settlement, to be among their kin in the heart of nature. (I will speak more of elven settlements further on in this text, in the section entitled *Where the Elves of Barsaive Dwell*.)

Though the specific details of many rituals vary from settlement to settlement and from participant to participant, I have described below the most common variations of the most significant elven rituals.

On the Rites Surrounding Birth

As with all Name-givers, elves value the birth of a new life beyond all other things. To an elf, the arrival of a new Follower along the Wheel of Life is cause for great celebration. From the moment of quickening, when the child first moves in its mother's womb, the expectant mother is showered with gifts and loving attention by all her kindred—indeed, by every member of the settlement, if she dwells in one. The sacred rites of birth, however, do not begin until the tenth month of the woman's confinement.

In the final month before the expected birth of the child, the closest kinswoman of the mother-to-be comes to live under her roof. This kinswoman, called the *dresner*, or "assistant," aids the expectant mother and fulfills most of her duties in the household. If an expectant mother has no close kinswoman, a dear female friend may act as *dresner*.

At the time of birth, the *dresner* and the midwife help the expectant mother walk to the birthing room. Once the door to the birthing room is shut, none but these three women may enter it until the child is born. To assure the special blessing of the Passion Garlen upon the newborn babe, the midwife clothes herself in the sigils of the gracious Mother Who Cares For All.

While the mother, her *dresner*, and the midwife labor to bring the child into the world, relatives and friends begin the ritual known as *Ar'laana*, or "the Wait." As early as a full week before the birth, these favored ones gather in the expectant family's home or a house nearby and pass the time telling tales and singing songs of the awaited child's ancestors. They also invent fanciful stories of the child's future exploits. To represent the child's first steps along the *Draesis ti'Morel*, every elf present during the *Ar'laana* adds some ornament or stitchery to a pair of boots crafted for the coming infant.

Once the child is born, the midwife takes it to its father. Whether presented with the child during day or night, sunlight or storm, the father carries his infant son or daughter out of doors and shows the new youngling the sky. As he holds the child up to the elements, the father announces the birth of a new Follower to the world.

On the Rite of Pronouncement

Each elven child is Named within three days of its birth, in the ritual known to elves as the Rite of Pronouncement. In my childhood, before the Scourge, Naming did not take place for twenty-one days in order to give the parents time to choose the child's Name well. The deprivations of life in the kaers, however, led us to shorten the time lest too many children die un-Named.

The child's parents choose three witnesses for the Rite of Pronouncement. Though all elves in the community may watch the proceedings, the witnesses play a special role. They bear witness to the child's Naming and also swear to care for and safeguard the child whenever its parents cannot. This responsibility lasts until the child takes part in the Ritual of Passage, which marks his transformation from child to adult.

Elves

A THORN MAN GUARDS THE **BLOOD WOOD** NEAR THE **QUEEN'S PALACE.**

A betrothal brooch from Sereatha, the City of Spires.

Living paintings, created as a reminder of what the world was, and a promise of what it will be again.

Jorealla, questor of Jaspree, ambassador from Shosara to the Blood Wood.

Portraiture showing the beauty of the Elven Court before and after the Scourge, painted by Doironn of Throal.

Pictured above is Niriame, Blood Warder of Alachia's court.
Pictured at right is the elven noble, Luxi Pannoor, painted before the Scourge.

This blood charm alerts the wearer to the presence of Horrors.

This ceremonial decanter reflects the corruption of the blood elves.

Karon Foll, reflects on the mysteries of the elven people.

The elven love of beauty is evident in the intricate craftsmanship of their weaponry.

The parents spend much of the three days between birth and Naming in seclusion, meditating on their hopes and dreams for the newborn babe and keeping their love for it uppermost in their thoughts. In this way, the parents ensure the choice of the right Name for the child, a Name that often represents some aspect of the infant's lineage. Once the Name is chosen, the parents bring the child to a place in the settlement that holds some significance for them. The witnesses and other attendees follow; when all are gathered, the parents pronounce the Name of the child to the witnesses. Each witness in turn then speaks the child's Name and pledges to protect him or her until the time of his Ritual of Passage. After this swearing of vows, the child's mother produces a small piece of fruit, either plucked from a nearby tree or brought with her to the Naming place. This fruit, called the *masa'e*, or "birth seed," is shared by parents, witnesses and child, with one bite for each. The sharing of the *masa'e* symbolizes the new life now shared between the ritual's participants.

On the Ritual of Passage

When an elf reaches the age of twenty years, he enacts the Ritual of Passage. Upon completion of this ritual, the newly adult elf takes complete responsibility for his own life's journey along the Paths of the Wheel. If he or she wishes, he may seek a mate, though few elves do so early in adult life. Indeed, many elves leave home soon after the Ritual of Passage, intending to help heal the world of the devastation left by the Scourge.

The Ritual of Passage takes place in two stages, with the first stage beginning seven days before the elf's twentieth birthday. From dawn until dusk on that day, the elf fasts, drinking water or a little wine if he desires, but partaking of nothing else. At dusk the elf goes out into the woods to sleep, and before slumber overtakes him he turns his thoughts to what he wishes to make of his life. Throughout the night, the elf dreams of his future. He returns to his home with the dawn and begins to make some item that represents his dreams. An elf who dreamed of becoming a healer might make a medicine pouch, an adventurer might make a weapon, and so on. Whatever the item, the elf must finish it by sunrise on his birthday. As he works, the elf thinks of his vision and discovers within himself his new, adult Name.

On the elf's twentieth birthday, the second stage of the Ritual of Passage takes place. The elf, his or her parents, and the witnesses from the elf's Rite of Pronouncement travel to a secluded place deep within the forest. The elf speaks in turn to each of the witnesses and to his father and mother, thanking them for the love and guidance they gave him throughout his childhood. Before them all, he declares himself an adult no longer in need of protection and tells them his new Name. Each of them speaks the elf's new Name, thereby welcoming him formally into the adult community.

In many elven settlements, the fasting day and the night of dreaming in the forest is combined with a challenge or test of courage. If the elf fails such a test, he must wait a year and a day before beginning his Ritual of Passage again. These ritual challenges are especially difficult because no elf who faces them has received any training as an adept; the changing of his name between childhood and adulthood would cost him anything he had gained in such training before reaching adulthood.

On the Two Rituals of Marriage

Though marriage rites among elves remain strikingly similar from settlement to settlement, the ways surrounding them differ considerably between the Sa'mistishsa and the Dae'mistishsa. Among the former, an elf may change his or her mate at the same time that he changes his Path and his Discipline; among the latter, the choice of a mate lasts for a lifetime.

Whether Sa'mistishsa or Dae'mistishsa, an elf wishing to marry must first court the mate of his or her choice. Courtship takes many forms; an elf may compose songs or poems praising the object of his love, or may fashion a special jewel for the loved one to wear. Often, a simple flower can become a token of undying affection (I speak more of this below, in the section entitled *The Custom of the Flower of Desire*). If the courting elf finds his or her affection returned, he must then seek permission to marry from the loved one's parents or guardians. In almost all cases, permission is freely granted, and the two families to be joined begin the preparations for the wedding feast.

In the marriage rite, the young couple pledge their love and fidelity to each other before their parents or guardians. In most elven communities, the vows take the form of a song, with the man and the woman writing alternating verses. The wedded pair each wear garments of leaves and flowers sewn together, with crowns of roses upon their heads. Once they have sung their vows, the woman takes a rose from her crown and gives it to her newly made husband. He in turn takes a blossom from his crown and gives it to his wife. The exchange of flowers seals the marriage contract, and the newly united families give the word for the feasting to begin. All members of the elven settlement are invited to the feast, which can last for one day or several, and which includes ballads sung and tales told in the newly married couple's honor. At the first breaking of bread, husband and wife weave the stems of their marriage roses together. They will preserve the twined flowers until one of the couple dies, or until one reaches the *Chaele ti'Désach* and chooses to end the marriage.

The Sa'mistishsa believe that the ending of one Path and the beginning of the next must be made manifest through great change in all areas of life. During the *Chaele ti'Désach*, elves who have married go into seclusion together to determine whether or not their lives are changing in complementary directions. If both partners agree that they are, they remain married until the next *Chaele ti'Désach*. If one or both of the pair discovers that his or her Path change requires a new mate (or no mate), the two engage in the ritual known as *Ke Seorach*, the Sundering.

All members of the settlement must witness this ritual, which is held at the site of the couple's wedding. Before the rite, the elf who is changing Paths chooses an Oathtaker from among his family, guardians, or friends. The Oathtaker must be Following the Path that the changing elf is about to tread. When all have gathered for the Sundering, the married couple stand before the Oathtaker. Each declares his or her intention to end their marriage and the reasons for it, and then together they hand the twined marriage roses to the Oathtaker. The Oathtaker gently separates the roses, handing one to the husband and one to the wife. The couple then throw down their roses and grind them to powder under their heels. This act symbolizes the Sundering, and from that moment the married pair are no longer husband and wife.

Among the Dae'mistishsa, the Sundering is regarded as an unfortunate holdover from less enlightened times at best, and as a deep disgrace at worst. Because Dae'mistishsa elves mate for life, many choose not to marry until at least the last few years of their first century. Though such late marriage may sound strange or even unnatural to other, less long-lived Name-givers, the reader must understand that marriage for an elf does not mean what it means for so many other races. For humans, t'skrang, windlings, dwarfs, and so on, marriage often means siring and bearing children as well as providing companionship. For elves, this is not so. An elven marriage exists for the purpose of providing companionship of the heart and soul as well as the body, and the begetting of children can just as well occur without marriage as with it.

In a human family, for example, a child whose mother is not married to its father can be said to have no father because the man who sired the child does not necessarily help to raise it. Among elves, anyone who begets a child helps to raise that child, whether married to the child's mother or not. We elves call the tie between unmarried parents the *niach mawr*, or the "child bond." Though *niach mawryn* often regard each other with friendship and affection, they are not soul-mates in the way that a married couple are, and may freely and easily break their bond when their child is grown to legal age. The *niach mawr* is particularly important among the Dae'mistishsa, whose members frequently choose not to marry until they are past childbearing.

The Custom of the Flower of Desire

When a male or female elf desires another elf of their acquaintance, the suitor customarily shows that desire by wearing a single flower pinned to the clothing or tucked into the hair. He or she wears the flower until it withers, or until the object of desire responds to it in some way. By custom, those who know the wearer of the flower must each determine if they are the desired one. The wearer of the flower need not state his preference; indeed, this custom works particularly well for elves who feel a certain delicacy about approaching the object of their affections. Persistent suitors frequently replace the flower with a new blossom once it has wilted; if the suitor leaves the withered flower in place, that act indicates a love that goes beyond desire.

On Rituals Associated With Death

Where many races regard death as a tragedy to be spoken of only when necessary, elves believe that the spirit of a fallen elf lives on in the memories and deeds of his loved ones. For this reason, elves speak often and with joy of their dead brethren, because only through such speech can the fallen live on in spirit. Though elves do see sadness in death, the sorrow is for the living, who will miss the physical presence of the loved one who has gone before. It is a gentle grief and carries no fear of death with it.

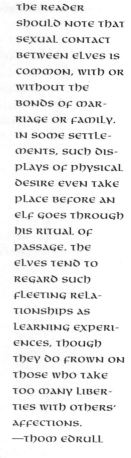

THE READER SHOULD NOTE THAT SEXUAL CONTACT BETWEEN ELVES IS COMMON, WITH OR WITHOUT THE BONDS OF MARRIAGE OR FAMILY. IN SOME SETTLEMENTS, SUCH DISPLAYS OF PHYSICAL DESIRE EVEN TAKE PLACE BEFORE AN ELF GOES THROUGH HIS RITUAL OF PASSAGE. THE ELVES TEND TO REGARD SUCH FLEETING RELATIONSHIPS AS LEARNING EXPERIENCES, THOUGH THEY DO FROWN ON THOSE WHO TAKE TOO MANY LIBERTIES WITH OTHERS' AFFECTIONS.
—THOM EDRULL

At the death of an elf, his or her loved ones perform the Ritual of Everlife. Many aged elves anticipate their deaths and spread word of their impending demise so that their families and friends may more easily prepare for the ritual. Because the Ritual of Everlife must include all those close to the deceased, this ritual often includes those not elven among its number. The Ritual of Everlife is the only elven ritual to do so.

The ritual takes place at midnight, in a place far from any habitation. Each participant holds a single, darkened source of light: a candle, a torch, or a light quartz crystal. Beginning with the mate of the deceased or his closest living relative, each participant shares a favorite memory of the departed. As each speaks, he lights his candle, torch, or crystal. The mate or chosen relative steps into the center of the softly glowing ring of light and speaks of the tales of the deceased that he will share with others, and which heirlooms the deceased has chosen to pass on to descendants. Once the mate or relative has finished speaking, all extinguish their lights as they speak aloud the deceased's Name in unison. In the renewed darkness, all participants leave the ritual site, none speaking a word to another.

An elf will always choose to die out of doors, within the bosom of nature. Should an elf fail to receive the Ritual of Everlife after his death, he still lives in spirit as long as even one person lives who remembers him in thought, word, or deed.

The Gift of the Ancestral Item

When an aging elf senses the approach of his death, he or she customarily makes a gift of one of his pattern items to someone in the youngest generation of his family. This gifting symbolizes the faith that the older generations place in the youngest, that the young will uphold elven traditions and customs. A young elf who receives such a gift regards it as a precious heirloom. To lose it, or worse, to cast it aside, is a fearsome omen of calamity.

Creating New Life From Death

In the years since our emergence from the kaers, the custom of creating new life from death has sprung up among many elven settlements. When an elf loses a good friend, he plants the seed of a tree in that friend's name. Once he has done so, he must return in a year and a day to see if the seed has sprouted. If it has not, the elf must plant another tree. Once the tree begins to grow, the planter Names it after his departed friend. Though it is not required that he return again to the tree, it is customary that the elf continue to watch over his living memorial. To my knowledge, no elf has engaged in this custom for a family member, nor has it ever replaced the Ritual of Everlife.

OF THE ELVEN ARTS AND CRAFTS

Unlike many other Name-giver races, elves nurture and perpetuate their arts and traditions from generation to generation. From his earliest days, each elven child learns of the arts of his people. He learns to paint, sculpt, dance, and sing even as he learns to walk and speak. This immersion in the elven arts ensures that each elven child keeps his people's traditions and heritage foremost in his thoughts from an early age, and it continues throughout each elf's life. Our race has an ancient history and traditions, which we must hand down to all generations. Only by so doing can we remain a people. In the years since the ending of the Scourge and the Corruption of the Elven Court, this cultural preservation has become even more vital to our spiritual survival.

IN TRUTH, MOST RACES TEACH THEIR CHILDREN OF THEIR TRADITIONS AT AN EARLY AGE. DWARFS CERTAINLY DO.
—MERROX, MASTER OF THE HALL OF RECORDS

Elven parents sire few children, but our long lives allow us to share our history, traditions, and culture with each succeeding generation firsthand in a way that other Name-givers cannot. I, for example, am the father of one child, who is the mother of one, who in turn is father to one more, and so on. I am the eldest of five generations within my family and have shared my knowledge of elven traditions with my daughter, my grandson, and with each generation born since. My daughter has taught what she knows of elven culture to her son, who has taught it to his son, and so on.

RETH'IM IS THE SPERETHIEL WORD FOR ELVEN CULTURE. TRANSLATED INTO THROALIC, THE WORD MEANS "TO BE ELVEN." LIANDRA'S VIEW OF RETH'IM IS SHARED BY ALL ELVES OF MY ACQUAINTANCE, AND THEY ARE MANY.
—KARON FOLL

Without *reth'im*, elves are no different from any other Name-givers. Unfortunately, the centuries spent underground and the Corruption of the Elven Court have harmed our culture and traditions. Because so much of our culture has its wellspring in the beauties of nature, many traditions could not be observed within the shelters. Now that our long imprisonment under the earth has ended, each elf devotes his life to restoring and re-creating our lost elven ways, as well as preserving those traditions and arts that have survived.

We elves consider ourselves the truest children of nature, and so we attempt to emulate its beauty and majesty in everything that we create. In the elven view, all the world's wonders exist in harmony and balance. Each work of art we create, each song we compose, each legend or tale we share reflects this balance and in some way connects to all the other arts and crafts that we practice. As an example, an elven weaponsmith does not simply forge a sword that balances well, fits easily in the hand and kills swiftly when it must. An elven sword is all of those things, but it is also a sculpture of surpassing beauty. In it, art and craft meet and become one.

OF DIVERSE ELVEN ARTS

The expression of the soul through various arts is a part of each elf's life from birth. This lifelong artistic training has given elven art a deserved reputation for unsurpassed beauty throughout Barsaive and the world. Because elven artistic endeavor takes so many forms, in the interests of brevity I have confined my text to observations on the most significant of the elven arts.

On the Noble Art of Painting

Elven painters tend to use a wide palette of colors, from sapphire blues and forest greens to fire-bright yellows and reds. The most common subjects of elven paintings are the many complex and beautiful forms of nature, and portraits of those who have achieved distinction among our people. Natural subjects include such beauties as a running stream or brook, the leafy canopy of the highest trees in a forest or jungle, an open field caressed by the sun, and so on. These subjects sound simple, but in truth they are not. The elven artist chooses them in order to test his artistic skill against the inherent difficulty of accurately portraying the full beauty of such "simple" wonders. As for elven portraits, these paintings bring out the inward soul of the subject as well as depicting outward features. In the days before the Scourge, elven artists considered it an honor beyond price to be allowed to paint the portrait of the Elven Queen.

As with many other aspects of elven culture, the Scourge and its aftermath have touched the art of painting. In many purely elven settlements, elven artists portraying the Horrors or the Corruption choose not to depict such dreadful subjects realistically, but instead to create images that symbolize them. Instead of painting a Horror's true appearance, such artists use certain colors, particularly dark grays and mottled browns and blacks, to represent the Horrors. Some artists portray a corrupted soul by giving such a subject a deeper shadow than other figures in the painting, or no shadow at all. A variant of this symbolic style has begun to appear in elven music, which I discuss below.

On the Creation of Sculpture

Most elven sculptors prefer to work with wood, as this abundant element is dearest to our hearts. On occasion, an elf sculpts with stone or even gems, and in some particularly elaborate pieces, even uses bronze or copper. Elven sculpture most often symbolizes elven spiritual beliefs; the Passions and their symbols are frequent subjects, as are aspects of spiritual Paths unique to the elven race. Intricate, complex designs, frequently calling to mind some aspect of the natural world, are a hallmark of the elven sculptor's art. Only the windlings come near to matching the quality of elven work in this regard, using their smaller hands and fingers to great effect.

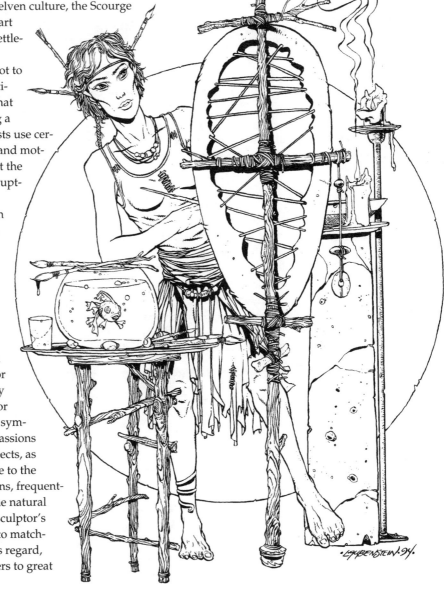

On the Creation of Tapestries

Elven embroidery, a popular method of decorating clothing, reaches its most noble expression in the making of vast tapestries that depict battles, legends, and tales. A famed example of this unique art, a finely stitched brocade hanging that depicts the grandeur of the Elven Court during the reign of the much-beloved Queen Dallia, is said to lie within Alachia's palace in Blood Wood. Queen Failla ordered the tapestry removed after the Separation of the realm of Shosara, and legend has it that Queen Failla ordered it burned. Most reputable scholars, however, insist that Alachia keeps the tapestry hidden within her private chambers.

On the Beauty of Elven Music

Of all the elven arts, elven music is best known throughout Barsaive for its unmatched loveliness and lyricism. The sweet sound of an elven air can calm even a frenzied troll or ork, and the royal musicians of the Kingdom of Throal love to play elven chamber music above all other types. It is said by many, and not only by elves, that the beauty and emotion of elven music makes even the Passion Astendar weep for joy at hearing it. The elves gave all Name-givers both the bardic tradition and the means for writing music, and many elves say that Astendar first gave these arts to us.

An elven composition, whether sung or simply played, is marked by sweeping melodies and rich, resonant harmonies. Because elven songs cover a wide vocal range, it takes considerable talent to sing one. Fulfilling the elven ideal of balance, the multiple harmonic lines common to elven compositions weave around and support the melodies at heights and depths beyond the ability of even elven ears to detect.

Among the many innovations that elven composers have produced is the combination of as many as ten or more different instruments rather than the combination of one or two instruments and a voice that is common to most races. Elven composers customarily combine five to ten instruments, producing a palette of sound which the composer uses much as a painter uses his color. Another innovation, one that owes its beginning to the ravages of the Scourge, is a symbolic style of composing that much resembles the similar style used in painting. In compositions inspired by events since the Corruption of Wyrm Wood, composers have begun to use certain themes or motifs to represent specific individuals, forces, or occurrences. Many musicians represent the Horrors, for example, with low-pitched instruments, somber melodies, and dissonant chords.

As well as composing melodies of heartbreaking beauty, the elven people create the most beautiful songs heard in all of Barsaive. Most elven songs speak of the glories of nature and of elven spiritual beliefs. So beautiful and finely wrought are the lyrics of these songs that even when translated from Sperethiel into less exalted tongues, they lose only a little of their loveliness and purity.

DESPITE LIANDRA'S OVERBLOWN OPINION OF ELVEN MUSIC, OTHER RACES DO CREATE TUNES WORTH LISTENING TO. GIVE ME A GOOD TROLL SONG ANY DAY—OR BETTER YET, A WINDLING HISTORY SONG. NO ELF CAN MATCH THE SHEER GORGEOUSNESS OF THE WINDLINGS' WING-HUM! —CHAG SKAT, TROLL TROUBADOUR

Of the Close Relation Between Music and Poetry

All elven lyrics take the form of verse, of course, and much of elven poetry is set to music. Where the two arts differ most is in length. Most lyrics are shorter than poems, and lyrics often contain repeated refrains. True poetry, by contrast, rarely contains repeated verses and is often several verses longer than most songs. Of course, exceptions do exist to these rules. The ballad of the Knights of the Crimson Spire takes several hours to sing in its entirety, whereas the poem of the healing of Blood Wood that most elves speak before breaking bread is a mere twelve lines in length.

In most elven poetry, each verse conveys a single idea, emotion or thought. Needless to say, poems pertaining to sweeping events or complex subjects need many verses in order to fully convey the poet's intent to the reader.

THIS POEM APPEARS IN "AN EXPLORER'S GUIDE TO BARSAIVE," AVAILABLE TO INTERESTED READERS IN THE LIBRARY OF THROAL.
—JERRIV FORRIM

On the Most Noble Art of Dance

Elven dance is a wonder to behold, one of the most graceful and elegant spectacles that one can be privileged to witness. Many dances created by elves combine movement with music and illusion magic to create flowing, ever-moving pictures of hypnotic beauty. Of all the Name-giver races, only windlings come close to matching elven dancers for intricacy and grace of movement, and even then only because their wings allow them to move in ways that we elves cannot.

In many elven settlements, dancers use their art to tell stories and legends, much as the windlings do. Such artists combine dance, lyrics, and music to tell epic tales of elven legend and history. I had the privilege of watching many such epic tellings during my years in the kaer, and these exhilarating, emotional performances did much to keep the lights of elven hearts burning in those dark days. In the years since our emergence from the kaers, such remembrances of our glorious past have become even more vital as a lifeline to pure, untainted elven culture.

On the Arts Magical

Magic permeates the arts as much as it does every other aspect of elven life. Though not all elves become adepts or magicians, all learn magical skills during the course of their lives, and almost all use such skills in their chosen art forms. Dancers and songsmiths, for example, create fantastic magical illusions during performances of their works. I know of several painters who use magic to make images or figures in their paintings move. In yet another example, many elven magicians embroider powerful magical sigils on their robes. Magic is also an art form in its own right, frequently used by so-called "minor" adepts in map reading and navigation, farming, and other tasks often considered not magical among other Name-givers.

In the years since the Corruption of Wyrm Wood, many untainted elves have avoided the use of blood magic, at least partly because of rumors that the Ritual of the Thorns was a blood-magic rite. Many elven settlements regard blood magic as so unsafe and repugnant that they forbid its use. Others allow it, but only under specific, limited circumstances.

A DISCOURSE ON CRAFTS

The distinction commonly drawn between arts and crafts means less to elves than to any other race, because elven craftsmen create their wares with an eye to beauty as well as function. Just as elven swordsmiths forge swords worthy of display in a royal audience hall, so do all elven crafts from armor to clothing to pottery exhibit uncommon beauty as well as cunning workmanship. I describe a mere handful of famous elven crafts below.

On the Glories of Elven Architecture

Many races prefer to beautify the insides of their homes rather than brightening a drab or plain exterior, but elves prefer beauty in all things. Elegant and practical, elven dwellings and other structures are often decorated with elaborate carvings and sculptures built into the walls and roof. Prominent elven buildings, such as the homes of those who govern cities and towns, are so elaborate as to rival the finest Theran architecture and design. In many elven settlements, of course, the ornamentation on the facades of buildings so closely mimics natural forms that only the eye of an elf can truly see it. The Queen's Palace in Blood Wood remains perhaps the finest example of this "naturalistic" style of building. The Palace is suported by eight enormous trees, and its walls and roof are woven of branches, vines, leaves, and the shimmering petals of violets and white roses.

On the Forging of Weapons and Armor

An elven craftsman makes each of his weapons and armor a work of art, but every decoration and ornament adds to the weapon's or armor's strength and resilience. Elven armor and weapons represent the ideal balance between beauty of form and efficiency of function.

Much of the decoration on elven arms and armor consists of runes in Sperethiel etched into the item's surface. From the

time of the Scourge onward, as the dwarfs' Throalic tongue gained prominence among all the peoples of Barsaive, elven weaponsmiths have combined the Sperethiel runes with Throalic symbols and icons.

On the Making of Clothing

Like all things of elven make, elven clothing is exquisite in both appearance and workmanship, whether simple or elaborate in pattern or design. In the dying of cloth, elven clothiers use as wide a range of beautiful hues as does an elven painter. The beauty of these colors requires a cloth fine enough to be worthy of them, and elven clothiers weave a fabric of a quality that no other weavers can match. Indeed, the cloth known as elfweave feels as soft as the petals of a flower or the kiss of a cloud and retains its luster far longer than any other cloth made in Barsaive.

Each garment made of such cloth is cut with an eye to beauty, hiding all flaws and bringing out the hidden loveliness of the wearer's body or coloring. (To those orks and dwarfs who claim that an elfweave robe never looks quite right on them, I can only say that some flaws are beyond the ability of even an elven clothier to hide.) Many elven garments are embroidered with intricate designs, using every color of thread imaginable. Some thread even resembles tiny bands of metal and gemstones. The combination of beautifully wrought stitchery, elegant cut, and finely woven and dyed fabric has made elfweave garments much desired among all the civilized folk of Barsaive.

ON THE UNIQUE BEAUTY OF THE ELVEN LANGUAGE

The elven language, called Sperethiel, is as beautiful to hear as the most melodious elven song. Its beauty lies not only in the grace of its sounds, but also in its complexity. Any truly devoted student of languages must surely admire the elegance of Sperethiel's intricate construction, especially when compared to the common and somewhat clumsy Throalic tongue. From his earliest days, every elven child learns to speak Sperethiel, just as he learns to paint, sculpt, dance, make music and make magic. Though Sperethiel graces the ear in whatever form it is spoken, the language is expressed most beautifully in song, where its flowing sounds combine with sweet melodies and harmonies to create the loveliest songs in Barsaive.

Though almost all elves can speak Sperethiel fluently, alarmingly few can write it fluently. The reason for this loss seems foolish—indeed, it arose from a problem so insignificant that no one foresaw it. A simple shortage of parchment on which to write and practice the intricate, Sperethiel runes came near to costing us a significant part of our culture! When we built the kaers to escape the Horrors, each kaer had only so much space for storage, and foodstuffs were judged more vital than writing tools. But without those tools, succeeding generations of elves could not learn to write the tongue of their people. In the years since our emergence into the light, elven scholars have made every effort to revive our written language and have met with some success. Many true elves consider it a sad circumstance that written Sperethiel is preserved in its purest form in the Elven Court, whose tainted inhabitants speak and write only the elven tongue. This state of affairs so perturbs many inhabitants of elven settlements that they have made a serious effort to re-learn our ancient language.

I have heard tales of a language that gave birth to Sperethiel, though I cannot vouch for the truth of the rumors. This language, supposedly spoken within the Elven Court and elven kingdoms throughout the world in the days before Alachia's reign, is said to exceed Sperethiel in both complexity and elegance. As a scholar, I should dearly love to find evidence of such a linguistic wonder!

THE LOSS OF WRITTEN SPERETHIEL DISTURBS MANY ELVEN SCHOLARS. ALL PEOPLES SHARE, TEACH, AND LEARN THEIR CULTURE THROUGH THEIR LANGUAGE, AND SO WITHOUT WRITTEN SPERETHIEL THE ELVES ARE MISSING A VITAL PART OF THEIR TRADITIONS.
—MERROX, MASTER OF THE HALL OF RECORDS

IN FACT, MANY ELVEN SCHOLARS CONSIDER THE VIRTUAL REPLACEMENT OF WRITTEN SPERETHIEL BY WRITTEN THROALIC AS A DREADFUL VIOLATION OF ELVEN TRADITION AND CUSTOM.
—KARON FOLL

25

ON THE TELLING OF STORIES AND LEGENDS

Storytelling, whether in verse or prose, is among the most valued of elven arts. My people's many stories include true accounts of events from elven history, legends, tall tales, and fables crafted to illustrate an important belief held by the elven race. As with the legends of other races, most elven folklore and tales have their origins in truth of some kind, whether literal or symbolic. Of the countless number of elven tales of heroes, tragedies, and triumphs, I have cited two examples below, one a well-known story of a legendary place and the other a fascinating tale currently making its way around Barsaive's elven settlements.

The Legend of the City of Spires

In the bright days before the Scourge darkened the land, there arose in the northwest a shining city. The elves who built it Named it Sereatha, the City of Spires, so called for the gleaming towers of alabaster and marble that surrounded the city and towered over every other building within its walls.

Within these shining towers lived the city's many adept guilds, all sworn to protect the city and to preserve the best and truest of elven arts and ways. Those adepts who followed a Passion Named their spire for that Passion. Oher guilds Named their spires for the elven ideal dearest to their hearts. All who lived in Sereatha spoke these sacred Names often, and with joy. The Universe, hearing their words, lent its magic to deepen the truth of the Names they spoke.

Three adept guilds claimed the greatest renown, not only in the City of Spires, but throughout all the lands surrounding it. The swordmasters of the Swords of Justice followed the ways of Mynbruje, Passion of Justice, Compassion, Empathy, and Truth. It was they who kept the laws of justice in Sereatha, and their members often traveled the land restoring the justice and mercy of Mynbruje to those kingdoms that had strayed from it. The Learners' Guild, a society of scholars, wizards, and troubadours devoted to the Passion Floranuus and the Path of Scholars, studied the ancient ways of the elven people and deepened the elves' knowledge of their inmost selves. And the warriors and swordmasters of the Knights of the Crimson Spire pledged their lives and hearts to the preservation and protection of elven culture and traditions.

During the most glorious days of elven culture, the City of Spires surpassed in beauty, grace, learning, and power every elven realm save the Elven Court at Wyrm Wood. Many an elf traveled far to reach the beautiful city, content to spend all his days practicing his art under the shadow of the spires. Musicians, dancers, painters, sculptors, tapestry-weavers, artisans, and magicians all came to Sereatha to learn from and teach others. It is said that the people of Sereatha often held contests to determine who among all the world's elves was best at his art, and that the greatest of elven troubadours learned their craft in that wondrous place.

Alas, the Scourge has taken the City of Spires from the elven people, as it has taken so much else. No one knows the fate of Sereatha, nor of any of those who dwelt in it. We have but a single, faint hope that the city may have survived the Scourge intact; a few travelers to Barsaive from the northern and western lands have spoken of the Knights of Crimson Spire, saying that members of the guild still live in those places. They also say that the Knights have come to Barsaive to help rid our land of the Horrors that remain.

How the Everliving Flower Came Again to Wyrm Wood

In the depths of Blood Wood, Named Wyrm Wood until the Corruption, lived the Elven Queen's chief adviser, Takaris. Now Takaris knew the tale of the Everliving Flower, the treasure that many claimed the Therans had stolen from the elves. It so happened that Takaris, who made it his business to know of the world outside the wood, heard rumors that the Everliving Flower had survived the Scourge and could be found within the ruins of the Forgotten City of Parlainth. Takaris wished to determine the truth of these rumors and to recover the lost treasure if they proved true. But his queen, unable to face the condemnation of the other Name-giver races, had forbidden direct contact with the outside world.

Now Takaris had also heard of a certain prophecy, namely that the return of the Everliving Flower to Blood Wood would be the sign of the tainted Court's redemption. If the Everliving Flower returned to its rightful home, Blood Wood could begin to become Wyrm Wood once more. Takaris, ashamed of the blight upon himself and his kindred, desired this redemption above all things. And so, in loving defiance of his sovereign's will, he secretly sent word to the city of Haven for a band of elven heroes to venture into Parlainth and reclaim the lost treasure.

The Passions fulfilled Takaris' unspoken desires, and three mighty elven adventurers answered his call for aid. The first was Le'ara, swordmaster of Balihan; the second was Kes'turah, beastmaster of Ennyskiel; and the third was Seosamh, elementalist of Urupa. Together, these three brave heroes ventured into the Horror-ridden depths of the ruined city of Parlainth, in search of that which would redeem their tainted kin and restore to the elven people the glorious heart they had lost.

The three faced and conquered many perils, until at length they came to a chamber whose walls were painted with runes that dizzied the eye and turned the stomach when any tried to read them. No magic could breach the chamber's sealed door, and Seosamh's astral sight revealed naught but a chill, black abyss with a tiny, warm glow at its heart. When Seosamh told his companions of this vision, they knew that they had found the Everliving Flower, and also the fearsome Horror that guarded it.

The Horror appeared to them in a cloud of bone-chilling mist, enveloping them all in a desperate attempt to slay them. It called every loathsome creature under its control to aid it, but to no avail. The three heroes slew every foe that the Mist sent, though it cost them dear in blood. Indeed, Kes'turah took a deadly wound, but dispatched her enemy even with her last breath. As Kes'turah died fighting and Le'ara battled the dreadful creatures that remained, Seosamh cast the spell that defeated the Mist. Upon the destruction of the Horror, the door to the sealed chamber fell open, and Le'ara took up the Everliving Flower from its resting place.

"As we have spent blood to claim you," she said, "so will you redeem the blood shed by our kindred."

Le'ara and Seosamh departed the ruins of Parlainth with the treasure and the body of their fallen companion and returned to Haven. After performing the Ritual of Everlife for Kes'turah, they traveled to Blood Wood with the Everliving Flower and presented the treasure to the Elven Queen. Alachia, sore angered that her trusted adviser had flouted her wishes, demanded of Takaris why he had dared to contact outsiders in a matter that so deeply touched the Elven Court.

Takaris bent his knee humbly before her and said, "Hear me, gracious sovereign. I know that I have transgressed, and I beg Your Majesty's pardon. But how could I send any of our own to reclaim the Everliving Flower? You know well how the other Name-givers of Barsaive regard us. Indeed, you have forbidden any blood elf to set foot outside Blood Wood, and I know of none who would disobey you. These outsiders were my only hope, and they are elven, my Queen. Though not of the court, they are our kin, and this matter concerns them also."

"They will not bow the knee to me, as all elves should," Alachia replied.

"That is true," said Takaris. "But they have brought you a gift beyond price. They have returned the Everliving Flower to its rightful home, so that our healing may begin. Is this not worth more than a few words of loyalty?"

ACCORDING TO
RECENT NEWS
FROM HAVEN, THE
EVERLIVING
FLOWER HAS
INDEED BEEN
RECOVERED FROM
THE RUINS OF
PARLAINTH. THE
CIRCUMSTANCES,
HOWEVER, DIFFER
CONSIDERABLY
FROM THE ABOVE
ACCOUNT. FOR ONE
THING, IT WAS NOT
SIMPLY ELVEN
ADVENTURERS WHO
RECOVERED THE
LOST TREASURE,
BUT HEROES OF
MANY RACES
WORKING
TOGETHER.
—THOM EDRULL

Hearing Takaris' words, Queen Alachia understood what he and the elven heroes had done. So moved was she by this knowledge that she forgot her anger and forgave Takaris his disobedience. The Everliving Flower now resides within the Queen's Palace, and it is said that its magic has begun to slowly heal the wounds of Blood Wood.

WHERE THE ELVES OF BARSAIVE DWELL

In the years since the Scourge, the elves of Barsaive have come out of their kaers to dwell in all manner of cities, towns, and villages, often alongside other races. As with most of the Name-givers, the Scourge taught the elves the value of living amid neighbors of all races. Though purely elven settlements do exist, they are much less common than they were in my childhood days. Of all the changes wrought by the Scourge, the mingling of the races is one of the few to bring good to Barsaive.

As a child, I did not understand why people of other races were not welcome in our village. I understood only that my elders seemed not to like them. The coming of the Horrors at first made people even more suspicious of the stranger. I was told not to trust others, because a stranger might carry a Horror's influence with him. Over time, as the great labor of building the kaers took more time and resources than any of our villages could muster, our village leaders were forced by circumstance to accept the aid of other races in nearby settlements and to aid them in turn. By the time of the sealing of the shelters, we had learned to trust the neighbors who had helped us, and we welcomed them into our kaers in the hope that greater numbers might aid in keeping the Horrors from destroying us.

Though the building of the kaers sowed the seeds of unity between the races, the dwarfs' Book of Tomorrow brought those seeds to full flower. All Barsaivians, regardless of race or realm, knew and shared its words and endured the Scourge by embracing the book's ideals. When it came time to re-enter the world, the varied races of Barsaive shared a true common ground.

Once we re-emerged into the world, the need to survive and to rebuild our beloved, ravaged land brought Barsaive's people together again. The return of the Therans both tested and strengthened our fragile, new-found unity. Led by the dwarfs of Throal, who had shown us the path to a united land, Barsaive's many races joined to throw off the Theran yoke and drive our hated, former overlords back to a tiny corner of southeast Barsaive. Had we remained diverse nations separated by mistrust, the Therans might have easily reclaimed Barsaive for their own.

Of course, there remain differences among the Name-giver races, and so there should. Unity does not mean uniformity, and there is no reason why an elf should live as an obsidiman does (or vice versa). The great good of our unity is the fact that the Name-givers of Barsaive can live in harmony no matter what our differences of custom, because we have learned not to see those differences as things that must divide us. In the spirit of this new unity, many elves have chosen to live among other races in towns, cities, and villages across the land. And those elven settlements that still exist work and live in peace with villages inhabited by other Name-giver races.

OF ELVEN SETTLEMENTS

Most purely elven settlements in Barsaive are found within its forests and jungles. Elves regard such places as the truest avatars of nature, and so prefer to live within them. Most elves use elemental magic to create their villages, many of which blend so well with their natural surroundings that one can walk into the center of an elven village without seeing it.

Those elves who wish to live away from other Name-givers value their privacy and guard it well. Every elven settlement that I have ever heard of posts sentries at its borders, almost always adepts of the beastmaster, scout, thief, or warrior Disciplines. In some realms, the elven adepts who serve as sentries follow a Discipline known only to elves, that of the woodsman or huntsman. This esoteric Discipline teaches union with nature and all the world's plants and animals. Whatever the Discipline followed by these sentries, they always know precisely who or what may be approaching their village. Rather than harm such unexpected travelers, the sentries send word to the village leaders, who then decide how to deal with the outsiders. In a few sad cases, however, a settlement's desire for privacy is so strong that the sentries attack and drive off intruders on sight.

Many elven settlements rival some of Barsaive's larger cities in size and are far more beautiful. Almost one in four true elves lives in these settlements. Though few in number, these elven cities play a vital role in the spiritual survival of the

elven people. For though many of us choose to live in towns, villages and cities inhabited by other Name-givers, we all retain our link to nature and value our brethren who live within nature's heart. These elves, who prefer the company of an oak tree to an ork cavalryman or a blossoming flower to a human troubadour, will most surely preserve true elven culture against the ravages of time and the warped ways of Blood Wood. If the Universe truly favors the elves, the woodland settlements may even restore elven arts and traditions to their former glory.

These elven cities also serve another important purpose in elven life by providing a site for rituals of birth, Naming, coming of age, marriage, and death. (I have spoken of these rituals earlier in my text, in the section entitled *Of Elven Rituals*.) Holding these sacred rituals in the elven settlements serves to link the elves of these villages with their kindred who live among the other races of Barsaive. Most elven families have ties with one or more woodland settlements and on special occasions visit their kin and join in elven rituals and festivities.

This practice of holding our most significant rituals and festivals only among our elven kin in the forests often leads others to think us secretive and aloof. Though it is true that we hold our traditions sacred and secret, I ask what race does not hide something of itself from those who are not of its blood? Surely it is our right, to preserve the history and traditions of our race as we see fit. Indeed, the Corruption of the Elven Court has made that need more urgent. Without the Court to act as the protector of elven culture and tradition, every elf must take this duty upon himself.

OF ELVES AND OTHER NAME-GIVERS

As is true of many other Name-giver races, elves as a race tend to share certain attitudes toward our fellow Name-givers. Sadly, the Corruption has led many races to mistrust elves, and this unwarranted suspicion has in turn affected the elven view of other races. Though we still desire to live in harmony with all Name-givers, it has become increasingly difficult to maintain tolerance in the face of distrust.

Many Barsaivians unfortunately see all elves as blood elves, and believe that we share the blood elves' corruption even though our bodies have no thorns. Unfortunately, too many outsiders fail to understand that most true elves have as little love as they do for the elves of Blood Wood, kindred or no. Blood Wood is a scar not only upon the world, but upon the soul of the elven people, and we more than any feel the pain of it.

For our part, I admit that we elves often do too little to change others' minds. We remain reserved and silent, even though we know that others mistake our quietness for arrogance. Perhaps we should open our hearts more, but we find it difficult to do so. After all, how can we truly share our spirits with those who do not understand us? And if they do not understand, is it not better to keep silent than to force our beliefs and ideas down others' throats?

The dwarfs tend to show the greatest distrust toward the elven people. Though the elves value the dwarfs' contribution toward freeing Barsaive from Theran domination, many of my people believe that the dwarfs' practical view of the world has left them bereft of spirit. As for humans, too many of them adopt the kind of arrogance toward others that we elves are said to have. I myself have made many human friends throughout my long life, but many more humans that I have met dismissed my worth at the first sight of my pointed ears. One of my friends, the human scholar Kallarian of Jerris, believes that his race pretends to belittle others in order to feel worthy of life themselves. If so, I can only feel sorry for them; to be unsure of your own worth is a tragedy, one that I know from personal experience.

I think it odd that
the race that
shares blood
with the denizens
of blood wood
can call any
other race
barbaric.
—Karoar, ork
troubadour

About such primitive races as orks and trolls, I can say little. Elves have so little in common with these young, often brutish peoples that friendships between us are difficult to foster and maintain. I do not, however, condemn their primitive natures as some of my brethren might. Orks and trolls are what they are, and it is to be hoped that in time they will outgrow the more barbaric of their ways.

The solemn obsidimen seem to share a depth of spirituality with elves, as well as the love of the natural world that shapes our very souls. More than any other race, the obsidimen understand how the Corruption of the Elven Court affected us, and they empathize with our loss. Some elves see their compassion as pity and therefore angrily reject it, but most of my brethren appreciate the sympathy that the obsidimen feel for our plight. Alone of all the Name-giver races, the obsidimen seem to understand the pain of losing a people's soul.

The t'skrang also share our spiritual nature, though their spiritual depth takes a different form than that of the elves. The t'skrang ideal of *haropas* resembles the state of balance, harmony, and power that all elves strive for, but where the t'skrang seem to embrace physical courage and even recklessness as a means of developing the soul, elves regard such physical challenges as merely the first, brief step on the five Paths that form the Wheel of Life.

Windlings share both appearance and a love of nature with elves, as well as the need to live a life of feeling. To the eyes of many Name-givers, windlings resemble tiny, winged elves. Indeed, so much do they resemble us that some scholars insist we are kin. For myself, I do not believe it, and would advise others not to make such comparisons aloud. Most elves find such speculations insulting; windlings are certainly an admirable race, but they are not elf-kin. To be elven is to see and hear and know certain things kept hidden from the hearts and minds of others, and the often-flighty windlings have not the depth to share such perceptions. It is possible, however, that they may one day develop something like it. Their reverence for nature and affinity for elven company certainly bode well

Both windlings and elves are capable of deep feeling, but where windlings exhibit a love of everything in life, we elves are selective about the object of our devotions. Also, unlike a windling, an elf does not lose interest and transfer his loyalties to some other thing or person or place or way of being. The devotion of an elf knows no bounds. All else becomes of lesser importance. Few other Name-giver races understand how much an elf's loyalty can consume him. Even windlings feel a mere shadow of elven devotion to a cause. They, like other Name-givers, often mistakenly judge us aloof and arrogant. In truth, most elves feel anything but aloof toward windlings; we enjoy their company. Because they share so much with us, albeit in faint glimmerings of understanding, many elves regard windlings as one might a delightful child.

OF TRUE ELVES AND BLOOD ELVES

Whether we will or no, the ties of kinship still exist between the true elves of the world and our tainted brethren of Blood Wood. Because of these ties, no elf of Barsaive—or of any realm—can ever put the awful reality of Blood Wood from his thoughts. The wood and its denizens are a blight on our world, for which all elves must bear some part of the burden. However much we untainted ones may wish to deny it, Queen Alachia was as much our queen as the ruler of the blood elves. It was our queen who chose to refuse the Therans' demands, who chose the soul-destroying Ritual of Thorns, and who has since embraced the dreadful thing that she and her folk have become. And though we true elves no longer heed her edicts, in a sense Queen Alachia still belongs to us.

We feel these unwanted ties of kin even more strongly through the judgment of others. Most of the world still looks to the Elven Court to judge what elves are, and far too many condemn us all as soulless. Far too many make no distinction between the elf who bears thorns and the elf who does not. We cannot escape the Elven Court, despite our efforts to divorce ourselves from it.

The truly tragic and frightening consequence of Alachia's terrible choice becomes clear when one considers the way in which the blood elves regard their purer kindred. Where we see them as the embodiment of corruption, they see us as unenlightened. Their souls have become so steeped in blood and pain that they have embraced their dreadful transformation as enlightenment. They celebrate it! Many true elves fear that the blood elves will someday act on their belief that they alone know the truth and will attempt to force us to adopt their ways. Such a catastrophe is one that any true elf would give his very life to prevent.

LIANDRA HAS RAISED A DISQUIETING POSSIBILITY. WILL THE BLOOD ELVES ACT TO SUBVERT THEIR BRETHREN, OR IS LIANDRA SIMPLY VOICING HIS WORST FEARS? UNFORTUNATELY, EVEN I COULD NOT SAFELY ASK THE ELVES OF BLOOD WOOD THIS QUESTION.
—KARON FOLL

AN ESSAY ON HUMANS

Humans are perhaps the most diverse and fascinating of all the Name-givers. Indeed, we found almost twice as much information on humans as on any other Name-giver race during the compilation of Volume III of this work. The following excerpt from this volume paints a fascinating picture of the unique nature that has made this peculiar race a favorite topic of study for Barsaivian scholars.
Of the multitude of documents we obtained that discuss humans, I thought this essay by Kallarian of Jerris especially well-suited for this anthology. Though the author writes from a human's view of the world, his vision seems largely unclouded by the distorting lens of racial pride, and his words honestly explore the human race's true nature.
—Presented for the edification of the reader by Thom Edrull, Archivist and Scribe of the Hall of Records, 1506 TH

ON BEING A HUMAN IN BARSAIVE

Of all the Name-giver races, the human race provokes the greatest number of different, often hastily formed opinions from Barsaive's other Name-givers. Elves think us crude. Dwarfs, obsidimen, trolls and orks think us fragile. The lizardlike t'skrang and ethereal windlings call humans slow-moving and dimwitted. Yet in my fifty years of wandering through our ravaged land, I have found no race more diverse, more colorful, or more dangerous of all that walk, fly, or slither across the earth than the Name-giver race called man.

My name is Kallarian, and some call me a sage. Once I lived in a kaer in the Scol Mountains. Now I pass my twilight days in Jerris, in the long shadow cast by our uninvited Theran guardians. I dedicate this work to those who come after me. May they learn from it what it was to be a human in Barsaive in the aftermath of the Scourge.

ON THE COMMON BEGINNING OF ALL NAME-GIVERS

Long before elf ears grew into points or the flesh of obsidimen hardened into stone, all sentient creatures that walked the earth were human. To the many who consider such an idea foul heresy, hear me out before you tear this page from the book. I have visited the libraries of the ancient realm of Landis and discovered the startling truth in the records. The archives of Landis tell us that all Name-giving races we know of were born of magic acting upon the human bloodline. It is the magical energies of the world that have created and that preserve elves, dwarfs, obsidimen, trolls, orks, windlings, and even t'skrang. Without magic, all Name-givers would swiftly return to their common, human form.

I believe that the tendency to become another race lies dormant within many humans, and these tendencies manifest when the tide of magic rises high in our world. I do not pretend to understand why this is so, but I believe that it explains human versatility and adaptability in comparison with other Name-givers. As for how it began, the Passions that inhabit our world may hold the key to the mystery.

Many sages believe that the beings we call the Passions once formed a single entity. In many things, the whole is greater than the sum of its parts, but not so the Passions. According to several ancient texts written by human scholars, this original, single being was far from omnipotent and found the many tasks that faced it overwhelming. To better attend to the needs of the mortal world that it loved, the being sundered itself into many parts. It became the thirteen Passions known in Barsaive, and each Passion devoted itself to a particular task or realm of influence.

I THINK NOT! AS AN ELVEN TRADER, I FIND THE VERY SUGGESTION THAT MY PEOPLE EVOLVED FROM MERE HUMANS ABSURD! WE ELVES HAVE NOTHING IN COMMON WITH SUCH CRUDE AND DISHONORABLE FOLK! I PROTEST THIS DISGRACEFUL, HUMAN SLANDER AGAINST OUR NOBLE RACE!
—GRIMMAS, MERCHANT OF IOPOS

At the same time that the separate Passions came into existence—perhaps because of this cosmic sundering—the level of magic in our world rose significantly. Human mothers began giving birth to babes with pointed ears and long faces or stout bodies and dense body hair. Seeing some of these infants as evil—those that would have become orks and trolls—their human parents unfortunately slew them. But as these unusual births became more common, humankind began to accept its strange and wondrous children, and created many a tale to explain their conception. Within a generation, men and women who had lived their entire lives as humans began to transform. Human husbands and wives suddenly hardened into obsidimen or shrunk into windlings; friends and neighbors evolved into elves or mushroomed into huge orks and trolls. Each different race of Name-giver swiftly joined its kin and, as is the sad way of mortals, began to war against the others.

These wondrous and tragic events occurred before written history, so no one can say for certain who ended the Great Name-giver Wars. I have heard sages from every race claim that honor for their own. I cannot say who is right, but it hardly matters. The only truth that does matter is that someone had the wisdom to end the bloodshed, and that the prejudices that spawned such an insane conflict have thankfully faded from our psyches along with the very memory of race war.

KALLARIAN SEEMS TO HAVE ACCEPTED AS TRUE THE BELIEF THAT DEATH IS THE THIRTEENTH PASSION. FROM SUCH A FLAWED BEGINNING, I THINK IT BEST NOT TO PUT TOO MUCH FAITH INTO THE REST OF THIS DOCUMENT.
—JERRIV FORRIM, SCRIBE AND SCHOLAR OF THE LIBRARY OF THROAL

ON THE VERSATILE NATURE OF HUMANS

To those still inclined to reject the notion that all Name-givers share a common, human ancestry, I bid you consider the unmatched versatility of the human race. Of all the world's Name-givers, only humans can learn talents and skills widely disparate from their chosen Disciplines. The longer-lived elves, dwarfs, and other Name-givers, by contrast, can only learn certain kinds of magical and non-magical skills. I know a human swordmaster, for example, who can pick locks. An elven thief of my acquaintance, however, has labored in vain to learn the whirlwind maneuver for many years. Some scholars explain this so-called Law of Versatility by theorizing that our fellow Name-givers are finely tuned, but limited, extensions of humanity. Magical energy heightens the particular attributes

of a Name-giver race, but also limits the number of inborn abilities they possess. And even these heightened attributes often express themselves as racial abilities, such as the ability to see in the dark or meld into liferock. Because humans carry within them the potential to become other Name-givers, they also have an affinity for a wider range of abilities.

The idea that all Name-givers derive from human stock provides the best answer to the puzzle of human versatility. For just as humans are the progenitors of all the Name-givers, the human ability to wield magic in varied ways is the font from which all the Disciplines spring. Magical texts describe how the Disciplines as we know them grew more sharply defined over time, as the adepts following these paths focused on certain talents in preference over others. And so, just as the human bloodline holds within it the seeds of all the other races, human magic contains the potential for all Disciplines.

In a particularly interesting example of the Law of Versatility, humans demonstrate a greater ability to adapt to their surroundings than does any other Name-giver race. Humans live in most any climate, whereas the other races have marked affinities for specific surroundings. The t'skrang prefer the rivers and the hot, steamy swamps; dwarfs and trolls prefer mountains; and elves love the woodlands above all other places. Humans have no such affinity and feel as much at home by the shores of the Aras Sea as in the foothills of the Thunder Mountains. In where they live, as in all else, humans demonstrate a versatility shared by no other Name-giver race.

ON THE GENERAL NATURE AND WAYS OF HUMANS

Though humans vary as greatly as do the Horrors that ravaged our world, members of my race nevertheless share many common traits. Our appearance, our physical nature, many of our customs, and much of the way in which we view the world remain the same or similar in otherwise vastly different human cultures.

ON THE PHYSICAL NATURE OF HUMANS

In many ways, humans resemble the other Name-giver races. A heart beats within each human breast, humans have two arms and two legs, we see with eyes, hear with ears, smell with noses, and taste with tongues. The greatest difference between humans and other Name-givers is outward, in skin color and texture. Human skin is thin and frail compared to the thick, rubbery flesh of orks and trolls, and as thin as the finest paper compared to an obsidiman's rocky hide. Compared to the silky skin of the elves, however, frail human skin is pitted and rough.

From accounts written in the years before the Scourge, I have learned that the color of human skin varied much more

If this is an example of human scholarship at its best, it's a wonder they survived long enough to give the rest of us birth.
—Grimmas

Human versatility with magic more likely has to do with the way humans view the world than with any special place humans occupy among Name-givers. Magic is everywhere in the world and touches us all equally. It shows no prejudice with regard to where it bestows its powers. If the opposite were true, surely the Horrors would not possess such powerful magic—unless one is prepared to believe that the life-giving universe secretly desires to destroy its own creations.
—Derrat, wizard of Yistane

widely in ancient times than it does nowadays. The humans of the south had skin the color of bronze, and northern-dwellers had pale, pink skin that looked as if only thin, winter sunshine ever touched it. In the wake of our four centuries spent living beneath the earth, these once-bright skin colors have paled considerably. The bronze-skinned Dinganni have faded to the pale tan of unworked leather, and the deep ochre skin of the Vorst has faded to the wan yellow of weak sunlight.

Interestingly, the same humans that can so quickly distrust their fellow Name-givers because of differences in appearance do not regard a difference in skin color as significant. Humans from Throal may draw steel on fellow humans who serve the Therans, and vice versa, but for one man to distrust another solely because he was brown and the other was pale would invite ridicule from all who heard of it.

On the Nature and Roles of Men and Women

The human race is divided almost equally between male and female, with the balance weighted slightly toward the female side. Ancient records tell us of dominance by men over women or by women over men in different times and places, but just as the races have learned to live equably together, so too have the sexes. In most human communities, men and women both raise food, make and trade goods, heal the sick, head villages, hold public office, and serve in local militias with equal chances for advancement. Because in many towns and villages the women do more of the child-rearing, however, men in the militia slightly outnumber women. Often, I have found women wiser and more patient than my more brash, coarse gender, and so perhaps it is as well for human children that their mothers frequently have the raising as well as the bearing of them.

ON MARRIAGE AND CHILD REARING

Most humans choose a single mate, though they do not always stay with their first choice. Few communities require anything more than a formal declaration of separation to members of a married couple's families if a husband or wife wishes to leave a marriage. After one partner or another has made such a declaration, most couples split their belongings and part ways. The only exception to this customary simplicity occurs in the case of a political marriage, a custom practiced almost exclusively among inhabitants of Barsaive's larger cities. Though most of these marriages take place and can be dissolved with the mutual consent of the married couple, they and their families must spend considerable time negotiating the circumstances of the split so that innocent lives are not adversely affected.

Though many older villages and settlements require formal ceremonies and a written record to recognize a marriage, less well-established towns and nomadic tribes regard any couple who have lived together for at least three or four years as married. Whether or not a marriage is formalized, the birth of a child usually engraves the relationship in stone.

Human women carry their unborn children for nine months, and most women only give birth to one child at a time. Cases of twin births occur on occasion, and I have read of women who carried three or four babes at once. Such multiple births, however, are highly unusual. In the best circumstances, human children are sheltered until they reach an age between their fourteenth and sixteenth years. At that time, they are considered of age and must make a contribution to the family welfare. In most cases, a newly grown son or daughter helps a parent in his or her business; on occasion, a young adult may take up arms in the local militia.

On Naming Rituals

Soon after birth, each human child receives from his parents a Name that remains with him for the rest of his life. Because this name is his first possession and everyone who knows him in childhood calls him by it, it contains great power. Some humans earn other names throughout their lifetimes, but only with the greatest of heroes or the worst of villains are these names as powerful as those they were born with.

ONE CHILD AT A TIME THEY MAY HAVE, BUT THEY NEVER STOP HAVING THEM! THESE HUMAN WOMEN CONSTANTLY STAY PREGNANT! THEIR SCREAMING WHELPS DRIP OFF THEIR ARMS LIKE A VILE FUNGUS, ALWAYS WHINING FOR TOYS AND TREATS. ELVEN WOMEN RARELY BEAR MORE THAN ONE CHILD IN A LIFETIME. WE HAVE TIME TO TEACH OUR CHILDREN DISCIPLINE AND RESPECT!
—GRIMMAS

I HAVE VISITED MANY ELVEN SETTLEMENTS, AND FIND FEW THINGS MORE OBNOXIOUS THAN SPOILED, SELF-INDULGENT ELF-BRATS. THEY BELIEVE ALL ADULTS EXIST TO SERVE THEIR WHIMS, OR TO SERVE AS THE BUTT OF THEIR OFTEN DANGEROUS PRANKS. I'LL TAKE A HUMAN "SCREAMING WHELP" ANY TIME, THANK YOU!
—STAUNCHUS FOSWORTH, MERCHANT OF THROAL

though the leg-
end is more than
likely untrue,
many popula-
tions still per-
form the ritual.
they feel it can-
not hurt.
—derrat

defensive?
pathetic! this
kallarian is no
better than any
other human,
explaining every-
thing from the
human point of
view. first he
decides that we
are all their
descendants,
then blames the
passions for his
race's own fail-
ure to behave in a
civilized manner!
—grimmas

civilized, indeed!
it may interest
readers to know
that grimmas has
spent years
studying
humans—so that
he might trick
them into paying
his exorbitant
prices. friend
grimmas owns
the largest black
market in
barsaive, selling
"elven" crafts,
weapons, and tal-
ismans for many
times their true
value.
—staunchus

All human cultures and nations have a Naming ceremony of some kind, though the details vary from one settlement to the next. One tradition found throughout Barsaive is the marking of the infant with the symbol of a Passion, usually Garlen. A parent or other leader of the rite then pours pure water over the babe's marked forehead or abdomen until the symbol washes off. Legend has it that the Passion's sigil actually passes through the infant's skin and remains with her for the rest of her life, bestowing some of the Passion's virtues on the child.

ON HUMAN SPIRITUAL AND OTHER BELIEFS

Like every other Name-giver race in Barsaive, humans hold certain beliefs, both about matters spiritual and about themselves. The belief we hold about ourselves that most greatly affects us is a certain insecurity about our place in the world, for which many a human feels he must compensate. In many ways, humans seem to spend their lives testing themselves, proving themselves. I theorize that this need to test and triumph comes from a tendency to see ourselves, albeit unwillingly, as a less-advantaged race. Orks and trolls are stronger than we, dwarfs and obsidimen able to endure more, elves and windlings swifter, and t'skrang fiercer warriors. But what we humans lack in brawn and speed, we make up for through sheer force of will. A human tries harder, fights longer, and gives his life more readily than any other Name-giver, at least when speaking in general. Many humans see such behavior as noble, even if it kills them; they feel a need to best those around them regardless of any natural handicaps they possess.

To my mind, this sense of insecurity and need to prove our usefulness springs from our subconscious knowledge that we are the wellspring of all Name-giver races. We wonder, I think, why the Universe chose not to transform us into a more powerful or exotic race. We are unfortunately prone to see ourselves as ordinary, and I believe that unconscious jealousy or even fear makes many humans naturally defensive.

Humans also tend to be far more wary of others than the realities of life warrant. Though many people put this sense of inadequacy down to the physical disadvantages humans have with regard to other races, I believe that the size of Barsaive's human population also plays a role. Though humans live in almost every place in Barsaive and outnumber such fellow Name-givers as elves, windlings, trolls, t'skrang, and obsidimen, humans are far fewer than dwarfs and orks. Dwarfs, in fact, make up

nearly a third of Barsaive's people, while humans measure only half that number. This sense of being outnumbered by the dwarfs, who play such a prominent role in Barsaivian life, and the orks, whose sheer physical power often outmatches a human's, do much to explain my race's unwarranted fears.

On the Desire to Control Our Destiny

One of the strongest human traits, for good or ill, is our desire to manipulate those around us. Sometimes this desire can make a man do great good for others. If the desire for power leads a man to seek office, as mayor of a hamlet, perhaps, the man must perform well and keep the trust of those he leads in order to stay in office. Such a man assumes power over others, but must respect the wishes of his people to sustain it. If he acts with honor and compassion, he can easily keep what he has gained.

On the other side of the coin, if a man cannot easily attain the power he desires, he often turns to violence or corruption. A man might attain office not by earning the respect of those he wishes to govern, but by bribing a certain number of his fellows to impose his will on every citizen, or by making false promises. Once in office, such a man fails to keep his promises, and the people protest against his rule. To stay in power, the ruler spends money meant for the public good to hire ruffians, so that he may keep dissenters quiet. Such a response only makes the people despise him more, and so he raises taxes in order to hire more minions. This act earns him even more enmity, and this pattern continues until the ruler either steps down or is overthrown. The sad fact that such things happen often among humans indicates the strength of our desire for power and superiority over our fellows. Though members of other races than humans also crave power, more humans desire it more often than does any other race as a whole.

On the Human View of Death

In perhaps the greatest irony of human beliefs about death, we humans seem to respect life only after it has ended. If Death truly exists as an entity, rather than simply as a fact of mortal life, humans excel at feeding its ravenous appetite. Wars over the boundaries of kingdoms, control of orichalcum, and petty local politics consume our youths by the thousands. Too often, no sooner does one conflict end than another looms on the horizon.

Every group of humans that I have encountered enacts a ceremony for the dead, not surprising for a race so prone to settling a dispute by killing the enemy. Some incinerate their dead in elemental fire, others bury them in earth, and still others give them over to the blue depths of the sea. In most mourning ceremonies, a mate, child, or friend speaks of the dead person's accomplishments, and all who have attended the ceremony add their own words of farewell. The simplicity of the death ceremony belies the emotional weight of it. Unlike such fatalistic races as elves, who regard death as a doorway to a higher plane of existence, humans see death as a tragic event. Human death ceremonies allow the bereaved a final testament to a loved one's life and endeavors, and so help them to overcome the pain of their loss.

On Human Belief in the Passions

As do other Name-givers, humans hold the Passions dear in their minds and hearts. But where other races often revere one or a few of the Passions over the rest, most humans hold all twelve (or thirteen) Passions in equal esteem. I believe that this equal reverence, like many other aspects of being human, springs from the human race's unique versatility. It is yet another way in which we humans can see and reach beyond the bounds that often restrict other Name-givers.

Of course, not all humans revere all the Passions. Indeed, many of the cults dedicated to the Mad Passions owe their beginnings to humans swayed by the ideals and emotions embodied only by those Passions. Sadly, many of these cults and other secret societies stem from the actions of humans wishing to further their own ends at any cost. The creation of destructive cults and secret societies are among the worst manifestations of my race's otherwise noble desire to prove themselves worthy of the world.

On Human Crafts and the Need for Usefulness

The human need to be worthy, to be of use, shapes the way we see the world and determines the nature of our crafts. Unlike many Name-givers much enamored of outward show, humans build and create objects to fulfill a purpose, rather than to impress the eye. A human swordsmith may forge a blade that looks plain and drab to dwarf or elven eyes, but such a blade is as durable and deadly as any made in Barsaive. Indeed, many human craftsmen eschew art altogether in the making of swords, armor, pottery, and suchlike, regarding decoration of such objects as a frill. If you want art, a human may

WINDLINGS RARELY
MAKE UP A SIGNIF-
ICANT NUMBER OF
A SETTLEMENT'S
POPULATION
BECAUSE MOST
WINDLINGS PREFER
TO LIVE IN
BARSAIVE'S
FORESTS AND JUN-
GLES. INTERESTED
READERS SHOULD
CONSULT VOLUME
VIII OF THIS WORK,
DEDICATED
TO WINDLINGS.
—THOM EDRULL

say, then look for it in a painting or a sculpture. If an item has any other function than to please the eye, art has no place in it.

Of course, many buyers mistake ornamentation for worth, and believe human-made wares of lesser quality than similar items crafted by members of other races. As is true of many things in this world, appearance belies reality. Human-crafted items are often equal to, or even better than, more decorative items available throughout Barsaive.

ON THE PLACES WHERE HUMANS DWELL

More than half of the humans of Barsaive dwell in small towns, villages, or such large cities as Travar and Iopos. The rest live in small enclaves of several families each, settlements really too small to be called villages. No matter the size of their community, many humans live with neighbors of all races—orks, dwarfs, trolls, elves, and t'skrang. A few human towns also boast windlings and obsidi-men among their number, though these unusual races are so few in number that few villages or towns can claim a substantial population of either. Aside from the human cultural enclaves that I describe later on in this essay, "human" settlements (in the sense of purely human communities) are quite rare.

Many types of humans live throughout Barsaive, and their ways are often significantly shaped by the world around them. Humans who live in the wildest and most dangerous places tend to be as savage as the lands in which they dwell, while those nearer cities and towns tend toward more so-called "civilized behav-ior." I say so-called because the civilized humans are not necessarily better or kinder than their more isolated brethren. In fact, many city dwellers show far more cruel and cunning in their dealings than humans native to the wild lands. Certain races, such as elves, regard the ability to scheme as a hallmark of sophistication, and many humans share this view. I am not so sure. I believe that a city-dweller's cunning rests on the simple fact that in a "civilized" setting, he has little to test himself against save his fellow Name-givers.

ON HUMAN ARCHITECTURE

I HAVE TRAVELED
WITH A HUMAN
COMPANION FOR
MORE THAN THREE
YEARS NOW, AND I
CANNOT IMAGINE A
MORE TRUSTWOR-
THY FELLOW—TO
HIS FRIENDS, AT
LEAST. I HAVE SEEN
THIS CLEVER ROGUE
SWINDLE MANY A
MERCHANT OUT OF
HIS GOODS, SELLING
THE SAME ITEMS TO
OTHERS FOR TWICE
THE PRICE. YET IF
WE BOTH ENDED UP
IN THE DESERT WITH
ONLY A CUP OF
WATER BETWEEN
US, I BELIEVE HE
WOULD LET ME
QUENCH MY THIRST
BEFORE HE DIED.
—VIRX, WINDLING
TROUBADOUR

Human architecture varies as greatly as every other aspect of human culture. In Theran lands, humans build great buildings adorned with carved pillars and mag-nificent sculptures, while human dwellings and businesses in Throal are built of plain stone along practical, almost box-like lines. Because many humans in Throal wish to make a clear distinction between their homes and places of business, the roofs of dwellings are often arched, while those of businesses are flat.

Village dwellings vary greatly, according to the materials available nearby. Along the Serpent River, humans build their homes of wood from the abundant trees, raising them up on tall timbers that reach well above the river's flood line. Humans dwelling in the Thunder or Delaris mountains often build homes on plateaus, or even carve cave-houses into the sides of cliff faces.

Many humans reject outward show in their dwellings, preferring to attract attention by their dwellings' contents. Most humans reserve

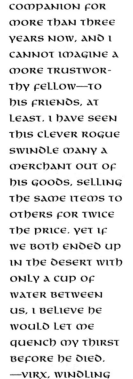

things of beauty and luxury for the insides of their homes. A human only invites those he considers friends into his home, and therefore displays his luxuries only to those who find him worthy without them. In extreme cases, a crumbling and ill-repaired exterior may hide a luxurious, even decadent interior.

ON DIVERSE AND UNIQUE HUMAN CULTURES

In our own time, human men and women are identified by their homeland rather than by the bloodline to which they belong. Humans from Throal are Throalic and those who hail from Thera are Therans, no matter whether they have Dinganni, Vorst, Galeb, or other blood running through their veins. According to the records of Landis, however, many distinct human peoples existed before the Scourge. Though the crossbreeding between these peoples in the kaers has largely abolished pure bloodlines, several culturally distinct peoples still remain in Barsaive. Some are remnants of ancient civilizations, and others are new peoples brought into being by the centuries spent in the kaers.

In order to understand the origins of these cultures, one must first understand the nature of kaer society and how it formed. When the Therans gave the Rites of Protection and Passage to the various kingdoms of Barsaive, small villages and hamlets within those principalities often banded together to build a single kaer. This melding of villages led to intermarriage between members of different human bloodlines, and so in these kaers the people either blended into new cultures, or retained the cultural characteristics of the dominant bloodline but lost such physical markers as skin color or eye shape. Other human settlements, such as large cities or isolated villages, built their own kaers, and their bloodlines and cultures remained largely unchanged by outside influences.

The following six populations that emerged from the kaers exemplify both the blended and the untouched human bloodlines, all influenced by the four centuries that the Name-givers spent buried alive.

OF THE CATHAN PEOPLE

The Cathan live in the Servos Jungle and take their name from the Cathan word for jungle, *c'athe*. Significantly smaller than most humans, Cathan males stand a mere five feet tall, females perhaps five feet and three inches. Their olive skins are extraordinarily tough, and many scholars believe that this trait came from countless generations of living half naked in a jungle filled with thick underbrush. Their hair is a mottled brown, and little of it grows on their sinewy bodies. A primitive race of hunters and gatherers, the Cathan are perhaps the only known people to have survived the Scourge without Theran aid. Without advice from Thera, Throal, or any of the other "civilized" nations of the world, the Cathan built kaers in the maze of natural caves under the floor of the Servos Jungle. When the Horrors descended on Barsaive, the Cathan fled to their underground havens, and their shamans worked powerful magic to seal the cave entrances. Upon the ending of the Scourge, the Cathan returned to the surface and took up their lives anew as if the intervening four centuries of hiding had never happened.

How the Scourge Touched the Cathan

As they did in ancient days, the Cathan tribes roam the Servos Jungle in small bands of forty to one hundred. The able spend most of the day gathering roots and berries, hunting when they can. The rest watch after the children, preserve meat and grains for storage, repair shelters, and perform other, similar tasks. Though

the Cathan have attempted to rebuild their ancient ways, the years of the Scourge did not leave them unscathed. One of their shamans, a woman named Mathari, spoke of the Scourge to me one night, and her words convey the dreadfulness of the hiding as my own cannot. (Note that in the following excerpt, the Cathan word *gitta* means "Horrors," and the word *tulan* refers to a wizard.)

"We went beneath the earth when the *gitta* came. They ate at the jungle like locusts; we found little left when we awoke to true life again. Many times during our little death, the *gitta* broke through the very earth to get at us. Our warriors fought the creatures off long enough for the *tulan* to close the wound in the rock, but many brave soldiers died. Once, the *gitta* possessed many of our *tulan*. Our wise men did not know of this evil for many years and so could not rid us of them by tearing out their hearts."

The Cathan's dark years beneath the earth served to intensify a way of thinking already made necessary by the everyday savagery of life in the Servos Jungle. Among the Cathan, every action and every decision springs from the need for each individual to survive. A Cathan captured by an enemy tells them anything they ask about his camp, his friends, even his own family if he believes it will preserve his own life, and the people he has betrayed expect no less of him. Many others find such a world view incomprehensible at best, appalling at worst. Before judging them too harshly, however, I would ask the reader to consider the reality of Cathan life.

The everyday fight for survival is so harsh for the Cathan that any act short of killing each other to ensure that survival is acceptable and even approved among them. If a Cathan tricks another out of his last fruit, the first Cathan has proven his mental superiority. The loser of the fruit has been foolish, and so deserves whatever fate awaits him. Only by testing themselves constantly in this way can the Cathan prove their ability to withstand the jungle's dangers.

The Cathan also exhibit an overwhelming, innate curiosity that can sometimes overcome the survival instinct in even the wisest of them. Up to a point, of course, their curiosity helps them to survive, because anything they learn may be of use. The Cathan see wonder in all things and wish to understand every new thing that they see. When I visited a Cathan village in the course of writing this essay, I held them in thrall for hours by the simple act of writing these words. They watched in fascination as the ink from my quill slowly leaked onto the paper, and asked why I was tattooing these pages. I told them that my "tattoos" would tell others all about the Cathan, information which provoked a long and animated discussion among them. The tribe I visited told me of what one might call "educated" Cathan, men and women who have left the tribe to explore the world outside the Servos Jungle. I cannot but wonder what will happen when these clever people discover the vices of their brother humans, and I greatly fear that their curiosity in this regard may spell the end of their simple society.

During the rest of my visit, the Cathan told me of all the wonders of their forest and related several of their ancient myths. I have recorded one of them below, which I believe reveals something of Cathan ways of thinking. The Cathan have a collection of stories about a wise youth named Duzami and a cantankerous old man known only as the Screaming Elder. I surmise that Duzami is a symbol of their survival instinct, while the Screaming Elder embodies those traits they regard as vices. In this particular tale, the fault is failure to mind one's own business.

The Tale of Duzami and the Great Race

One day, the village held a great race. All the young men and women competed, and many of the people made bets on the runners they believed would win. The race was very close, and Duzami, the village's swiftest runner, ran ahead of only one other man. When Duzami passed the finishing tree that many others had touched before him, he did not seem winded, nor was there the sheen of sweat on his skin. The Screaming Elder walked up to Duzami and cursed him, for he had bet all of his food that Duzami would win. But Duzami only shrugged at the Screaming Elder and walked away.

That night, a terrible *gitta* rampaged through the jungle. Every Cathan in the village fled from the thing, including Duzami and the Screaming Elder. As Duzami ran, he saw that the Screaming Elder was right behind him, shouting angrily at him as always.

"Why do you not run faster, Duzami?" the Elder shouted. "The *gitta* is right behind us!"

Duzami did not speak, but kept up his steady pace. When he heard the *gitta* catch the Screaming Elder, Duzami yelled over his shoulder, "You do not have to be first to win the race. You must only outrun one man."

Too late, the Screaming Elder recognized Duzami's wisdom as the *gitta* ate him.

On Cathan Spiritual Beliefs

The Cathan have their own religion, serving a spirit they call the God of the Tree. I believe that the Cathan "god" is the Passion Jaspree, who sees the Cathan as caretakers of the Servos Jungle and commands them to protect it from fire and other harm. Because the Cathan see this duty as part of their own survival, they willingly fulfill Jaspree's commands. In etchings that I have seen, made by Cathan holy men, Jaspree takes the form of a giant tree. A knothole serves as his mouth, mighty branches are his arms, and his eyes are huge, yellow slits in the trunk, well above the tallest man's head.

A Few Interesting Aspects of Cathan Culture

The Cathan are both curious and friendly, as long as friendship does not imperil survival. Though they hunt well, they have little talent for warfare, and the heroes in many of their campfire tales run from threats or slay enemies from ambush. Perhaps predictably, the Cathan see killing from ambush not as murder, but as an efficient use of resources to protect their tribes from danger. To make such killing easier, the Cathan tattoo their olive skins with elaborate patterns in white pigment; this patterning helps them blend with the light-dappled leaves of the underbrush.

A young Cathan rarely goes anywhere without his bow, which he uses to bring down prey from high branches. The Scourge left the Cathan with one positive legacy that improved their hunting; because they spent their time underground almost entirely in the dark, many of the last few generations of Cathan have been born with the ability to see in very little light. To catch large fish and reptiles, Cathan warriors will often tie strands of giant spider webs to their arrows, using the lines to drag in the catch. I saw one Cathan kill an enormous, swimming reptile with a single shot; I suspect his arrow was poisoned, though I know not with what.

A DISCOURSE ON THE DINGANNI

The Dinganni travel the plains between Kratas and the Mist Swamps. They take their name from their word for a slow-running river, *d'inga*. When applied to themselves, the word "Dinganni" means "wanderer." Despite their relative poverty and the constant danger they face in their roamings, the Dinganni are one of the most hospitable and friendly peoples in Barsaive. A Dinganni always welcomes a stranger into his or her camp, offering food and water in exchange for news or campfire tales.

A tall people, the Dinganni also have large builds; indeed, they nearly match the bulk of orks. In temperament, the Dinganni tend to be quiet, friendly, and respectful. When angered, they often use their height to intimidate opponents, hoping to extract an apology for an offense without resorting to violence. Once weapons have been drawn and blood spilt, however, a Dinganni attacks without mercy. The Dinganni believe that to let an offender go free only encourages him to repeat the offense.

When not girded for hunting or war, the Dinganni wear soft, leather hides decorated with bone jewelry. Though primitive, their garb is anything but rough; indeed, I have seen no more finely worked leather even in the bazaars of Bartertown. The Dinganni offer excellent proof that primitive and simple do not mean savage; one has only to speak with them to see their intelligence and compassion.

On the Origins and Daily Life of the Tribe

The Dinganni revere freedom, and the life of the kaers suited them ill. At the end of the Scourge, they vowed never to live within walls again and have forsaken cities and villages ever since to live the life of wanderers. They have prospered since that day, and the Dinganni people now number more than a thousand.

The Dinganni tribe comprises seven or so wandering bands, each anywhere from seventy-five to two hundred in number. Through hard experience the Dinganni have learned that allowing any band to grow too large can devastate the land around them, and so if a band exceeds 200, some of its members leave to seek a new foraging ground. All bands are considered part of the tribe, and little enmity exists between them. They live in tents made of beautifully tanned hides lashed to stout sticks; during my stay with the tribe I weathered more than one storm in warmth and comfort beneath a tent-hide roof.

Though every Dinganni child learns to ride a horse soon after leaning to walk, only ten to twenty people in each band have steeds to ride. The horses belong to those riders with the greatest skill whose mounts also show an affinity for them. The Dinganni believe that their horses are near humans in intelligence and pay close attention to their preferences. A Dinganni rider can fire a bow and wield a spear from horseback, skills they use to hunt and to fight off any enemies foolish enough to attack them.

Reflecting the harsh realities of a nomad's often dangerous life, every adult Dinganni carries a longbow and a long knife, and even children as young as eight years carry small daggers. A privileged few carry metal blades, but the scarcity of metal in the Dinganni lands forces most to make do with knives of stone or bone. Having seen them use such blades to skin a jaguar, I can testify to their sharpness. Under no circumstances do the Dinganni draw weapons against each other.

On the Dinganni Code

The laws that comprise the brief Dinganni Code allow the members of the tribe to live in harmony with each other and the land. All must follow the code or be cast out of the tribe. The five laws of the Dinganni Code are as follows:

One will never cause harm to another member of the tribe.

One will never steal what belongs to another.

One will learn the ways of war, so that he may protect the tribe.

One will never kill the creatures of the air, for they are our kindred.

Death awaits him who betrays the tribe to enemies.

Though far shorter and simpler than any other text of law that these old eyes have read, the code of the Dinganni contains far more wisdom than the complicated laws of Throal.

The law against harming flying creatures springs less from a belief that such creatures are sacred than from the Dinganni tribe's love of freedom. Birds and other flyers, particularly the hunting hawk, are in a sense living symbols of the Dinganni people, and a tribesman would no more kill a bird than an ork scorcher would defame the standard of his warlord. The Dinganni design much of their armor with an avian motif, adding beaks to their helms and painting flying birds on their leather armor. On the rare occasions when they make war against others, many of them wear manes of brightly colored feathers. One of their favored weapons is inspired by the hunting hawk: the talon, a set of bone claws strapped to the wielder's forearm that extend far beyond the knuckles. The Dinganni are deadly proficient with this weapon; I saw one hunter use it to tear the spine from a full-grown swamp lizard.

Any violation of the precepts of the code leads to banishment or death, and no circumstances can soften these penalties. During my visit, I witnessed the trial of a youth accused of stealing my own carving knife! I use it only to skin small game and peel fruit and could easily have replaced it, but my words to that effect mattered not to the tribesmen. After the boy's banishment had been pronounced, even his parents turned their backs to him, deafening their ears to his pleas for their help. The oldest and wisest of the horsemen tossed a bag of dried meat and fruit, a bone knife, and a waterskin at the boy's feet, and from that moment no tribesman spoke to or even looked at him.

A WEAPON DESIGNED TO PRY FLESH FROM BONES! HOW UNSPEAKABLY VULGAR! IF HUMANS SPENT HALF AS MUCH TIME TRYING TO BETTER THEMSELVES AS THEY DO TRYING TO KILL EACH OTHER, THEY MIGHT YET ATTAIN A MODICUM OF CIVILIZATION—BUT I CANNOT BELIEVE IT WILL EVER HAPPEN!
—GRIMMAS

Though I shall never tell my Dinganni friends of this, the boy sought to slay me in revenge. I had left the tribe to return to Throal and sat camped beneath the open night sky, ready to feast on the dried meat and fruits that the tribe had given me. The boy crept up soundlessly behind me, but the bright moon cast his tall shadow on the earth as he closed for the kill. Forewarned, I struck first. It still saddens me that the carving knife the boy tried to steal wound up between his ribs.

ON THE STRANGE ORIGINS OF THE GALEB-KLEK

The Galeb-Klek are an interesting example of a new people created from a blending of distinct human bloodlines during the Scourge. According to tomes in Landis that date from before the Scourge, the ancient Galeb were a short, stout people with craggy faces and ruddy skin. The name Galeb means "boulder" in the tongue of Landis and refers to this people's short stature, stocky build, and rocklike strength.

The Klek differed greatly from the Galeb, being tall and lithe of build and tending toward pale hair, skin, and eyes. My mate, Shadras, is one of the few Klek of pure bloodline still living, according to the voluminous records of her family historian. Slightly taller than myself and extraordinarily agile, Shadras made her livelihood as a dancer in Iopos. She has had silver hair since the age of twenty, and her eyes are of a pale gold color much like a hawk's. The name Klek derives from the word *kahlek*, meaning "vine," and came to mean "dexterous" in the tongue of Landis. Though a few Galeb and Klek still exist as distinct bloodlines, most of the descendants of these peoples owe their heritage to both. Many scholars, myself included, regard the Galeb-Klek as a new people.

In the years before the Scourge, the kings of Landis determined the best sites for kaers within the kingdom and sent the people of Landis' villages and towns to build and live in them. Several large villages in the foothills of the Delaris Mountains were told to build a kaer nearby, that all these villages would share. Half of these villages were Galeb, the other half Klek.

Now the Galeb were a warlike people and had often coveted the beauty of the Klek as a greedy noble covets a valuable bauble. Many among these Galeb villages admired the Theran practice of slavery and took slaves from those villages that they defeated in war. Throughout the history of Landis, these Galeb villages had only refrained from making war against the Klek because the Galeb feared that their Klek neighbors would call upon their kin in the other parts of Landis to liberate them. Apart from desiring them for their beauty, the Galeb knew little of the Klek and did not know that violence was unheard-of among them.

The Scourge changed this uneasy balance of power, as it changed so much else in Barsaive. The Galeb, deprived of other foes to war against, took their Klek neighbors captive. The Klek, bewildered at this armed conquest and unable to respond in kind, yielded without a fight. The Galeb forced the Klek men to farm for them and carve chambers for them from the rock walls of the kaer, and the Galeb men forced the Klek women to bear them children. When the children of the two peoples came of age, the Galeb married them to each other to ensure a steady supply of slave labor for the kaer.

Now the first generation of Galeb-Klek, born to purely Klek mothers, were raised by them and learned from them in secret the arts of reading and writing. They taught these arts to their children, and each generation of Galeb-Klek passed on this forbidden knowledge to the next. Each generation also nursed within their hearts a desire for freedom, and for revenge against their oppressors. As the centuries of the Scourge passed, fewer and fewer pure Galeb or Klek were born, until the Galeb-Klek "slave race" far outnumbered their Galeb masters. Aided by the few remaining pure Klek, the Galeb-Klek rebelled a generation before the Scourge's ending, and emerged a free and sovereign people into the light of the new Barsaive.

On the Nature and Ways of the Free Galeb-Klek

Though caused by unfortunate circumstances, the melding of the Galeb and Klek bloodlines has had fortunate consequences for Barsaive. The unique characteristics of the Galeb and the Klek have combined to produce a people both dexterous and amazingly strong, with the lithe build of elves and the endurance of orks. The Galeb-Klek are somewhat taller than many other humans, but often by a mere few inches. They have retained the Galeb ruddy complexion, though their skin tone is a much paler shade than that of their Galeb forebears. Muscular and well-proportioned, the Galeb-Klek in many ways combine the best traits of their progenitors.

This fortunate blending carries over from their physical natures into Galeb-Klek minds and hearts. They have retained the patience, forbearance, and gentle nature of their Klek ancestors, but their Galeb blood and their awful history of enslavement have tempered their gentleness with an iron will to fight when necessary. After the Scourge ended, the Galeb-Klek dispersed throughout Barsaive and so have less in the way of a distinct culture than many peoples bound together by geography. But I have noted that many Galeb-Klek show a marked preference for the bright colors and loose tunics favored by the Klek, and they revere learning above all else. This strong, handsome, educated, freedom-loving people have provided more than a few of Barsaive's heroes in the brief generation since emerging from the kaers and may well continue to do so.

OF THE OUTLAW RIDERS OF THE SCORCHED PLAIN

Though the Riders of the Scorched Plain are as unique a people as any other of which I have written, I have included them in this treatise principally because they pose a certain danger to travelers in northern Barsaive. Needless to say, I myself spent no time among these people, but gleaned what I know of them from ancient records and modern-day tales.

In the years before the Scourge, this bandit band roamed the plains between Wyrm Wood and Lake Vors, waylaying travelers and relieving them of their goods. As the Scourge drew nearer and the first Horrors began to arrive in Barsaive, the roving bandits schemed to get the knowledge of how to build a kaer. Knowing that the Therans would never willingly offer their Rites of Protection and Passage to a band of outlaws, the cutthroats stole the plans through treachery and built their kaer in a maze of hidden caves by the shores of Lake Vors. To understand how the Riders accomplished their treachery, one must know the history of their king, Gerrik of the Mask.

The Tale of Gerrik of the Mask

Beginning in the last century before the Scourge, the Riders of the Scorched Plain concentrated their thieving (and occasional murdering) on trade caravans plying the routes into Blackcliff, a proud and rich city that lay on the edge of Lake Vors. The Riders had a knack for waylaying the most valuable cargo at the most opportune times, and the city's merchants were sorely distressed that Blackcliff's leader, Warden Garshin, seemed to have no luck in catching the Riders' mysterious leader.

Warden Garshin had served Blackcliff for more than fifteen years, and the people loved him well. Even the merchants, though disturbed by his inability to catch King Gerrik of the Mask and put an end to the Riders' depredations, granted that in all other things he was a just and able ruler. None in Blackcliff suspected the dreadful truth: Warden Garshin was none other than the bandit king. When leading his people on raids, Gerrik wore a mask to hide his face, and the Riders' raids brought them untold plunder because "Warden Garshin" told them which rich caravans to strike. Warden Garshin might well have continued his charade until his death, had not the Scourge demanded drastic action of him.

Gerrik loved his bandit followers and was determined to gain for them the safe haven of their own kaer. When a Theran emissary arrived in Blackcliff bearing the plans for building and magically warding a kaer, Gerrik murdered him in his sleep, then escaped with the plans to the bandit encampment in the wilderness. Taking his Riders with him, Gerrik fled into the Scol Mountains. In the foothills of those forbidding heights, the vagabonds built their kaer.

The remaining authorities in Blackcliff, meanwhile, sent a panicked message to Thera telling of their plight. They had already delayed too long in accepting the Empire's distasteful bargain, and the theft of the kaer plans proved their undoing. As the Horrors began to appear in force, the doomed citizens of Blackcliff tried everything they knew to protect themselves, to no avail. The Horrors fell on them like a black rain and devastated the city. These days, little remains of Blackcliff save for the following inscription on the keystone of the city's prison, that damns Gerrik of the Mask to the darkest of fates. The inscription is known as the Curse of Blackcliff.

The Warden let the foul creatures reign,
The Coward led the cursed into the hills,
The Scarlet Mask left us to our cruel fate,
But Garshin stays forever in dead Blackcliff.

Among residents of villages and settlements near Lake Vors, rumors persist that a wailing man wearing a tattered mask haunts the ruins of Blackcliff. A few believe that Gerrik still lives, close to five centuries after his disappearance into the Throal Mountains. Most believe that his spirit haunts the ruins, trapped there by the powerful curse of the innocents that he condemned to death.

Of the Riders Since the End of the Scourge

The depredations of the Horrors showed the Riders of the Scorched Plain the truly dreadful consequences of evil and destruction, and so the Riders of today rarely kill those they steal from. Their number has recently passed one thousand, of which perhaps a tenth actually ride out to raid caravans. Most often, bands of ten to twenty Riders waylay lone travelers or extort money from nearby villages. Because their livelihood depends on stealing, they do not regard it as a crime. Indeed, a clever scheme for parting a traveler from his belongings is met with the greatest approval.

Aside from those Riders who actually go raiding, the rest of this strange clan lives in wet-season camps that dot the woods south of Lake Vors. These woodland dwellers do not openly proclaim their ties to the Riders, but the abundance of horses and stolen goods in their encampments mark them as the homes of this odd, bandit nation. The Rider camps gladly share food and wine with passing strangers in exchange for information, especially news of trade routes, caravans and wealthy travelers in the area.

The people who emerged from the Riders' kaer vary in appearance, but most are of average height and solid build. Though they are no more muscular than other men, many of the archers among them have well-developed forearms from

constant use of the longbow. Though the original Riders were of human stock, outcasts from many other races have swelled their ranks in the years since the Scourge. These days, an obsidiman named Grannic is particularly infamous in Throal for striking the dwarf kingdom's land-barges. Most Riders favor the dwarf sword or longbow, and a few wield spears. Some horsemen use lances stolen from ambushed patrols, because acquiring such weapons is a mark of courage among them. They wield lances with little true skill, however.

The hardiest of the Riders spend anywhere from two to three seasons of the year roaming the plains north of the ruins of Blackcliff. They spend the rest of the year in the wet-season camps repairing their weapons, plotting new escapades, and occasionally hiding from authorities. While roaming the plains, the Riders steal what they can. Often they disguise themselves and enter the cities of Throal, where they sell their stolen goods, spend money, and make mischief. Some believe the Riders a romantic, lusty lot, but most shun them as common thieves.

ON THE STRANGE HISTORY OF THE SCAVIAN PEOPLE

Many generations before the Scourge blighted our land, the mighty city of Scavia arose between the Scarlet Sea and the Mist Swamps. Built on ruins of a truly ancient civilization, of which its citizens knew nothing, the city of Scavia grew in power and riches for many years.
Like their unknown ancestors, the Scavians loved ships, and they ruled undisputed over the Scarlet Sea and the narrow strait between the Scarlet Sea and Death's Sea known as Dead Man's Gullet. In barges of stone warded with enchantments, the Scavians mined the Scarlet Sea for elemental fire, keeping close the secret magics they used. Only the shipbuilders knew of them and taught the magics to a chosen few.

When the King of Scavia accepted the Rites of Protection and Passage from the Therans, he chose to build Scavia's kaer in Dead Man's Gullet. He knew that the cliffs of that pass were riddled with vast mazes of caverns and passages, and that lava from the Death's Sea blocked the lowest caves. The Scavians mistakenly believed that the layers of molten stone would protect them from the Horrors, and that they need only build and ward strong walls and a roof for their kaer. Earlier than most other city-states in the realm that became Barsaive, the Scavians began to build their magnificent kaer in the cliffs of Dead Man's Gullet.

Because their wise monarch had begun the building so early, the Scavians had time to build one of the most beautiful, unique kaers in Barsaive. Within a mere five years, Scavian workers had carved canals beneath the kaer proper and flooded them with lava, and sculpted elaborate dwellings up the cliff sides. Sadly, the

SOME LEGENDS INSIST THAT THE KAER BUILT BY GERRIK AND THE RIDERS REMAINS SEALED IN HIDDEN CAVES NEAR LAKE VORS, AND THAT GERRIK STILL LIVES WITHIN IT. OTHER RUMORS CLAIM THAT THE BANDITS HAVE MADE A RAIDERS' FORTRESS OF THEIR KAER.
—JERRIV FORRIM

King of Scavia did not know that many of the Horrors found the molten sea as hospitable as we might a cool pond. The Theran wards kept the Horrors from entering the Scavian kaer from above ground, but nothing could stop many of them from swimming up through the fiery canals and breaching the magnificent city's defenses from below. At first, the dreadful creatures simply eyed the Scavians from the blazing canals and devoured any vessel that came too near them. When they tired of this macabre game, the Horrors used their power over human minds to lure the kaer's residents to the burning shores and make them throw themselves in. The Scavians hid in their rocky chambers, but the Horrors came after them and slew them with fire. As the death toll mounted and the smell of burning flesh filled the air, Prince Darl Hilloman of Scavia took command from his ailing father, gathered the Imperial Guard, and led them against the Horrors in a campaign that the people called the Retribution.

Though many Scavians died in the Retribution, so too did many of the Horrors. In the three and a half centuries after the campaign, the Imperial Guard kept Scavian citizens from destruction, though occasional Horrors slipped through the Guard and wreaked havoc on the kaer. Even after the death of Prince Hilloman, the Imperial Guard maintained their vigil. And though the Kingdom of Scavia sank beneath the Mist Swamps during the Scourge, the noble Order of the Scavian Guard exists to this day.

On the Descendants of the Kingdom of Scavia

Though Scavia always had and still has members of other races among its people, I include Scavians in this treatise because the vast majority of them were (and still are) of human stock. Their numbers, however, are decreasing. Scavian humans have begun to intermarry with other human peoples, thinning the Scavian bloodline; every year, fewer pure Scavians are born to carry on their people's heritage. Also, hostility between the Scavians and the t'skrang that travel the lower Serpent River are slowly eroding the number of Scavian barge-towns (which I describe below). Within another generation, I fear the once mighty Scavians may dwindle to nothing more than memory.

The Scavians of our time exhibit their ancestors' love of sailing. They live on vast barges that travel the lower Serpent River, from the Mist Swamps as far north as the edge of the Servos Jungle, trading where they can and battling their t'skrang rivals when they must. Many of these barges are large enough to be called villages, and serve as such for those who ride them. Each of the more than forty Scavian barges is an independent, floating town, providing a home for four to ten extended families. The population of each barge, therefore, numbers between thirty and one hundred. Though most Scavians are human, the rest are an odd mix of elves, dwarfs, and even occasional windlings.

The head of each town, known as the helmsman, is usually the patriarch of the largest family aboard. In cases where the helmsman has died raiding the t'skrang, I have seen the helmsman's woman take command, and all obeyed her orders without question. The Scavians appear to have a stricter separation of roles and responsibilities between men and women than do many other human cultures, at least with regard to fighting. But their women serve equally well as sailors, and I had no sense that they value women less because fewer women wield swords.

ON MANY OCCASIONS, THE SCAVIANS HAVE COME INTO CONFLICT WITH THE HOUSE OF THE NINE DIAMONDS, A T'SKRANG AROPAGOI THAT CONTROLS MOST OF THE LOWER SERPENT RIVER. INTERESTED READERS MAY WISH TO REFER TO VOLUME VII OF THIS WORK, DEVOTED TO THE T'SKRANG.
—THOM EDRULL

Humans

DINGANNI WARRIORS DEFEND THEIR ENCAMPMENT FROM BRITHANS.

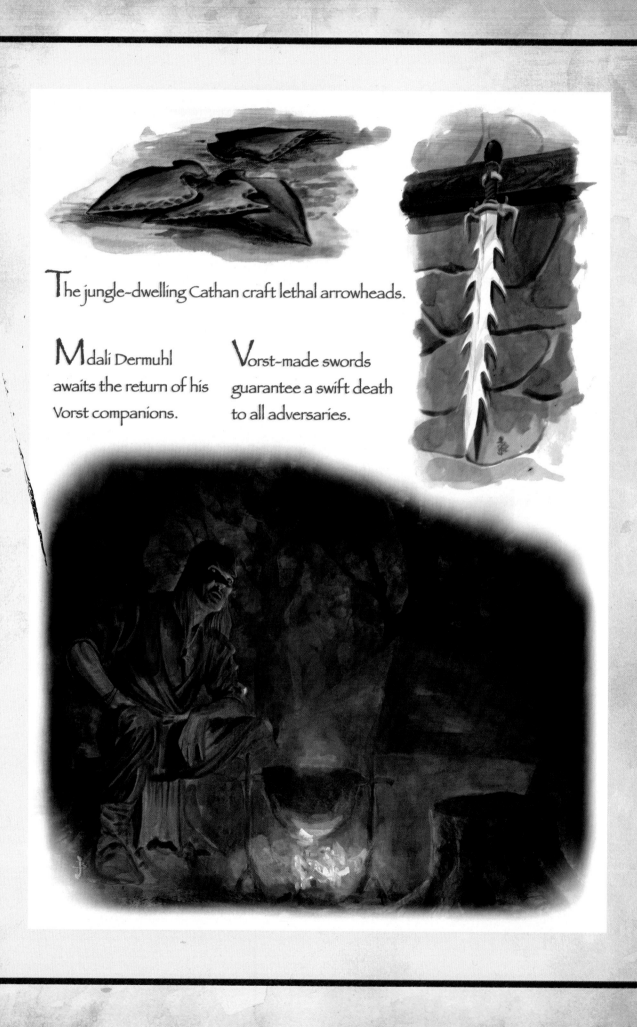

The jungle-dwelling Cathan craft lethal arrowheads.

Mdali Dermuhl awaits the return of his Vorst companions.

Vorst-made swords guarantee a swift death to all adversaries.

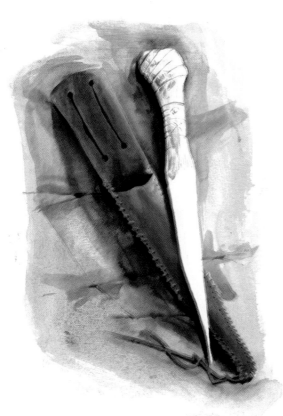

A ceremonial bone knife and eagle sculpture, tools of Dinganni magicians.

A Scavian miner lights his way with a heatstone, fueled by elemental fire.

Trelaria, troubadour
of the Galeb-Klek.

The Cathan of the
Servos Jungle camouflage
themselves with face paint.

The
keystone
of Blackcliff
gives mute
testimony
to the
treachery
of Garrik of
the Mask.

Both men and women among the Scavians dress in flamboyant colors, particularly favoring scarlet and brilliant white. Both genders also wear their hair long and often wrap scarves around their heads to keep the long strands from blowing into their eyes as the winds whip over the decks of their barges. Though both men and women wear jewelry, the men are particularly fond of it, especially of earrings and bracelets. The Scavians regard ornaments taken from conquered or slain foes as badges of honor, and many a helmsman wears ornaments at the neck and wrists that together might weigh as much as ten pounds.

The Scavians with whom I stayed seemed all too aware of their people's dwindling numbers and therefore fought against any threat to it—whether real or perceived—with a ferocity that borders on recklessness. Having survived a vicious river battle between the Scavians and a fleet of t'skrang merchant vessels, I can tell you that no other folk in Barsaive could have fought so bravely—or taken so many foolhardy risks. Indeed, the Scavians (to my way of thinking) even surpass the t'skrang in this regard.

Sadly, the Scavians have come to see the t'skrang with whom they share the lower Serpent River as a threat to their very existence rather than as mere trading rivals and have embroiled themselves in a race war of sorts with the serpent-men. The Scavians truly hate the t'skrang and will kill a defeated one rather than take him prisoner.

The Scavians see themselves as a besieged people and so teach even their small children to be deadly marksmen with the crossbow. Adult Scavians use all manner of weapons, including magical fire cannons mounted aboard their tremendous barges. The long centuries of the Scourge have cost them their ancient knowledge of how to forge the fire-resistant vessels that enabled their forebears to sail the Scarlet Sea. One man I met claimed that his grandsire ten times removed had been a shipwright in Scavia, but said that the family had long ago sold the manuscripts that held the old shipwrights' magical knowledge. (To be frank, I place little credence in his tale.) Some believe that the builders of the first Scavia sailed on seas of water, but this claim is preposterous. All records that we possess from ancient days speak of the Scarlet Sea as a sea of molten stone.

ON THE EVILS THAT BEFELL THE VORST

The Vorst, a once-proud people who built thriving cities in the lands east of Lake Ban before the Scourge, have become a grim and fatalistic lot. They suffered greatly during the Scourge; a Horror breached their kaer in a most subtle and awful manner many generations after they had sealed themselves in what they believed was a safe haven. The Vorst survived, but paid a dreadful price. One aging Vorst to whom I spoke, a man named Cho Shimmus, fought this Horror in his youth. I have recorded his horrible account as I remember it.

The Corrupting of Kaih Lia

"The dark time we know as the Long Death began nearly four hundred years after my people went below ground. It began with our greatest wizard, Kaih Lia, who often used his mystical powers to spy out the ravaged lands above our kaer. Alas, Kaih Lia was old, and a Horror found his aging mind as easy to vanquish as a young warrior might have found Kaih Lia's frail body. This Horror entered Kaih Lia's mind and ate his soul as if it was an overripe fruit. The Horror then inhabited Kaih Lia's empty shell. When we knew what had happened, we mourned Kaih Lia and named our enemy Tendris 'al, or Black Mind. But it took us many years to see the dreadful truth, and we nearly saw it too late.

"Over the years, the Black Mind began to sow the seeds of madness among my otherwise enlightened folk. Our art, once bright and joyful, turned to morbid scenes of the macabre. Our buildings became warped and ugly, our stories told of blood, murder, and betrayal. The Black Mind meant to drive us all insane, and his malign scheme might have succeeded had not the Disciples of the Black Mind, a group of guards utterly devoted to Tendris' al, breached one of the kaer's main passageways to let in the rampaging Horrors.

"Those of us who remained sane fled to a retreat deep within the kaer, from which we fought an endless battle with our dreadful foes. They could not kill us all, nor could we slay enough of them to retake the kaer and rebuild our sanctuary. Our retreat, perhaps the size of a small keep, became our prison for eleven years—two hundred of us remained locked within its magical walls like sheep in a pen.

"The warriors among us often raided the outer kaer in attempts to steal food from the rampaging Horrors. We lost many men to these desperate forays. I survived several of them and would sooner die than suffer such experiences again. Mindless spirits lurked in every corner of our home, along with even worse beings. Intelligent Horrors, things with red eyes and bony hands, also lurked in the shadows—we called these walking nightmares the Plotters and feared them above all others. They knew how to set traps for us and often directed the actions of their less intelligent kin. We dared not confront these Horrors in pitched battle, for we could not afford to lose.

"The Horrors wreaked havoc on our kaer, and this destruction posed its own dangers for us. The great inner cliffs, that once gave homes to so many of our people, had been broken and crushed as an enemy's battle-ax might crush a skull. Often, we had to climb the pitted and scarred cliff faces in search of food; more times than I can count, a sickly arm lashed out from the crumbling windows and broke or cut our ropes. My comrade Cho Kether lost his life that way, as he scaled the cliff wall a scant finger-length from me. A Horror snapped his rope in twain, and Cho Kether plunged to his death. I still hear his screams on sleepless nights. Our best bowmen guarded the climbers, but all too often an arrow missed its mark. On every raid, we knew that half of us would meet death. I accepted that risk, but I curse the Horrors that made us pay such a dear price for our lives."

Of What the Scourge Wrought on Vorst Society

When the dwarfs of Throal reached the Vorst's inner retreat, they found less than 100 survivors, many of them children. The terrible experiences they suffered have been burned into the racial memory of all the Vorst, and have shaped every aspect of their lives. They extended civility to me when I visited their one, small village, but without warmth. And they never ceased to watch me, waiting for a hint of betrayal.

The village, named Vorst after its inhabitants, comprises thirty homes and nestles on the eastern shore of Lake Ban. Extended families in this tiny settlement link their stone-walled, wooden-roofed huts together by way of crude, underground tunnels. The tunnels hide their movements from prying eyes, a concealment that they value.

The Scourge taught the Vorst to leave nothing to chance. Their every action is done thoroughly, even excessively, with a furious energy. They build walls, not of one row of stones or bricks, but of double or even triple rows, cementing them with fire-hardened mortar. They roof their houses with no other wood save the stoutest oak. If one of them slays a foe in battle, the victorious Vorst warrior dismembers and burns the body, then scatters the ashes over the earth. I believe this behavior stems from their dreadful imprisonment in their ravaged kaer, when the slightest neglect of a precaution might lead to untold deaths at the hands of the Horrors. Were the Vorst to put their fierce determination to bettering their lot, they might yet become as proud and mighty as were their ancestors. As long as the grim will to survive is the only thing that sustains them, I fear that the glory of the ancient Vorst culture can never return.

On the Appearance
and Dress of the Vorst

Only the physical nature of the Vorst has remained the same since the Scourge. A small but sturdy people, the Vorst have thick, tough, yellow-tinged skin and thick, black hair. Most wear their hair cut short; those few Vorst men who grow beards keep them short as well, lest long hair or beards somehow impede them in combat.

Vorst dress, once elaborate and beautiful, has become simple and drab. Vorst men wear tight-fitting garb that does not restrict or entangle their limbs, and the slighter Vorst women wear somewhat looser tunics and trews to make themselves look bigger. Weapons have become everyday ornaments, and a Vorst would as soon appear without one as I might go naked in a blizzard. Many of the men carry great axes with blades as sharp as a Vorst warrior's stare. Men and women both bear barbed swords, which (as Cho Shimmus told me) can tear out a foe's guts at a stroke. Bows are another favored weapon among them, and many wrapped their arrows in oiled cloth. The arrows also often sported barbed heads, and could easily be set alight. The brutality of their weapons clearly show the dreadful legacy of fear left to them by the frantic, eleven-year struggle they waged against the Horrors beneath the earth.

I have heard more of the horror Tendris'al than Kallarian seems to know. Rumors persist that the horror still lurks in the depths of the old Vorst kaer, and that Tendris'al's possessed disciples still serve him. I know of at least two groups of adventurers that have gone into the kaer in search of treasure, but know of only one survivor: a dwarf, Bannon by name. He passed on the rumors of the horror to me, but would say little else. He spends his days wandering from tavern to tavern in Bartertown, often in a drunken stupor, presumably living off what little spoils he carried when he fled the Vorst kaer. If Bannon found treasure in that awful place, what more might lie beneath those haunted ruins? And what dreadful thing guards it?
—Staunchus

A BRIEF TREATISE ON THE T'SKRANG

How this document found its way to the Great Library of Throal remains a mystery, for the t'skrang author begins by relating that the text was written at the behest of then Theran Overgovernor Kypros. From other references, we glean that the author was a troubadour taken captive by the Therans, but we do not know the details of his captivity or if he ever returned to his own people. We may never know the tale of this scroll's journey to our archives, but its origins are less important than the wealth of information it contains. The author of this scroll dated it in the year 1044, using the Theran calendar system. That date would correspond to 1487 of our own Throalic calendar, indicating that this document was written 19 years ago.
—Humbly presented for the edification of the reader by Thom Edrull, archivist and scribe of the Hall of Records, 1506 TH

In the beginning the Spirit Mother, the Great Encircler, took root in the Void that existed before time began. In time, she grew full of life and she planted four eggs into the emptiness of the Void. When the first egg opened, she was called Shivoam, the Birth Mother, the Serpent River. Then the second egg opened, and she was called T'schlome, the Light-bringer, the Sun. When the third egg opened, he was called Shivos, the Earth Father, the Land. And when at last the fourth egg opened, he was called Syrtis, the Nightwatcher, the Moon. And the Spirit Mother nursed her brood in the circle of her embrace, the circle without beginning, without end, which we call Houros, the worm that eats its own tail.

Now Syrtis looked into the skies and saw the beauty of his sister, the Sun. He was filled with the longing of a man for a woman, and grew wings to follow T'schlome. When Syrtis caught up to her, the skies caught fire as T'schlome resisted. Seeds of flame rained down upon the earth, and where they broke open, out sprang the Firebrothers, the dragonkind. Again Syrtis caught her, again T'schlome struggled against him. The Heavens trembled with the great storm, and from the clouds burst the Skysisters, the windlings. You can look up into the skies and see them chasing still, and with each new mating is hatched another star.

Shivos lay near Shivoam, and from their first mating came a small brood of eggs. And there was a sadness, for the shell did not shatter, the young did not break forth. With a second mating came a second egg brood, but once again no hatchlings came. And the River looked to her sister, the Sun, and the many children of Syrtis and T'schlome, and she sang and she wept. At the sound of her song, the eggs trembled, and at the touch of her tears they broke open. And the children of the first brood were called the River-daughters, the t'skrang. The children of the second brood were the Earthsons, the obsidimen. With each new mating of Earth and Water, a new mountain is born, a new river runs forth. These are the generations of the four Founders.

ON THE NATURE OF THE T'SKRANG

My name is T'chal Siandra K'vechnalonika V'strimon, and for sixteen years, I was the weaver of the Yearsong in the Great House V'strimon. By order of my new lord, Overgovernor Kypros of Skypoint, I now undertake to recount all that I can of my people, the t'skrang. Though I have been given but short space, I will try to make my story both brief and concise, giving special attention to those matters that might be of especial interest to the Theran reader.

If asked to describe the physical appearance of my people, most members of other races might say that the t'skrang are the lizard-men of Barsaive. But unless offense is intended, pray do not compare our race to creatures such as the lizard or snake in our presence. The t'skrang are a Name-giving race, and deserve to be treated as such. As with all the other races, all that sets us apart from the rest are certain unique physical characteristics. A typical t'skrang stands no taller than six feet, for example, an average comparable to that of the human race. It is our tails that makes us longer, adding some six feet in length and another forty pounds to our weight. T'skrang skin is hairless and as supple as soft leather, and its color varies widely, from green to blue to russet red, often patterned with spots and stripes.

Among the Name-giving races only trolls show a wider range of natural physical variation. Some of my race also display spectacular crests of cartilage that sweep up from the base of the neck to the center of the skull. Others have spikes or plates on their tails or along their vertebrae, while still others have flattened, scoop-shaped snouts like a duck. A rare few are born with a leathery membrane stretching from either wrist to hip that can serve as wings. T'skrang mature at age ten, and seldom live past eighty years.

We t'skrang are creatures of sweeping motion and great passions. Indeed, for grace of movement, lightness of step, and innate sense of balance the t'skrang are often compared to the elven race. But it is not dancing that is our great delight, as it is with the elves. No, if the t'skrang have a favorite pastime, it is the spinning of tales and the pleasures of conversation. As the dwarfs are fond of saying, "Every t'skrang was born a troubadour, and some wander from the art." No matter that the dwarfs intended the words as insult, we t'skrang have always taken it as high praise. Outrageous fictions produced at a moment's notice are a time-honored tradition among the t'skrang—and the more fabulous the tale, the greater the honor to the storyteller.

We t'skrang navigate the waters of the Serpent River in wondrous riverboats, trading up and down the river, and then returning to our underwater villages with needed goods and honestly won profits.

Generations of expert haggling in pursuit of favorable trade has made my race tolerant and amicable, and we t'skrang bear no racial prejudice against the other Name-givers of Barsaive. Most dwarfs, especially those of Throal, seem unable to set aside their instinctive distrust of the t'skrang. But perhaps this is only a healthy suspicion for one's major economic competitor, for their attitude seems not to possess any rancor. The t'skrang themselves trade willingly with anyone who speaks a language they can understand.

Most t'skrang live on or near the Serpent River and its tributaries. Though Shivoam, the great mother goddess of the Serpent River, has blessed us with gills, we t'skrang can only remain underwater for ten minutes at a time before needing to come up for air. We prefer to swim near the water's surface, using our powerful tails to travel as quickly in the water as on solid ground. Water holds such importance for our species that bathing has evolved almost to the height of ritual. A t'skrang without his daily bath is a disgruntled t'skrang indeed!

If asked which two words of our own tongue best describe the t'skrang race, I would choose *niall*, our word for family, and *jik'harra*, usually translated as fearlessness or bravery. These two concepts encompass the true paradox of what it is to be born t'skrang, for a t'skrang spends most of his or her life torn between the craving to live surrounded by family in the village and the longing to sail the river, trying each day to find the truth of *jik'harra*. Strung between these contradictions, the t'skrang are like the taut string of a well-tuned chitarra. The music that emerges— that is the beauty of life for a t'skrang!

SHORT SPACE?
THIS SCROLL RUNS
MANY, MANY
PAGES. IF THIS
T'SKRANG THINKS
THE SPACE
ALLOWED WAS
INADEQUATE, THE
IMAGINATION
BALKS AT WHAT
LENGTH HIS
T'SKRANG LOQUA-
CIOUSNESS MIGHT
HAVE THOUGHT
SUFFICIENT. . .
—JERRIV FORRIM,

ON THE T'SKRANG OF THE SERPENT RIVER

Though t'skrang live all across Barsaive, the greater part live in and on the Serpent River. Because this group represents the center of our culture, much of what I describe is based chiefly on the Serpent-dwelling members of my race.

OF THE IMPORTANCE OF THE NIALL

Each t'skrang takes great pride in the heritage and bloodline of his or her *niall*, or foundation. The *niall* is a large communal family consisting of thirty to sixty kin, from infants to ancients, all living under a single roof. Lineage is traced through the maternal line. When a woman takes a husband, the male leaves his familial home to join the *niall* of his mate.

Before I continue further, I must explain that a single *niall* does not a village make. Most villages consist of three to eight foundations. If the village owns a riverboat, the group is known collectively as a *t'slahyin*, or crew covenant. Sometimes, several *t'slahyin* join to form an *aropagoi*, or Great House. This is the way of the t'skrang, to gather in ever-larger groups.

Governing each *niall* is the six-member Women's Council. At its head is the foundation's eldest female, who is given the title of lahala, or Honored One. Tradition forbids men to sit on the Council, but in practice, wives and sisters commonly solicit the advice of their mates or siblings before attending a meeting.

T'skrang society is communal, with food, clothes, wealth, and village chores distributed fairly and systematically throughout the *niall*. I suppose this seems sensible to the sons of man, who rarely put ten kin under the same roof, but I assure you, even the t'skrang sometimes consider fifty relatives too many people with whom to share!

Each week, the women's council makes up a work list and posts it near the communal dining area. The list describes the tasks necessary to the maintenance of the foundation and assigns each task to pairs of members by name. The Council, I should point out, makes certain that every member of the foundation performs his or her fair share of the onerous tasks, such as fertilizing the crops, dredging the latrines, or scrubbing pots in the kitchens. An extra shift at such undesirable tasks is often assigned as punishment to members who commit minor offenses or who deliberately disrupt the fabric of life within the *niall*. Many riverboat crews insist that the Council always assigns the worst chores to returning crew members, but the Councilwomen merely smile and say that life on the river always makes crew act like hatchlings. At least, so went the customary exchange in my *niall*.

ON THE HONOR OF BEING THE LAHALA

We honor the eldest female member of a foundation with the name lahala, or Honored One. The lahala holds considerable power within her *niall*. As head of the Women's Council, she arbitrates disputes within the family—and truth to tell, with forty relatives all living in the same house all the time, it takes a wise woman indeed to sort things out! The lahala also represents the *niall* in the village council, or Council of Lahalas, and in dealings with outsiders, and presides over the essential rituals of t'skrang life, including birth, Naming, marriage, and death.

When the time draws near for the current lahala to travel down the river to the sea, the next eldest woman is consecrated as Honored One in an intricate ritual of threadweaving and blood magic. The ritual grants to the new lahala all the racial memories of her predecessors, extending all the way back to the *niall*'s first lahala. In becoming lahala, the elder lays aside her Name, breaking all threads attached to it and taking the name of the *niall* as her personal name. This ritual is called *k'soto ensherenk*, the Name-passing.

Only a woman may bear the title of lahala. Though they must sacrifice all they were previously, these Honored Ones seem to gain serenity from the grave responsibilities of their position, an inner peace that eases the sacrifice and teaches them the wise use of their authority. The rare lahalas who speak of *k'soto ensherenk* say that the racial memories are like a vast library of wisdom into which one may reach in time of need.

Because of the blood magic entwined in the nature of the Name-passing ritual, some risk does exist that a Horror-tainted lahala might corrupt the new lahala, but such an abomination has occurred only rarely. The ritual also prolongs the life of the lahala beyond the normal span by as many as thirty years. Other races may scoff at stories that some t'skrang live to ripe ages of one hundred years or more, but the lahala bear witness to the truth of these tales.

OF THE MIRACLE OF NEW LIFE

Very few t'skrang could tell you the name of their mother and this is why. The word *niall* means foundation, in much the same sense as the first row of stones form the base of a house, but it also means eggshell. T'skrang females lay eggs rather than giving birth live to their young, as do most other races of Barsaive.

A t'skrang egg is the size of a large hand-span, and twice that measure around the widest part. Sometimes speckled, sometimes plain, the eggs range in color across a pastel spectrum. T'skrang women believe that the color of the eggshell predicts the destiny of the life within, but I have heard that scholars from other races speculate that the egg color is a product of the mother's diet, not of fate. T'skrang females may lay as many as ten eggs at one time, but seldom lay more than three times in a year.

The heart of any foundation is the hatchery, where eggs are kept moist and warm as they await coming to term. Once a t'skrang lays her eggs, she will carry them to the hatchery of her foundation as soon as possible. If females are traveling away from the foundation at the time they lay their eggs, they wrap them in cloth and protect them in a wicker basket known as a *creshenkta*. The sooner the eggs arrive in the hatchery after being laid, the greater the chances of their fertility.

A foundation's hatcheries are the strict domain of the women—indeed, few men ever learn or understand what goes on inside. (By nature, of course, the men have invented all manner of outrageous tales about what the womenfolk really do inside the hatcheries.) The only thing men know for certain is that an egg takes eight to ten months to hatch. Near the end of each egg's hatching cycle, the women entrust its care to a male of the foundation. In most *nialls*, men vie with good-natured rivalry for egg-tending duty, while the women try to make the assignment of the honor as fair as possible. Because egg-tending is considered both a responsibility and a privilege, foundations never lack for volunteers.

The male t'skrang provides the milk a hatchling needs to grow and survive. Six to eight days before an egg's hatching, the eggtender's body chemistry changes, and he begins to provide a regular supply of milk for the hatchling. This change, known as *t'chai kondos,* or egg bonding, combines significant psychological, emotional, and magical elements. Hatchlings nurse for three months, during which the male carefully attends to the infant's needs and development. At the end of the first year, everyone in the foundation begins to take responsibility for the child's development, but the eggtender maintains a close relationship with his charge up to the child's second Name-day. Youngsters refer to their tenders as *chaida*, and the memory of an egg-parent can bring a sentimental tear to the eye of even the roughest river pirate. A t'skrang's feeling for his *chaida* is something akin to a human's love for his mother.

When a woman reaches egg-bearing age, she is brought to the hatchery and shown the fate of most t'skrang eggs. The eggs are covered with a rich ooze dredged from the river bottom and imbued with magic, then tucked into large cauldrons of heated mud. There they remain for up to a year and a day. After seven months, the women in the hatchery begin checking the eggs for signs of life by setting a bright light behind the egg. If the egg is fertile, the embryo appears as a dark shadow. Germinated eggs are watched carefully, to properly time the assignment of an eggtender. Even ungerminated eggs are checked periodically to see if they are simply late bloomers. After a year and a day, ungerminated eggs are removed from the hatcheries to the kitchens, where they are used in various recipes.

We t'skrang have a saying, "Many are dreamed, few are born." This is the way we express the sad truth of our inefficient fertilization process. Only about one in every hundred t'skrang eggs germinates. Moreover, many women will never lay a good egg, while others will lay dozens. The t'skrang foundation is itself a direct response to our uneven, unpredictable fertilization pattern. By virtue of our social structure, no one knows whose eggs have hatched and whose have not, and thus the joys of child-rearing are known equally throughout the community.

Many lahala believe that the already low fertility rates of our race have taken a dramatic downward turn since the time of the Scourge. This subject is virtually taboo among my people, and it often proves dangerous for an outsider to raise the issue of t'skrang fertility in the presence of members of my race. The sons of man have a saying: "When t'skrang talk, nothing is forbidden." Whoever coined this phrase must never have tried to get a t'skrang to speak about the birth rate of his foundation.

ON GROWING UP T'SKRANG

The eggtender is charged with a hatchling's care from the moment it cracks its shell to the day it is weaned from the tender's milk. (Let the reader note that until the age of twelve years t'skrang are neither male nor female, but sexless, so the neutral "it" is indeed appropriate here.) Though half a year will pass before the hatchling learns to walk, every t'skrang is born knowing how to swim. The confines of every *niall* contain a large shallow pool where the newborn happily play. Of course, what is shallow water to a t'skrang hatchling could easily drown a human infant, so beware when ordering a t'skrang slave to give the baby a bath.

Humans eagerly await their children's ability to walk, while we t'skrang care far less about a hatchling's first step than his first swing. It is our custom to drape the interior of our dwellings with nets, rope ladders, and swing lines. It is in this maze that our children learn to swing and play, while visitors to our domes often stand aghast at the risks we encourage our hatchlings to take on the ropes.

Outsiders who have known only adult t'skrang are probably not aware that all t'skrang are born with a fear of heights that is as strong as their love for the water. Knowing that a hatching must overcome this fear, we swell with pride at the sight of one swinging across the dizzying heights for the first time. All hatchlings must learn discipline in the face of fear. That lesson holds such importance that the t'skrang call it *jik'harra,* our word for bravery or fearlessness, literally translated as "brave passion."

Life is not all fun and games for the young t'skrang, however. In its third year, the hatchling begins to attend the foundation's school, a classroom that migrates from dwelling place to dwelling place throughout the village. The youngster's formal studies, which include spoken and written language, history, music, and mathematics, continues until the age of twelve. In my travels, I have found no other race that teaches mathematics so early or so thoroughly as the t'skrang. As with all other tasks, the teaching is done by a rotating staff of adults assigned to the work by the Women's Council. All adults share in teaching the hatchlings, and even the riverboat captains are drafted into instructing the hatchlings when they put into port for a few days,.

At the age of seven, the hatchling joins the foundation's labor force, working alongside adults to perform the foundation's daily chores and the other tasks that maintain the village as a viable economic enterprise. The Council of Lahalas carefully assigns each hatchling to a full turn of duty; that is, each child spends at least a week at each of the village tasks. We do not expect children to work as hard or as long as adults, but neither do we allow them to grow up ignorant of their responsibilities. The Council reserves a number of especially undesirable tasks for disciplining unruly youngsters. At this stage, many villages group hatchlings from neighboring foundations by age and continue classes to the age of twelve.

> MOODY AND BELLIGERENT IS A RATHER FAINT DESCRIPTION OF THE HUMOR OF A T'SKRANG DURING KAISSA. IT IS AN UNPLEASANT SIGHT FOR AN OUTSIDER TO WITNESS!
> —MERROX

T'skrang begin *kaissa,* the change from child to adult, at twelve years of age. This is the moment when hatchlings become male or female. The change from sexlessness to a specific gender, and from child to adult, is a difficult time for t'skrang, as I suppose it is for all younglings, regardless of race. Among the t'skrang, no one knows the hatchling's sex until the onset of *kaissa.* On the one hand, this permits the child to grow up unrestricted by the expectations of a certain role in society. On the other hand, the lack of practice, so to speak, only serves to make the process stranger and more complicated for the hatchling. *Kaissa* can last for up to a year and a day, and during that time, there is nothing so moody, belligerent, or obstinate anywhere in Barsaive as that poor, confused hatchling. I have raised six, so I should know.

Two t'skrang customs help hatchlings through *kaissa.* The first is the Festival of Names. Each year on the first day of spring, a foundation acknowledges its twelve-year-olds' passage to maturity by allowing each hatchling to take a Name of his or her own choosing. It often happens that a child will honor its egg-parent by adopting the *chaida's* name as its own. In a simple, but moving ritual, the child stands before the gathered members of the foundation and states its new name. (As this custom usually takes place before *kaissa* has even begun, a t'skrang name never even hints at gender.) Then, one at a time, the members of the foundation approach the hatchling, join hands, and exchange names with the new adult. After the last foundation member has presented this honor, the ceremony transforms into a great celebration, in which it is each person's duty to get their new comrade outrageously drunk—at least, thus do I recall my own coming of age.

The second custom actually offers relief from the physical and mental chaos of *kaissa* by sending the hatchling off to the river for ship duty. These recruits are called *khamorro*, which means "he who scrubs the deck." As the name indicates, *khamorro* draw the most demeaning, physically demanding tasks on the boat, while the adult t'skrang generally treat them like galley slaves. Despite this rigorous ordeal, most hatchlings leap at the chance to work on a riverboat and to live an adventure on the river. Fresh air and hard work offer the perfect distractions from the pangs of *kaissa*, and many *khamorro* return from ship duty without even realizing that they have completed the change.

ON THE COMPLEXITIES OF VILLAGE LIFE

The foundations of the Serpent River t'skrang join together in groups of four to twenty to form villages. The typical t'skrang village has five important features: the domes, the towers, the *refs,* the *t'slashina,* and the riverboat. Most outsiders do not realize that skilled t'skrang engineers produce these five structures using the five elemental substances. Indeed, elementalist adepts of other races constantly request permission to study our villages to divine the true nature of their construction.

I shall start with the towers, for they are the visible evidence that people are living beneath the surface of the Serpent River. The towers of a t'skrang village consist of large, rounded spires of rock raised up from the bottom of the river using elemental magic. From shore, the towers look like thick, circular posts set into the river by a giant hand. Water sprays from their upriver face as the Serpent's mighty current crashes against the stone. Although each village chooses a unique shape and structure, most towers rise at least 30 feet above the water's surface. Other towers, however, remain hidden below the surface of the water, for reasons I shall explain.

T'skrang builders arrange the village towers in groups of four set into a diamond pattern. The long axis of the diamond aligns with the river's current, and the two flanking towers usually lie just beneath the surface of the water. Larger villages link multiple diamonds together to form a larger pattern. House K'tenshin, or the House of Nine Diamonds, for example, takes its name from the unusual size of its tower array, nine interlocking diamonds framed by sixteen towers. Villages that can afford fire cannons mount them on the tops of their towers to protect against marauders. The side of the structures that faces the inside of the diamond provides docks for our riverboats. The towers are hollow within, with a cunning system of ramps and pulley-driven lifts leading down to their base.

The dwellings of the t'skrang lie partially buried under the muddy bottom of the Serpent, sheltered by domes scattered across the area within the diamonds and linked by underground tunnels. We live perhaps a hundred feet below the surface of the river, and many people wonder how we keep the air from going stale. Remember, some towers are submerged just below the water's surface. The force of the current moving swiftly across the tops and sides of these hollow towers creates a vacuum that draws air *up* through the tower, through the underground tunnels and through the domes, and also *down* through the towers that extend above the surface. This feat of engineering keeps our air fresh and clean. Visitors to our villages are always surprised to feel the constant pressure of a gentle breeze against their faces.

Each dome is large enough to house a *niall*, up to forty or more members of an extended family. At first glance many outsiders might consider a typical dome cramped and cluttered, filled with all sorts of outlandish structures. The space inside is usually divided by wooden beams, paper walls, huge sleeping-baskets dangling from the ceiling, and a maze of ladders, nets, and rope swings crisscrossing in every direction. Most villages also build one especially large dome, sufficiently large to hold all members of the village during festivals and meetings.

A system of invisible, magical barricades called *refs,* an abbreviation of *refselenika,* protects the open spaces between the towers. We fashion the *refs* from elemental water, shaping it into big, thick spikes sharp enough to rip a hole in the hull of a passing riverboat. Most villages also place *refs* in a pattern radiating outward from their towers to prevent approach from the water (perhaps considering the fire cannon too little protection!). Sentries in the towers may raise and lower the *refs* so that boats can safely approach and then dock in the village. We also create a second kind of *ref,* called a curtain *ref,* that extends up to the surface of the river to deflect the force of the current away from the area inside the village diamond.

I have deliberately avoided describing the building material of the domes, because the choice of building materials varies. Primitive t'skrang in the far reaches of the Serpent's tributaries still use mud and sticks to build their domes. In times long ago, foundations on the main river constructed their domes of carefully hewn stone, and any dwarf who musters the courage to cross the open waters to visit our villages marvels at the fine workmanship and engineering skill of our ancient stonecutters. Long before the Scourge, the t'skrang discovered a method of weaving elemental air with elemental water to form beautiful, translucent structures unique in all of Barsaive. We call this kind of building material *durc,,* and any adept with the talent to weave a *durc* can name his own price.

We call the space sheltered from the current by the combination of towers and *refs* the *t'slashina,* or village diamond. The surface of the water within the *t'slashina* is tranquil, still, and smooth as glass. On the river bottom, the nearly still water allows the village to use the fertile mud to grow crops. The curtain *refs* break up the force of the river's current, which would otherwise sweep both the planter and planted downstream. On the edge of the *t'slashina,* t'skrang fisherman cast their nets into the current of the Serpent River. The *t'slashina* forms the heart of t'skrang industry, for without it, my people would be completely dependent on trade for their daily bread.

Even the most productive villages find it hard to be self-sufficient. What cannot be grown or caught or created must be obtained through trade, and trade is only possible using the riverboat. So much has been made of the t'skrang and their riverboats that I think the people of Barsaive believe that my people live their entire lives, from birth till death, aboard ship. Quite possibly, they have drawn such a false conclusion from overhearing the talk of t'skrang sailors, some of whom behave as though they were full-grown the day Shivoam the Great River Goddess tossed them out onto the deck of a riverboat. The fact is, riverboats are just another thread in the pattern that is t'skrang, and no doubt there will be t'skrang left in the world long after the last riverboat engine sputters and dies and sinks to the bottom of the Serpent River.

OF THE T'SLAHYIN

Villages share responsibility for crewing a riverboat. These groups of foundations are bound together by an ancient tradition of oaths and regulations called *t'slahyin,* or crew covenant. A village can subsist on fishing and farming, but to truly prosper, the t'skrang also rely on trade.

Since time out of mind, the t'skrang have depended on the extraordinary memories of our lahalas to maintain the tradition of *t'slahyin,* though my people have been attempting since the time of the Scourge to set down in writing the body of law that comprises it. It was House V'strimon that initiated this great task, which is now into its thirtieth volume, with much yet to be recorded.

Some t'skrang factions on the river propose using this document as the legal basis for regulating trade all across Barsaive, similar to way the dwarf courts function in Throal. I personally believe that such an attempt would be disastrous, for one simple reason. The courts of King Varulus make judgments based on a cohesive system of general laws that can be applied to a variety of circumstances. The t'skrang

covenants, on the other hand, are a collection of regulations that are much more specific than general, making it difficult to interpret them broadly. This system works for the t'skrang because of the wisdom of our lahalas, who can draw on centuries of practical experience in interpreting precedent.

Perhaps the clearest example of the difference between dwarf law and t'skrang tradition is the simple concept of the covenant share. Each member-*niall* of the crew covenant participates equally in the profits of its riverboat trade. In prosperous times, the whole village shares in the wealth, just as in lean times all share the burden of scarcity. Because no single foundation is big enough to crew an entire riverboat, this principle of equal shares keeps covenants together through all manner of tribulations—at least in theory.

The ship's captain is elected for a term of one season from among the ranks of all adult members of the village. Elections are a grand affair, conducted with many speeches and much tail-thumping before the village's gathered population. Every member of the *t'slahyin* over the age of twelve is expected to vote in the election in which two candidates are finally chosen. The Council of Lahalas then decides which of the two will become captain. The chosen captain must assemble a list of officers within two hours, and each officer must choose five crewmen. That same day the Council of Lahalas reads the list aloud before for the rest of the village, usually at the conclusion of a huge communal banquet, then the Council members take turns appointing additional crewmen to fill any vacancies.

Though a village may elect a new captain each year, most captains keep their position for many years by scrupulously and honestly fulfilling their part of the covenant. Because a captain often chooses the same officer core from year to year, captains and crews can remain on ships for decades despite a system designed for change.

The next step is the heart of the matter. Once a year, the people of the village gather to present the fruits of their year of labor to the crew council (the captain and his officers). Each trade offering is counted, verified, and added to the cargo manifest. After the cargo manifest has been declared, the Council of Lahalas presents a list of all the goods and materials the village must obtain through trade in the coming year. The two councils then forge the covenant, an oath that binds the crew to provide for the needs of the village by the time their ship returns from its journey while binding the village to receive the returning crew.

Once the crew council and the Council of Lahalas have completed the covenant, the riverboat sets out to trade on the river. The crew's first goal is to fulfill the terms of the covenant. Having accomplished that, they then turn to increasing the village's profits. This goal is usually accomplished by buying and selling goods along the river along with offering passage to merchants and adventurers seeking to travel any portion of the Serpent.

OF LIFE ON THE GREAT RIVER

Life on the river is my people's great passion—the gentle rocking motion of a ship beneath your feet, the ever-changing vista of the distant shore, the mystery and fascination of unfamiliar ports of call. The discipline of life in the village gives way to the joy and freedom we find on the Great Mother River we call Shivoam, the Serpent.

It is not that the details of life on the river are so distinct from life in the village. Just as the Women's Council manages the communal workload and task assignments in the village, the officer corps delegates shipwork. Instead of a lahala to act as final arbiter, the ship's captain performs that function. And though crew members may have more time to call their own while on board the ship, the riverboat is a cramped little world offering as little privacy as life in the domes. Despite all this, the river provokes an undeniable change in the average t'skrang. His eyes gleam brighter, his tail swings more proudly, his voice booms, and his heartbeat quickens like a man whose heart has been struck by Astendar's darts. Our word for this feeling is *shivarro*, the river passion.

ON THE AROPAGOI

The largest political units among the t'skrang are the *aropagoi*, or Great Houses. Just as a crew covenant consists of several cooperating foundations, so each aropagoi consists of numerous villages and crew covenants. Each Great House coordinates trade operations to the benefit of the crews and villages that compose it. The main purposes of the aropagoi are

INDEED, TO APPLY THE LAWS, IDEAS, AND PRACTICES OF THE T'SKRANG CREW COVENANT TO ALL OF BARSAIVE WOULD BE LUDICROUS!
—MERROX

IT IS AN INTERESTING DISTINCTION THAT THE PROFITS BROUGHT HOME ON THE RIVERBOAT ARE SHARED BY THE T'SKRANG VILLAGE, WHILE MOST THROAL TRADING COMPANIES ONLY PROFIT THEIR OWNERS.
—ARDINN TERO

profit and trade advantage. Political ambition, especially as understood in Throalic and Theran terms of military alliance and land control, has no place among the t'skrang aropagoi.

Each of the aropagoi controls a section of the Serpent River and regulates trade and passage in that territory. The aropagoi do not control the entire length of the Serpent; some villages do not belong to an aropagoi, but most see the advantage of that system.

The core of each aropagoi consists of a central *niall* numbering as many as one thousand members. In its strictest sense, the word aropagoi refers to this central foundation, but over time has come to represent the entire allied structure. Unlike traditional foundations, membership in the central foundation is not based on a family relationship. Instead, each crew covenant nominates new members to the central foundation. Election to the foundation of an aropagoi brings distinction and honor to the t'skrang chosen, the kind of recognition from his peers that every t'skrang yearns for. Some estimates have nearly a third of all the t'skrang in Barsaive belonging to an aropagoi of crew covenants and foundations, but less than one in a hundred of these are true *aropagoinya*, that is, members of the central foundation.

Upon joining the central foundation, new members adopt an additional name, the *g'doinya*. Usually more an epithet or label than a name, the *g'doinya* is descriptive of its wearer, giving rise to such rubrics as "Seadreamer" or "Orkfriend." The *g'doinya* is rarely used outside the membership of a particular aropagoi. This taboo is so strictly observed that use of the *g'doinya* in other situations takes on deeper meaning. In combats between rival aropagoi, for example, opposing central foundation members speak each others' *g'doinya* as a way of announcing that they intend to duel to the death.

During a *g'doinya* ritual, the new member of the aropagoi foundation also receives a token of identification. Each aropagoi has a unique token, usually imprinted with the House symbol and colors. These tokens hold great value in the t'skrang river communities. Any non-t'skrang carrying an aropagoi token is accepted as having received the blessing of the House, and any t'skrang carrying one is accorded the same rights as a member of the aropagoi. Of course, carrying a stolen token into the aropagoi to which it belongs is almost as perilous as falling into the hands of one House while carrying the token of its rival. T'skrang consider possession of an aropagoi token under false pretenses to be a criminal act and punish offenders of their own race by cutting off their tails. For other races, an arm or a leg will serve as well.

The eldest woman of the central foundation is called the shivalahala. The shivalahala receive the same kind of ancestral memories as the lahalas of the smaller foundations and are also believed to possess supernatural powers. The last documented case of an elementalist casting a spell higher than tenth circle took place during the siege of House V'strimon in Lake Ban, when the Shivalahala V'strimon changed the elemental air to earth in every airship of the Theran fleet threatening her home. Theran ships may fly, but Therans left to their own devices are indeed subject to the laws of gravity.

The smallest of the five known aropagoi can field a fleet of thirty riverboats, including eight to twelve riverboats controlled by the central foundation rather than the crew covenants. Easily the most splendid vessels on the Serpent River, the aropagoi riverboats are armed to the teeth with fire cannons, powerful engines, and veteran crews. Aropagoi flagships patrol the river to keep the waterway near their headquarters safe for trade. But some others trying to make a living on or near the Serpent consider the aropagoi to be little more than pirate federations who did not ask either their approval or participation in setting up these patrols. While it is true that aropagoi crews sometimes charge exorbitant tolls or wring exorbitant coin for protection services, they rarely engage in traditional "board-and-storm" pirate tactics except against ships of a rival House. Indeed, *aropagoinya* actively seek out and engage pirate ships as a preventive measure to protect their trade routes along the river. I can describe certain facets of each of the five aropagoi, but there is much I do not know and much I cannot say.

Syrtis Aropagoi is called the House of the Moon. Its colors are blue and silver, and its symbol is an S-shaped silver dragon set against a deep blue background. The token of the *aropagoinya* of House Syrtis is a silver ring with a cameo of a dragon set against a faience stone. The Syrtis central foundation gathers at Lalai Canyon, one of the ancient wonders of the t'skrang race. Steep and wide, this magnificent canyon was carved out where the Serpent River bends around the northern spur of the Throal Mountains. On the canyon's south face my people long ago carved out a city that rises above and drops below the surface of the river. That a small colony of obsidimen still lives here adds strength to the legend of the city's origins, which tells that it was constructed through the efforts of obsidimen and t'skrang working together. The Shivalahala Syrtis enjoys great renown as a prophetess.

The House of the Nine Diamonds, or K'tenshin Aropagoi, takes red and gold as its colors and the image of nine red diamonds against a gold background as its symbol. Every *aropagoinya* of K'tenshin wears in his left ear a token in the form of a large gold earring studded with rubies. The name of the House refers to the arrangement of its sixteen village towers, which form nine interlocking diamonds. K'tenshin boasts the tallest towers on the river, their extraordinary height making them visible for miles around. In addition to the Shivalahala K'tenshin's traditional duties, she also leads one of the more famous schools for warrior adepts.

The name of my own house, V'strimon Aropagoi, roughly translates as the House of Reeds. Our colors are blue and green, and our symbol is a stylized clump of green river rushes against a background as blue as the river. We *aropagoinya* wear a simple bracelet of river reeds around our right wrists, a token that will remain green and supple for as long as its wearer remains alive. Our trading house lies in the center of Lake Ban and is called the Floating City. It is set on a floating island of interwoven reeds and is considered by the people of all Barsaive to be one of the province's most remarkable sites. The reed island measures nearly thirty feet thick, and is anchored to five towers arranged in the shape of a pentagon. Shivalahala V'strimon has a reputation as the most powerful elementalist in Barsaive, and, among the leaders of the Great Houses, I suspect she possesses the greatest political ambitions. This headstrong woman also outranks other shivalahalas in pigheadedness, and though it is by her command that I sit here, a prisoner in this Passion-forsaken pit of a Theran dungeon, I love her dearly just the same.

Henghyoke Aropagoi is the House of the Otter. Its symbol is an otter carrying a silver egg in its mouth, and its colors are brown and white. The *aropagoinya* wear a platinum band around their necks as a token, and it is believed that they cannot remove the token without destroying it. Many theories attempt to explain the mystery of the Shivalahala Henghyoke, but my favorite is the version that claims that she is an illusionist who has hidden her home with an enchantment.

Ishkarat Aropagoi is the House of the Wheel. Its colors are crimson and white, its symbol a white paddle wheel against a red background. As their token the *aropagoinya* carry a ritual dagger made of black obsidian. The only thing the other *aropagoinya* know of the Ishkarat's headquarters is that it lies on Lake Vors, for anyone not of the aropagoi is condemned to immediate execution if discovered in the city. Members of the Ishkarat generally keep to themselves, though members of associated crew covenants seem to be the usual gregarious group. Apparently, the only people who ever see or talk to the Shivalahala Ishkarat are members of the central foundation, and members of that select group become very surly if asked to discuss her. As a word of warning, I would mention that the most dangerous swordsmen on the length of the Serpent River are Ishkarat *aropagoinya*.

ON UNIQUE ITEMS OF TRADE

My people practice many crafts and support several industries peculiar to our way of life, producing goods that command premium prices in the river trade. For those people in Barsaive who are not familiar with my people's skills and craftsmanship, I will describe a few of the more interesting and unique items created by the t'skrang.

FISH OF SURPASSING DELICACY

As I mentioned, t'skrang foundations catch fish by stringing a maze of nets between their domes. From there the fish are sent for processing with a secret combination of spices and magic, packed carefully in layers of reeds and preservative oils, then sealed in pottery or baskets for transport. The result is among the finest delicacies available in Barsaive, and with proper care the fish will last for months without spoiling.

As fish are the most profitable of our trading goods, we t'skrang take our fish recipes quite seriously. Revealing the secret's of a village's recipes is one of the few crimes punishable by the death penalty among our people. The t'skrang tell a story that one overgovernor of Skypoint, a gourmet of great renown, became so enamored of the little yellowtail fish prepared by the Sokriosh village that he sent a raiding party to capture their cooks. After a short siege, Therans breached the village's defenses and enslaved the whole community. When one of the Theran crew let slip the purpose of the mission on the voyage back to Skypoint, the captives immediately launched a desperate, bloody rebellion. When the Therans finally put down the revolt, they were dismayed to discover that the first captives to die had been the cooks, who had preferred to take their secrets to the grave rather than divulge them under interrogation to the Therans.

SPICES OF GREAT DIVERSITY

The t'skrang cultivate many of the spices necessary to prepare their fish in the fertile mud of the protected area between a village's towers. These same spices have other uses as well. The people of Barsaive are just rediscovering the virtues of t'skrang spices for their medicinal and curative powers. In many cases, however, the spices one buys from a t'skrang merchant represent mixtures of several compounded herbs and often require many intermediate preparation steps to reach their final state. Indeed, two of the best-selling spices on the river, *d'janduin* and *kuratai*, provide a subtle variety of flavors and various side effects, depending on the village that made them. In the interest of maintaining an absolute monopoly over this facet of their trade, t'skrang rarely, if ever, sell unprocessed spices.

ROPE OF INCOMPARABLE STRENGTH

Used for everything from kite string to ship hawsers, t'skrang rope is considered the best money can buy. Unfortunately, some t'skrang rope makers take advantage of this reputation to sell second-rate merchandise. Because ropes play such an important role in our society, whether for rope swings, boat lines, or netting, we t'skrang have had much practice in the making of rope.

Our many uses for rope have inspired my people to experiment with various materials and braiding styles. One type, made exclusively by the Ishkarat Aropagoi on the Upper Serpent, is called clingor in the dwarf language, a word that describes the rope's unusual properties. When fastened securely, clingor will bind itself to any other material without sticking to itself. If clingor is fastened correctly to a post, the fastened end will bind tight, while the other end can move freely around the post. Riverboat crews and mountaineers alike appreciate clingor's unique properties.

BASKETRY OF EXCEEDING CUNNING

Few people realize that more than fifty varieties of reeds grow along the Serpent—and the t'skrang have a word for each one. We weave reeds into countless shapes and sizes, creating many of the containers, utensils, and other items needed to make our lives easier. Many cultures in Barsaive use our baskets to store solid objects, but the t'skrang have also mastered the art of weaving watertight baskets. Lighter and more resilient than wooden barrels, these baskets keep food, wine, and ale safe from spoiling. Our weavers bring great skill to their art, weaving beautiful patterns into their creations by varying the texture and color of various types of reeds.

FINE INSTRUMENTS OF WRITING

Our artisans also weave reeds into paper. Because it is so durable, t'skrang paper has become the standard for Barsaive's magic-wielders, though the finest paper in the land still comes from the reeds that flourish in the Mist Swamps. The same craftsmanship that produces watertight baskets is also used to create water-repellent paper, and a scroll made of t'skrang paper will last more than a month underwater without disintegrating or losing the ink inscribed on it.

Naturally, water-resistant paper is of little value unless used with inks that will not smudge or run. In another example of certain villages dominating the market, several t'skrang villages specialize in extracting the base for such inks from the glands of certain fish, creating a unique product with a large demand. The folk of Sessipau village long ago discovered a way to make certain inks invisible except under special circumstances—for example, when the paper is soaked in blueberry juice or only under the light of a full moon. These conditions may seem frivolous, but, in truth, it was invisible ink which allowed House V'strimon to safely exchange diplomatic letters with the dwarfs of Throal during the Theran War.

One of the finest products the t'skrang manufacture from reeds is pens. At the very moment of this writing, I am using a remarkable pen made by House Syrtis. The tip of the pen will last a year and a day, and the inkwell is built into the reed to provide a constant flow of ink to the tip. I have never used a better writing instrument in all my days, and I recommend it highly to the scholars who will doubtless someday be forced to copy this scroll ten times over.

MUSIC OF JOY AND PROFIT

The t'skrang make one other trade item from reeds: musical instruments. Even as a troubadour, I must bow to the elves as the undisputed masters of music in all its forms. Though everyone knows that elven instruments are considered the finest available, not everyone can afford to own one, and the heart of the matter is that music belongs to everyone. The t'skrang fill the basic need of all Name-givers to own inexpensive, tuneful instruments. In particular, t'skrang craftsmen create extraordinary reed flutes capable of expressing two and sometimes three notes at the same time.

Beyond even the sale of musical instruments, the t'skrang have won spectacular success selling music itself as entertainment. The riverboat crews have always used music to fill the tedious hours that plague any long voyage. No one can say just where or when it began, but the townsfolk in some community along the river's edge must have heard a t'skrang crew playing, and lured them off the boat with the promise of money. Today, some villages do only minimal trading, instead sending their riverboats to give performances in exchange for money or goods in town after town along the river. I personally organized the first showboat for House V'strimon, which to this day remains one of the most profitable ships in the aropagoi.

POTTERY OF BEAUTY AND USE

The deep mud of the Serpent River's bottom contains rich deposits of elemental earth that t'skrang potters use to create unique and wondrous things. These skilled artisans incorporate small quantities of this precious substance into their raw materials to make sturdy plates and cups that will stay warm for hours, lidded urns that do not shatter, and spouts for watertight baskets. The t'skrang also have developed unusual crockery that remains cool to the touch on the outside yet hot enough to cook food on the inside.

It is said that the obsidimen taught the t'skrang the art of working with glass in return for a quantity of elemental earth. I do no know whether the obsidimen still fashion art and other objects from glass, but certainly the t'skrang are still among the most serious practitioners of the art. One of the few t'skrang land caravans that operates on a regular schedule belongs to House K'tenshin, whose hardy prospectors scour the shores of Death's Sea for the rare pearlescent sand deposits that give K'tenshin porcelain its characteristic luminescence.

ART OF ELEMENTAL NATURE

The greatest source of pride for t'skrang artisans, and deservedly so, lies in their renowned elemental art. Statuettes carved of elemental water, bead necklaces that change shape and color as the wearer moves, spiral-shaped bracelets that flow up and down the wearer's arms—all these are marvels of t'skrang skill. Villages that have lost their riverboat to piracy, mutiny, or accident often manage to sustain themselves by selling and trading such jewelry. Whenever possible, Great Houses offer such villages full membership in the aropagoi as *krohyin*, or trade covenants.

ON THE T'SKRANG LOVE FOR ART

While t'skrang take craftsmanship quite seriously, art stirs their souls. Indeed, t'skrang accord to fine art a reverence that is akin to the spirit of *haropas*, or communion with the Passions. Such artwork so affects the t'skrang that we enshrine the finest examples and dedicate them to the Passions. Beloved tales speak of riverboat crews who, in the course of a trade mission, discover a statue, painting, tapestry, magical talisman, or some other work of such arresting beauty that they do whatever is necessary—even to the point of selling everything on the boat—to bring it home to their village. Other common tales describe crews risking life, limb, and ship to steal objects of beauty and wonder from their rightful owners. It is quite true that t'skrang sometimes hold an unusual notion of ownership.

If anything good can be said to have come of the Scourge, the truly impressive leaps forward in complexity and craftsmanship of artistic endeavors would be that thing. When the citizens of Barsaive decided that the mental focus and creativity needed to create a work of art provided proof that a person had not been corrupted by the Horrors, their artistic efforts not only proliferated but reached unexpected and wondrous levels of skill and beauty. Even the simplest, most utilitarian items are created with a careful eye to detail. But beyond mere intricacy, the t'skrang appreciate the artful combination of elegance and usefulness. In fact, a shared taste for beauty in functionality may be one of the keys to the successful commerce between t'skrang and dwarfs.

Where other races believe that the person who makes a new and original object in some way holds special rights to profiting from his creation, the t'skrang find no shame in faithfully copying another artist's work as long as the final product is well crafted and beautiful. As might be expected, this has led to some ill will between master artisans of other races and the admiring t'skrang who copy their work. When a t'skrang sees something in the world that pleases his eye, he is as likely to try and copy it as he is to offer to buy it. And the object's creator usually becomes further outraged when the t'skrang begin large-scale production of their work.

T'Skrang

PALE ONES TRAVEL THE MINES OF RAZHIKHUL.

An elemental water sculpture depicts the legend of the Old Man of the Nets.

Riileska, servant of Earthroot, King of the Pale Ones.

Young k'stulaami embrace their natural fear of heights.

Cunningly crafted jars hold unique spices, magically prepared by the t'skrang.

The t'skrang of the Servos Jungle wear elaborate battle masks into war against Theran slavers.

A T'SKRANG BOATMAN SHOUTS A CHALLENGE TO AN ATTACKING PIRATE SHIP.

One example of the strain this can cause is clearly illustrated in the case of the earthenware necklaces known as "shapeshifters." A human named Erin Laszlo of the riverside town of Tansiarda claims that his family has been fashioning elemental earth into ever-changing jewelry for three generations. He made the mistake of demonstrating the secret of these necklaces to the captain of a riverboat from House Ishkarat whose hobby was elemental magic. Two years later, an Ishkari trade covenant began producing a thousand of these trinkets each year. Today, Erin Laszlo no longer earns enough to feed his family because the Ishkari flooded the market and drove down the price for this jewelry. No doubt King Varulus and his legal system could sort out this dilemma, but not without interfering with Ishkari profits—and declining profits are exactly the sort of thing that keeps riverboat captains from supporting the widespread adoption of Throal's laws.

ON THE T'SKRANG BEYOND THE SERPENT RIVER

Over the past century, the t'skrang have spread far afield from the banks of the Serpent, joining communities all across Barsaive. It may surprise the reader to learn that the loudest supporters of Throalic influence in Barsaive are these t'skrang foundations thriving in Barsaive's towns and trading posts. T'skrang, more so than other races, readily recognize that trade controlled by the Theran Empire would be lopsided and barely profitable.

Most every town in Barsaive founded since the end of the Scourge possesses a t'skrang area. Humans unfairly complain that town t'skrang cluster together too much and refuse to live among their fellow races, but other races usually do not understand that our large, extended families virtually require communal living arrangements. Town t'skrang tend to live in dwellings connected like rabbit warrens and centered on the hatcheries and the gathering circles. If the town lies near a river or lake, the t'skrang will build their homes as close as possible to the shore, using stilts to extend their homes over the surface of the water when allowed. If the town lacks open water, the t'skrang often take to the trees, sometimes collaborating with windlings to build truly remarkable dwellings. Where the forest meets the river's edge at Axalalail on the Coil River, the t'skrang and the windlings have created one of these astounding structures and named it the Swinging City. More than one elf has expressed a grudging wonder at its beauty.

The town t'skrang have introduced the other Name-givers to many new enterprises. The very idea of what we call a *trisnari*, an inn that provides food but no rooms for guests, was enough to send most folk into gales of laughter. Despite this initial reaction, t'skrang *trisnari* now command a loyal following in larger towns, and many humans seek advice on establishing such businesses for themselves. It was t'skrang engineering that first dammed streams and set that power to work

JANET AULISIO DANNHEISER 1994.

milling seed to flour. And, of course, the idea of the "covenant share," where all who help create a community's profit share in that profit, has spread from the foundations into the mines and merchant caravans, opening up the possibilities of entirely new methods of business and trade.

My impression of town t'skrang is that, as a group, they seem less high-strung than their compatriots on the river. In the towns, our race's emphasis on *jik'harra* and *p'skarrot* gives way to acceptance and cooperation. Some *aropagoinya* claim that t'skrang grow soft with city life, but their words are little more than beating a shield with one's spear. We survived the Scourge, and now less action and more introspection might do our race some good.

ON THOSE T'SKRANG KNOWN AS THE PALE ONES

The tributaries of the Serpent River flow from sources deep within the heart of the mountains of Barsaive. As with all parts of the Serpent, t'skrang live on these underground rivers. Known as the Pale Ones, these t'skrang shun the light of the sun and have never tasted the wind. Their name describes the tone of their skin, which is much lighter than the range seen among other t'skrang. Some have silvery scales like a fish, others actually glow with luminescence. Many legends say that their huge popeyes are blind and that they use other senses to "see," but I have met the Pale Ones myself, and I assure you that their vision is as keen as any dwarf's in the dark. They also rely on their extraordinary sense of taste for information about their surroundings by rapidly flicking their long, forked tongues in and out of their mouths.

The dwarfs consider the Pale Ones something of a mixed blessing. On the one hand, the Pale Ones' boats and extraordinary knowledge of the underground waterways provide dwarf miners with readily available transportation for their ores. On the other hand, the dwarfs' endless quest for new veins of minerals inevitably invades the Pale Ones' territory, arousing bitter hostility toward the dwarfs. Tribes of Pale Ones often wage hidden, vicious wars against those same mining dwarfs for whom they have been providing transport services.

Like the dwarfs, my own reaction to the Pale Ones was decidedly mixed. Throal requested a legate from House V'strimon to negotiate with a group of underground t'skrang living near Razhikhul. I do not recall how my name came up before the Council as a candidate for the task, but I'd had a falling out with the shivalahala over some triviality shortly before, and I was inconveniently close at hand. I spent two lightless months lost in the mines of Razhikhul (dwarf guides notwithstanding) before we caught

even a glimpse of a Pale One. By that time, of course, they considered me guilty of dwarf sympathies by association. The next day, following a merry, night-long game of hide-and-seek, I found myself a bound captive in the Pale Ones' camp, my erstwhile dwarf retinue roasting over a fire in preparation for the forthcoming victory feast.

When the Pale Ones capture a t'skrang from another tribe, they will, by custom, set him free if he can spin a tale that no one among them has heard before. They say that every t'skrang loves a good story, but my task was not so easy as it first appeared. Accomplished troubadour though I am, I was unable to find a tale that someone among the audience could not finish. The Pale Ones may live forty leagues beneath the surface of the earth, but they know their legends. The War Against the Elves, the Breaking of the Earth, the Old Man of the Nets, the Founding of Thera, the Coming of the Horrors—all these tales they knew by heart.

Just as I despaired of finding a story they did not know, the perfect solution came to mind. I made up a tale out of whole cloth, relating details of the voyage of Vaare Longfang and the fate of her ship the *Earthdawn*. The tale won me my freedom, and incidentally, in the light of day the same song won me first prize at the Lernaean bardic contest. But this is all somewhat off the sweep of the current! I so impressed the Pale Ones with my tale of the fall of the *Earthdawn* that they insisted I must meet their king. They took me down the deep watercourses that run through the depths of the mountains of Throal in their boats, which are themselves marvelous affairs. These craft float on inflated, watertight bags that the Pale Ones fashion from the dried intestines of a subterranean creature they call *iyoshkira*. It must be that they cure these skins in a way that makes them tough enough to resist puncture, because the floats held up even when I tried the sharp edge of a sword against them. Using the bones of the *iyoshkira* as a frame for the boat, the Pale Ones stretch tightly woven mats across the frames to make a raft. These t'skrang rely on their knowledge of the currents to take their boats where they want to go, but willingly jump into the water and tow their raft by swimming when necessary.

Far below the Throal Mountains, deeper even than the dwarfs have yet delved, the underground rivers drain into a system of vast caverns to form lakes and seas. The Pale Ones call this place Shuss Halima, which roughly translates as "glittering home." The glitter refers to the light given off by a phosphorescent moss that flourishes in the warmth and humidity of the caverns. I have never seen a stranger place in the world, for all manner of flora and fauna thrive there, the likes of which I could barely have imagined—plants with leaves colored every hue but green, mushrooms that grow tall as trees near the water's edge, and fish that burn like fireflies moving under the surface of the water.

The greatest surprise of my journey to the glittering caves, however, was the discovery that the king of the Pale Ones was no t'skrang! My escort maneuvered our craft out to the center of a brightly lit lake where the king held his court. The walls of the cavern all around the lake shore were carved into homes for the Pale Ones, and the place rang with the bustle of busy t'skrang and darting boats. As we waited patiently in the center of the lake, a fleet of boats sailed toward us, each laden low to the water line with food.

Suddenly, our raft pitched uneasily, the waters churned, and less than ten feet away surfaced the head of a dragon, its jaws alone large enough to swallow every boat present in a single gulp. This was Earthroot, King of the Pale Ones. My audience was mercifully brief.

NO OTHER LEGENDS OR FIRSTHAND ACCOUNTS WE HAVE COLLECTED CONCERNING THE PALE RACE OF T'SKRANG SO MUCH AS HINTS THAT THEY EAT OTHER NAME-GIVER RACES. I SUSPECT THAT OUR AUTHOR WAS DELIRIOUS WITH PAIN FROM AN INJURY, OR SUFFERING THE EFFECTS OF SOME HERB OR POTION USED BY THESE UNDERGROUND T'SKRANG, OR THAT THE ROASTING WAS A TYPE OF TORTURE.
—MERROX

OUR SCHOLARS HAVE GIVEN THIS TALE CAREFUL SCRUTINY, AS IT CONTRADICTS MANY COMMONLY HELD THEORIES AND BELIEFS ABOUT DRAGONS. AS WITH MOST MATTERS, HOWEVER, THE WHOLE TRUTH REMAINS ELUSIVE.
—JERRIV FORRIM

Though most legends tell that dragons loathe the water, I suspect this one arranged his lair underwater because it was the only way to support his immense weight. Earthroot is quite fond of fine foods, and his court is less preoccupied with governance than with the provisioning and feeding of their king. Apparently Earthroot protected the Pale Ones from the Horrors during the Scourge, and so the t'skrang treat him with worshipful respect. He seemed most amicable for a dragon, and I did more than merely survive my encounter with him—I extracted certain concessions from him regarding the dwarfs, allowing me to fulfill my mission and the Pale Ones to return me to the land of the sun.

OF THE T'SKRANG WHO FLY

On rare occasion, a hatchling is born with a thin membrane, which we call the *k'stulaa*, that stretches from each wrist to each hip. During the Scourge, the women tending the hatchery considered such a birth a bad omen for the foundation, and for very simple reasons. Children of the *k'stulaa* become completely unmanageable when they enter *kaissa*. They think only of flight and the promise of the open sky and lose the ability to speak our language. It is very strange to see a t'skrang at a loss for words! During the Scourge, when no one was permitted to leave the village domes, many *k'stulaa* went mad locked up in the kaers.

My fifth hatchling was *k'stulaa*. Other than having an unusual advantage when swinging on the ropes of our dome, Gamal was very much the same as any other hatchling. Sometime during her eleventh year, however, she began to change. Instead of performing her assigned tasks for the village, she would be discovered on the roof of a village tower. Neglecting her chores won her nothing but punishment, but the disciplining she suffered only made Gamal more distant and unapproachable. One day the sentries fished her out of the river after she had jumped from the tower in an attempt to fly.

No sooner had she healed from her injuries but she tried again. I tried to find a post for her on a riverboat as a *khamorro* in hope that the usual distractions from *kaissa* would help her, but no crew would take her. No one quite knew how Gamal survived her fourth fall, but witnesses say she leveled into a glide after checking her fall with her wings, only to crash headlong into a neighboring tower. After that, we were so afraid that she would die in the attempt to fly that we kept her virtually imprisoned in the village. She became violently ill, then forsook speech altogether and began to twitter and whistle like a bird.

At my wit's end, I implored an old comrade in arms, a windling named Jennalee, to teach Gamal to fly. A few days under Jennalee's tutelage settled Gamal down dramatically, and we even managed a brief conversation, though it consisted mostly of Gamal babbling uncontrollably about the joys of flight. Jennalee called Gamal's obsession the "flight passion;" apparently many young windlings experience a similar phase as a youngster.

A few weeks into Gamal's "training," Jennalee suggested that the three of us take a trip to the southern spur of the Throal Mountains. Though Gamal could successfully glide for long distances, she was as yet unable to take off from the ground under her own power, and Jennalee guessed that the mountain heights would provide the perfect remedy for Gamal's insatiable flight passion. I was so impressed with the changes in Gamal since my friend had taken her in charge that I arranged passage on the next boat going upriver.

Gamal herself made an extraordinary impression on the crew of the *Waverider*. Each day of our journey, she would soar off the top deck under Jennalee's guidance. Most t'skrang are terrified by the idea of flight, and Gamal's relentless, exuberant pursuit of the experience made the crew believe that the child possessed a heroic measure of *jik'harra*.

When we left the river and headed into the mountains, I agreed with the crew. Jennalee would scout ahead in the mornings for a nearby pinnacle or cliff, then Gamal and I would follow her up outrageously difficult terrain. No sooner would we reach the top than Gamal would run and throw herself over the precipice. Standing a safe distance from the

edge, I would struggle against dizziness and even vertigo to watch Gamal find her wings and rise toward the clouds. I cannot lie to you. Never once did I feel the least desire to join Gamal, to hang poised between earth and sky, but her limitless joy made me believe that this was what the sages meant when they said, "*Haropas* resides in the heart that embraces every fear and every passion."

Near sunset of our fifth day in the mountains, the *k'stulaami* entered our camp. Each of the strangers was a t'skrang with the *k'stulaa*, and they had tattooed their wingflaps with intricate patterns and pictures in a way that bore a striking resemblance to the decorations on the robes of a magician. At first, they said very little, but after sharing our evening meal, they began speaking to Gamal in the same birdlike language that she had used when confined in the domes. The next day, they led us to a well-used footpath that climbed one of the highest mountains in that region. The path soon narrowed to a precarious ledge along a frightening precipice that curved away out of sight. Afraid to look down, we gazed at the sky, and could see what appeared to be a family of eagles circling majestically in and out of the clouds.

As we rounded a bend in the path, we entered the cliff dwellings of the *k'stulaami*. The home of these winged t'skrang is carved deep into the face of a sheer cliff rising thousands of feet high. The *k'stulaami* need take only two steps out their front door and they have launched themselves into thin air. Several hundred of them lived in this place, but it seemed large enough for a city of several thousand. Our guide introduced me to a wizened t'skrang woman who called herself the Shivalahala Sesslakai. She said that before the Scourge, hers was one of the Great Houses of the t'skrang, the House of the Spirit Wind. With the coming of the Horrors, however, the aropagoi had dwindled, for her house depended on the people of the river to send *k'stulaa*-born hatchlings to their mountain citadel.

The Shivalahala did not yet know that the Scourge was ended, for Sesslakai Aropagoi had never acquired one of the elemental clocks that signaled the retreat of the Horrors back to the infernal domain from which they came. Our visit, therefore, proved to be an occasion for great celebration. Jennalee and I received a hero's welcome as the bearers of glad tidings and were sent off with more gifts than we could possibly carry. My dear Gamal, of course, stayed with the *k'stulaami* in their cliff dwellings, and no doubt is there still, tossing herself off the edge of the world with nothing but a scrap of skin between her and a steep plunge to the ground. I still shudder to think of it, but what's a *chaida* to do? Hatchlings grow up, you know.

SINCE THE TIME THIS ACCOUNT WAS WRITTEN, SEVERAL OF THE RIVER AROPAGOI AND SOME MERCHANT COMPANIES IN BARTERTOWN HAVE ESTABLISHED TRADE COVENANTS WITH THE HOUSE OF THE SPIRIT WIND.
—ARDINN TERO

OF THE T'SKRANG WHO LIVE IN THE JUNGLE

Under the green canopy of the Servos Jungle live tribes of t'skrang who remain close to their origins. For the jungle t'skrang, there are no crew covenants, no riverboats. Their domes are huts made of mud and sticks, half-submerged in the shallow waters of the Serpent's tributaries. They struggle to survive by hunting the jungle's most fearsome creatures with their stone-tipped spears. I know of no other people in Barsaive, except perhaps the Tamers of the Liaj Jungle or the Cathan of the Servos, who live in such a primitive state.

Their crude weapons do not prevent the jungle t'skrang from being accomplished hunters, and many of the finest hides and furs in Barsaive pass through the trading posts that the river t'skrang maintain in the jungle. As I may have mentioned before, the Shivalahala V'strimon has not always treated me with the greatest respect, and one particularly bitter argument landed me a tour of duty at a Servos trading outpost.

I remember that on the voyage downriver, the crew of the riverboat took perverse delight in telling stories about the jungle cannibals, how they sharpen their teeth on a whetstone, how they have a special knack for curing the hides of Name-givers. I spent most of the spring trading for a stack of hides, all the while wondering if one of them could have belonged to a t'skrang. That summer the Therans mounted the campaign for Travar, and the trading post was overrun by the Theran navy, as were most other civilized settlements on the Serpent below Lake Pyros. Much to my surprise, the jungle t'skrang opened their homes to those who had lost their shelter in the Theran action and found themselves homeless in the Servos. During my stay with the jungle t'skrang, I learned a deep and lasting respect for these people we are too quick to dismiss as mere primitives.

The domes of the jungle t'skrang are much smaller than ours on the great Serpent, but they make up in sheer numbers what they lack in size. The village of a hundred t'skrang where I and my companions found sanctuary contained more than forty-four domes connected by underground tunnels. Most married couples lived alone in a dome. The community used a central hatchery, but quite unlike the anonymity of motherhood in my foundation, the women of the jungle tribes personalize their eggs by painting them with patterns that identify the parentage of each egg.

We were able to follow the course of the Theran campaign throughout the summer by way of the drum signals the jungle t'skrang use to relay messages over long distances. Five feet in diameter, each drum requires three skilled musicians to create a proper message, and the drumming itself is complex and pleasing to the ear. The drumming constitutes an amazingly comprehensive language, and carries for miles through the humid jungle air. We could easily plot the exact numbers and locations of Theran troops throughout the jungle as signals converged from miles away in every direction. Of course, sorting out and interpreting the signals was another art in itself, but I found the whole concept so intriguing that I was inspired to apply serious efforts to learning as much as I could.

The Theran troops rarely came near the community where I was living, but one day the drums told us that a Theran vedette had gone to ground about three miles beyond the river. Before I could suggest that my companions and I investigate the situation, the tribe's lahala called for a hunting party, and I quickly understood that the Therans were our prey. The end of the Scourge had brought the Therans of Skypoint out in force to scour the villages of the Servos in search for slaves for their domain. But Therans who commit the error of entering the Servos unprepared seldom leave the jungle alive.

Still, as our war party jogged through the dense jungle undergrowth toward the fallen airship, I doubted that forty t'skrang armed with primitive weapons and no armor could actually threaten the Overgovernor's trained soldiers. But by the time we reached our target, seven other equally large hunting parties had also arrived. The airship squatted in the jungle growth like a poorly engineered fortress, and the faces of the sailors manning the fire cannons all along the decks clearly showed their terror. I remembered the stories of the riverboat crew, and wondered what tales the Therans might also have heard about the "jungle cannibals."

Rendered completely invisible by the lush vegetation, we crouched among the trees and waited. After a time, the Therans sent ten men and a brigade of slaves out to find fresh water. I expected simple, straightforward war tactics such as an immediate, full-strength attack from the jungle t'skrang, but instead they shadowed the supply party as it hacked its way toward a stream. A small team of t'skrang ranged out in front of the main body of our force, setting cunning snares that snatched the Theran soldiers one by one, but left the slaves unharmed. When only one sailor remained, forty hunters uttered shrill war cries in unison and swung out of the trees, sending the soldier back to his ship in a blind panic. We freed the slaves and gave each a spear, then returned to our posts out of sight of the ship and waited for nightfall.

While we waited, the jungle t'skrang gathered leaves and sticks and mosses and began to craft their battle masks. I felt tempted to laugh at the crude results of their labor, convinced that the leaves would fall into the warriors' eyes, the sticks would catch on the surrounding branches and vines, and that the whole contraption would peel off their faces before the first exchange of melee. But as twilight crept through the trees and the weird sounds of the jungle's night-dwelling

creatures swelled into full chorus, the warriors slipped their masks over their faces, and it suddenly seemed to me that I was gazing not upon t'skrang, but upon the visages of hundreds of Horrors.

I have fought in battles before that one and since, and many times have I heard the screams and shouts of dying men. But never have I heard men's voices so filled with terror and despair as I did that night. The t'skrang spared a few Theran lives, for their own ends. A few survivors they dragged up the river, leaving them where a passing Theran patrol might pick them up a few days later. In my opinion, those survivors were surely as mad as any Name-giver touched by a Horror.

The events had turned my thoughts to the Scourge, and when we returned to the village I asked the lahala how her people had survived the time of Horrors without benefit of either a citadel or a kaer. She looked at me sadly and said only, "For us, the book of memory is closed. We do not speak of the time of darkness, nor can we reach beyond to the bright days that came before, except to say we bled and we wept, bled and wept."

The jungle t'skrang are indeed cannibals, my friends, but they do not hunt to eat. The foundation took those of their members who had fallen in battle against the Therans and prepared the bodies of those who shed blood at their dying for the feast. The whole tribe came to the victory feast and ate the flesh of their fallen sisters and brothers. Much to the horror of my companions, I joined the feast. As I ate, the shadows of the surrounding trees came to life, the sounds of the jungle took on meaning, and I felt a drumbeat as though the earth itself was stretched taut and some dark gods were beating upon it. The feasting gave way to a dance. The things that happened during the dance I will not describe here; songs were sung that I will not sing; and stories were told that I will not retell. I can only say, "We bled and we wept."

And that is all I will say about the jungle t'skrang. My memories of these members of our race hold my heart in a powerful grip that I will feel until the end of my days. Though I returned to V'strimon the next spring and begged the shivala-hala to send me back to that tiny trading post in the Servos Jungle, I was sent instead to the court of Varulus in Throal, and I have never stepped foot in the jungle since.

ON THE T'SKRANG LOVE FOR LANGUAGE

The t'skrang firmly believe that no other Name-givers love the spoken word as well as we do. The elves gave us the bardic tradition, of course, but where elves devote their most passionate efforts to poetry and philosophical discourse, we t'skrang more often wax ecstatic over trivial conversation, as long as wit and humor prevail. Dwarfs, being a taciturn lot, are fond of saying, "An elf will bore you to tears, but a t'skrang will talk you to death." Though I have never seen a dwarf die from listening to too much talk, I freely admit that my people often speak when silence would suffice.

Like most Barsaivians, the t'skrang embraced the ideals of the Book of Tomorrow, and so speak Throalic quite fluently. This greatly benefits our trade efforts, because at least half of Barsaive's population cannot even pronounce the complex sounds of T'skrang, much less muddle their way through our difficult syntax. During the Scourge, our language developed as many dialects as there are villages on the river, making our native tongue even more difficult for an outsider to learn. Still, we cling to the ancient racial language, even in our settlements above water and among other Name-givers. Certain concepts, such as *t'chai kondos* and *jik'harra* and *haropas*, simply fail to translate.

My people also retain our own written language, though we use the simpler dwarf script for everyday tasks. The T'skrang script consists of pictures and is an art form in itself. One can express distinct moods and subtle innuendo using the brush strokes of certain, key characters in a phrase. Masters of T'skrang script often deliberately leave the exact interpretation of many words in a manuscript to the reader's imagination. From personal experience, I assure you it is no small feat to piece together the right words to an ancient spell from a t'skrang elementalist's grimoire, especially with a hungry Horror knocking at your door.

Though fewer t'skrang know our written language than ever before, we can still take credit for the widespread use of two systems of notation. The first, our numerical system, greatly simplifies arithmetical calculations, and many people who trade with the t'skrang learn this system. Jen Damritsar Syrtis found a way to translate some of the classic t'skrang mathematical texts into Throalic using a limited set of the original t'skrang characters, a system we expect to continue to spread across Barsaive. Because our number system represents an important part of our culture, more adult t'skrang can use it than can read our texts.

Our method of musical notation, which is closely tied to our number system, makes it possible to easily and concisely write out multiple instrumental parts simultaneously. As a troubadour, I admit that the elves originated formal musical notation, but their system can hardly be called either effortless or concise.

ON CUSTOMS PECULIAR TO THE T'SKRANG

All t'skrang, regardless of their physical location or lifestyle, share several customs collectively. Though Naming rituals, marriage rites, and death rites are common in other Name-giver races, the customs applied to tail etiquette are unique to my people.

OF LIVING IN HARMONY WITH A TAIL

The t'skrang believe that all other Name-giver races must somehow have angered the Passions, which is how they come to be born without a tail. Indeed, many foundations along the river maintain the ancient practice of cutting off the tails of individuals who commit minor acts of lawlessness. Such a mark no t'skrang can conceal, but it is an injury easily survived and soon recovered—our tails grow back after a year or so.

The reader might then think, quite logically, that the t'skrang consider all other people criminals. That is not so. We simply find it difficult, in fact, nearly impossible, to grasp what it would be like to be born without a tail. How does one run and keep one's balance without a tail for counterbalance? Without a tail to lean on, how does one rest feet weary of standing in one place? And why learn to swim unless one has a tail to sweep through the water and propel oneself forward? A tail is such a useful thing, yet others seem quite happy to be born without one. We have a saying, "The tail-less hatchling nonetheless learns to walk."

Naturally, other Name-giver races have very little awareness of tail etiquette. In crowds, someone invariably forgets that our tails occupy the four to six feet directly behind us. Because a t'skrang's tail constantly moves, the offending fellow usually takes a swift jab in the ribs or a slap to the head, all because he's in too much of a hurry to be polite. Unfortunately, cities seem full of folk ready to start a fight on the slightest pretext, even over an involuntary reflex—a completely barbaric attitude, really.

Non-t'skrang must understand the most important principle of the tail: if a tail obstructs your way, never attempt to move that tail yourself. To "pull someone's tail" is to challenge a t'skrang to a formal duel, and enough high-strung t'skrang follow the discipline of the swordmaster to make taking hold of any t'skrang's tail a calculated risk. Furthermore, to be "handed one's own tail" means to insult a t'skrang beyond recourse or retribution. Both these considerations mean it is difficult to escape from a tail-holding situation without a fight. My advice to those who will listen: if a tail obstructs your way, ask the owner's pardon and wait for the tail to move of its own accord.

When a t'skrang's tail lies still, it is usually a sign of impending violence or other emotional distress. Indeed, one sure sign of a t'skrang who will kill casually and in cold blood is that the individual's tail remains relaxed and mobile right up until the moment he attacks. Beware such folk, for they are not completely right in the head.

A t'skrang who suddenly slaps his tail on the ground is amused, and dragging one's tail back and forth in the dust means one is tired. A t'skrang who comes to you holding his tail in his hands wishes to formally surrender. A t'skrang who points his tail at you from between his legs is making an obscene gesture. (I'll say no more, for children may someday read this.)

A t'skrang's tail never stops growing. As a result, the tip of the tail regularly becomes brittle and breaks off. This is not at all painful or a sign of ill health, for there is very little blood flow to the tip of the tail. In fact, a t'skrang can lose three or four feet of tail in combat and regenerate most of that length within a year.

A passerby in the city once stopped me to return a piece of my tail that had just fallen off in the crowd. I must admit that I had no idea what to say. Was I being "handed my own tail"? The fellow, a young dwarf by the name of Ghizhon, seemed quite sincere in his concern for my loss. But I would hardly stop a son of man on the streets in the interest of returning to him a handful of his fingernail clippings. The best advice I can give you is to leave a fallen tail lie.

No t'skrang would consider this accounting of the tail complete without some reference to our race's fighting styles. The more bloodthirsty among us prefer to dwell on the martial advantages of the tail attack rather than attending to the social aspects of the tail I have described. As Warrior Shen Harsi once put it, "The tail is just another weapon," and for every crew covenant on the river there seems to be a school of the warrior arts willing to use the tail a bit differently. For example, in the celebrated Ch'tard fighting form, the warrior straps a four-inch knife blade to the end of the tail. Never stand behind a Ch'tard in a crowd, for he is likely to cut your throat without realizing his mistake. The Edo school focuses on strength and suppleness, and students of that style can use their tails like a crude tentacle to grab stray ankles or weapons. The Skora wear a special piece of armor on the end of their tails and use it almost exclusively to parry.

A t'skrang's tail serves as a source of pride and practical utility, and represents everything courageous and unique about the t'skrang. When an egg parent wants to brace a hatchling against anxiety or danger, he always says, *choth edo k'tan var*, which means, "Up tail, out of the mud!"

OF THE WAYS AND HONORS OF NAMING

An old t'skrang riddle states, "Before it starts, it has two. It then changes and picks three. Honored makes four but sometimes just one. What is it?" The answer is a t'skrang's name. All t'skrang begin life with two names, one chosen by their egg parent before the hatchling breaks its shell, and the second the name of the foundation into which it is born. At *kaissa,* when the hatchling becomes an adult, it chooses its third Name. A t'skrang who earns the honor of entering an aropagoi gains a fourth name. The honored t'skrang who undergoes *k'soto ensherenk* and becomes a lahala accepts the foundation's name as her only name.

Our personal names may seem complicated to outsiders, but the names we give our boats reach pinnacles of complexity. Once every twelve years, we honor the Passions by adding a new name to each riverboat's lineage. Though few riverboats survived the Scourge, we honor those earlier crews and their ships by giving their names to newer riverboats. Because some of the resulting names have existed for centuries, a formal reciting of a boat's name may last nearly an hour. Some ship names consist of nothing more than lists of the names of famous captains, while others chronicle events in the history of the village. Others, when spoken, please the listeners' ears as poems and stories.

Another type of naming ritual offers a way to honor the *niall* each year. Much to the misfortune of future generations, this ceremony, called the Yearsong, is rapidly fading from the traditions of our society. Couched in a highly formal bardic style, the Yearsong condenses into five lines of ten syllables each the most important events that have occurred in a foundation over the course of a year. In winters past, the lahala chose one member of the foundation and honored him or her by asking that member to compose the Yearsong. The final version is sung on the first day of spring at the crew election. The lahala always memorizes the Yearsong, so that all future lahalas will know it through the ritual of *k'soto ensherenk*.

ON THE REASONS FOR MATING

Courtship and marriage play a small part in t'skrang society. It is far easier to say what marriage does not mean to a t'skrang than to describe its effect on his or her life. Because the t'skrang value every egg as a potential hatchling, we do not discourage coupling outside of marriage. And because we live from birth to death as part of an extended family, we need not marry simply to have a helpmate. Finally, because our political organizations create collective prosperity rather than personal power, there is nothing to be gained by arranging marriages between members of aropagoi.

To outsiders, t'skrang hatcheries and foundations seem to make marriage between members of our race unnecessary. They arrive at this conclusion quite naturally—people of one race who observe the rituals of another rarely understand the nuances. Astendar blesses each race in individual ways, and the t'skrang are no exception. Marriage offers a t'skrang the chance to create a hatchling in the women's every season as well as an opportunity to discover the joy found only in the most intimate emotional and mental relations between men and women.

Because our race suffers from an erratic fertility rate, it becomes very important for a man and a woman to couple each time the female's body creates eggs. Marriage makes such regular fertilization possible; an unmarried woman who comes into her cycle cannot feel so sure that her potential hatchling will have a chance to achieve life. Because t'skrang sexual urges are driven by the phases of the moon, a woman's cycle is fairly easy to predict, but even for the t'skrang, mating is a larger, more complex issue than the availability of the nearest male and female.

Frankly, it seems to me that human men will cheerfully go at anything with two legs and long eyelashes. Further, I am always surprised by how quickly humans conclude their business. I traveled with a long-married human couple while mapping the passes through the Tylon Mountains, and found their sexual behavior very illuminating. I watched their eyes meet over the evening campfire, exchanging what at first seemed cryptic glances (I later understood their meaning), followed immediately by them retiring to their tent. They would return to the fire a scant fifteen minutes later, smiling and flushed with exertion. For a t'skrang couple, reaching the stage of moving into the tent would take at least an hour, and they would remain there until sunup.

Coupling between two t'skrang takes place for a very practical purpose, and so, over the centuries, we have created elaborate rituals to reflect the special meaning the act has for our race. These rituals remind us each time of the great privilege and responsibility we carry for creating hatchlings, and allow us to periodically reaffirm our marriage relationships.

When a t'skrang couple marries, the husband leaves his foundation to enter the foundation of his wife. When possible, both foundations gather to celebrate the marriage ritual, though the t'skrang passion for travel often means that t'skrang from different villages and aropagoi meet and marry. In this case, each foundation celebrates separately, the man's foundation sending him off, and the woman's foundation welcoming the couple. A married couple then joins the extended family of the woman's foundation and shares the communal quarters. Town t'skrang are currently experimenting with providing separate housing for families within a foundation while maintaining a central hatchery, and so far the system seems to be working. In my opinion, however, the immediate presence of an extended family is sometimes the only thing that can help a couple through a difficult patch in an unhappy marriage, of which the t'skrang have their share.

OF THE T'SKRANG RITUALS AT DEATH

When a t'skrang dies, the foundation gathers to remember the dead. If he dies on the river, the crew performs the passing ritual. Presided over by the lahala or captain, depending on the circumstances, the passing ritual consists of each mourner telling a story about the deceased. Because the ritual allows foundation members to express their grief, no one judges the tales told, and no one censures those whose stories fall short of usual t'skrang standards. Some of the finest t'skrang stories ever told have sprung full-blown from the speaker's mouth during a t'skrang memorial service, the truth and fiction, humor and pathos of the tale welling up from the inspired heart of the mourner. The only rules governing events at the ritual are that one should tailor the length of one's tale according to one's intimacy with the deceased, and that all in attendance must speak.

When every member present has told a tale, we burn the body in elemental fire, place the ashes in a small paper boat, and let the current of the Serpent carry it away. The ritual ends when the lahala or captain pronounces the words, *amotla shivoam ga'nai,* which means, "down the river to the sea." The tiny boat carries the ashes to the end of the Great River to Death's Sea, where the Passions have imprisoned Death and the waters change to molten earth.

The death of a lahala is observed somewhat differently. Because lahala usually know the time and place of their own passing, they plan their own passing ritual and arrange for the *k'soto ensherenk* to transfer their ancestral memories to the next eldest female in the foundation. No one can say how the lahala know such things. Instead of the living spinning tales of the dead at the lahala's passing ritual, the new lahala tells a story about each of the gathered mourners by drawing on the memories of her predecessor. The foundation then carries the old lahala's body into the part of the *t'slashina* where the village grows its crops; here they bury the body in the thick mud of the river bottom. I do not know why we honor the passing of the lahala in this fashion, but it may be to help the members of the foundation to understand and accept the passing of the Honored One, and to reinforce the cyclical nature of life.

A DISCOURSE ON THE SUBJECT OF HAROPAS

Haropas is the word the t'skrang use to describe a state of being in complete communion with the Passions—and even that definition fails to create an accurate idea of the concept. In his own attempt to clarify the meaning, Mitlas of Kratas translated *haropas* as "purity," but mankind's idea of purity is more unyielding and self-righteous than any philosophical view the t'skrang would accept. One thinks of questors as pure, for example, dedicated to a single Passion. *Haropas* allows us to embrace all the Passions at once, taking us outside ourselves and the present moment to experience something more. Obsidimen use a word that we can neither pronounce nor write to describe an apparently similar concept, and they seem satisfied with the word "enlightenment" when speaking of this experience with other races. Perhaps *haropas* is the t'skrang path of enlightenment, and perhaps not.

The t'skrang base their notion of *haropas* on four more fundamental ideas: *jik'harra, kiatsu, p'skarrot,* and *kyaapas.* Loosely translated, these mean fearlessness, discipline, measure or destiny, and balance. As these are the four cornerstones of the t'skrang view of life, I shall at least attempt an explanation.

The t'skrang word *jik'harra* was originally translated by the dwarfs as "bravado." As the general understanding of bravado relies on the idea of pretense, of a mere show of fearlessness, this translation is unfortunate. Indeed, from an outsider's point of view, the bluster, swagger, and headlong recklessness of a typical t'skrang riverboat crew member must seem absurd. The actual meaning of *jik'harra* is quite different. Breaking the word down into its component parts, *ji* means courage and *k'harro* means the heart, but we also use *k'harro* to describe the Passions. Thus, *jik'harra* means a courageous heart, a brave passion. To live according to *jik'harra,* all t'skrang must strive to live beyond the reach of fear.

Most Barsaivians believe that the effortless, almost casual devastation the Horrors caused during the Scourge should have made it more difficult, if not impossible, for the t'skrang to embrace *jik'harra* and live beyond fear. Yet many say that the years spent in hiding made my people more fearless, not less. The lessons humankind learned from the Scourge make the foolish bravado of the t'skrang seem sheer effrontery. The t'skrang, of course, know the truth of how we survived the Scourge with our *jik'harra* intact.

As the tale goes, when the Theran predictions of the coming Horrors reached the banks of the Serpent River, Shivalahala Syrtis called together all the lahalas in the land. Together, this Great Council of Lahalas sifted through the fragments of their collective memories of the First Age, searching for some scrap of knowledge that would help defend against the Horrors. Though this effort failed to produce any solutions, the council learned that the race of Firebrothers, the dragonkind, had once before come to the aid of the t'skrang in a time known as the Spreading Fear.

Asking for aid from the Firebrothers has ever been a proposition filled with risk, and one unlikely to yield many rewards. Keeping this truth in mind, but determined to seek help from any possible source, the Council at Syrtis fashioned twelve riddles to both entertain the dragons and glean from them the information the Council desired. Armed only with these pleading questions disguised as riddles, emissaries traveled to dragon lairs across Barsaive to learn what they could. Few of these ambassadors returned to their foundations, and only one returned bearing a message. The Esteemed Suthparalans answered our cry for help with a cryptic message known as the Thirteenth Riddle of Suthparalans. It states, "The Horrors know what you most fear—do you, O river daughter? The river cannot hide you, the Therans cannot bind you, the kaers cannot hold you. What is left for you, courageous heart?"

The answer to this riddle reveals a closely held secret. The kaers and citadels were built to keep the Horrors out, but could never have held a restless t'skrang within. Further, we saw no way to alter our river-bottom homes to withstand such a siege and still provide the fresh air and food needed from outside.

The Council solved the great riddle, and the dragon Suthparalans taught them magical rituals that allowed us to hibernate throughout the dark centuries of the Scourge. These rituals, and the Theran Rites of Protection and Passage, guaranteed that the t'skrang would survive the Scourge without being forced to endure centuries of confinement.

When the Scourge ended, we woke from our slumber and, like many others across Barsaive, began to re-explore our world. While the vast majority of Barsaivians were forced to spend years cowering in their kaers and citadels, we t'skrang emerged unscathed, unchanged, ready to confront the Horrors, our *jik'harra* intact.

It is said that when the *Earthdawn* and its crew returned home to Throal after her first voyage, the ship carried the Lahala Desti-denvis and an embassy from V'strimon Aropagoi. When the lahala received an audience with the court of Varulus, the king immediately asked if the t'skrang had encountered the Horrors since emerging from their kaers on the river.

"I left V'strimon on the first of spring, and we had slain five by that time," said Desti-denvis.

The tale tells that the court fell silent as the deepest water, then Varulus laughed, a great dwarf guffaw from deep in his belly. "After all these years, still none can match the t'skrang for an idle boast or an impossible tale!"

The expression on the face of Desti-denvis was enough to curdle milk, and the entire court of Throal burst into embarrassed laughter. With a flourish of her plumed hat and a sweeping bow that put the courtiers to shame, she replied, "As you say, my lord, an idle boast." Shustal! Nothing more need be said. We t'skrang refuse to waste a good tale on the skeptic.

Kiatsu, or ritual preparation, represents another cornerstone of *haropas*. *Kiatsu* forces a t'skrang to achieve discipline by seeking out and confronting his fears one by one. This usually helps explain to outsiders the extraordinary single-mindedness with which my people pursue apparently irrational acts. We often use swinging, climbing, and back flips to achieve *kiatsu*, not because such deeds are difficult, but because most t'skrang instinctively loathe heights and shudder at the thought of flying. If this seems unbelievable, try to coax a t'skrang onto an airship. I guarantee that unless you suggest that staying behind might be interpreted as an act of cowardice, you will not succeed.

Confronting one's fear takes as many forms as t'skrang have fears. A quiet, retiring fellow may sell goods in the marketplace to confront his fear of strangers. A homebody might undertake a long and perilous journey to dispel his attachment to familiar places and faces. T'skrang may be as fallible as the next race—much as it pains us to admit that fact—and many a traveler on the road to *haropas* steps over the line from discipline to vanity.

The always present pitfall of vanity finds ample reinforcement in *p'skarrot*, the third cornerstone of *haropas*. Like most words in our language, *p'skarrot* has two meanings. The first is "measure," a word that applies to our food preparation and recipes to indicate ingredients added to taste. *P'ska nala p'skarrot* means a little of this, a little of that. In a philosophical sense, *p'skarrot* represents the measure of the man. To take the measure of a man, however, one must compare the individual to something. In many other societies, the basis for comparison turns out to be someone, rather than something else—I am a greater man than he, but not so great as that other. T'skrang measure themselves by nothing less than the universe itself. The universe presents a challenge, and the t'skrang prepares himself to meet it. To be equal to that challenge—that is *p'skarrot!*

The second meaning of p'skarrot is "destiny," though the t'skrang view destiny in a different light than other races. The sons of man often speak of destiny in terms of divine providence, as if the Passions cared to plot men's lives on some etheric mandala board. The t'skrang believe that each man casts his destiny like a net into the waters. The events that befall us are like fish caught in the net: beautiful, nourishing, and sometimes strange.

For the t'skrang, building one's destiny requires craftsmanship. Woven well, the destiny net catches big fish. A man with a weak net goes hungry. Unfortunately, the necessary craftsmanship is often accompanied by a sense of self-importance that gets in the way of true learning. It is the current fashion among young t'skrang to choose a rival for life and then call the struggles against that opponent *p'skarrot.* Mind you, I realize that they borrowed this idea from the alleged ork custom of striving against a life enemy, but these hatchlings should not then insist that the tradition belongs to our ancestors. Further, I hear that many young t'skrang choose an elf as their rival, basing their choice on our epics of the t'skrang War Against the Elves. It's all piddlefinnegary in the first degree, I say! A specific someone offers far too little challenge to a t'skrang seeking the true meaning of *p'skarrot;* he or she must struggle against a larger, more impersonal force to truly achieve this aspect of *haropas.*

The fourth cornerstone of haropas is *kyaapas*, or balance. In this sense, *kyaapas* refers to the balance between the individual and society. T'skrang live in a communal society more tightly woven than any other in Barsaive. The qualities that make up *haropas*—discipline, fearlessness, and destiny—often conflict with close-knit clannishness. *Kyaapas* recognizes this natural tension and calls for balance.

The t'skrang must evaluate every moment of their lives for *kyaapas*, because the balance can change quickly. The last tale of Yustraa Piaan plainly illustrates this point. It is said that disguised as a hunter and armed only with a hunter's bow and arrows, Yustraa Piaan traveled alone to his home after an absence of ten years. Upon arriving, he learned that during his absence his beautiful wife had been besieged by the attentions of some three dozen men, each of whom was eagerly awaiting her announcement of which one would take Yustraa's place in her bed. Yustraa went to greet his wife, but so changed was he by his journeys that she did not recognize her husband in the man standing before her.

Struck by this strange turn of events, Yustraa says, "My life has fallen out of balance. What power in the world can right it?" He returned to the great hall where the suitors were feasting, and fell upon them suddenly to avenge the dishonor they caused his wife. Soon his wife was cutting a path to his side, having realized that the stranger who had greeted her was actually Yustraa, her beloved mate. Everyone in the hall perished that day: the suitors, Yustraa, and his wife. Yustraa's fate is what t'skrang mean by the price of *haropas*. Communion with the Passions is not for the timid, my friends.

ON THE T'SKRANG AND THE PASSIONS

Because *haropas* implies direct contact between the individual and the Passions, the Passions themselves figure prominently in t'skrang spiritual tradition. What does it mean to "commune" with a Passion? Ah, my friend, that is a question against which t'skrang philosophers have beat with their intellectual swords ever since first we learned the power of Name-giving. Is it true communication, measured with words? When we achieve *haropas*, does the spirit of the Passion enter into us, as the questors believe, or do we rather enter the spiritual place wherein the Passions dwell? Indeed, if true *haropas* is communion with all the Passions, what use is there in trying to answer these questions at all? I do not suppose we will ever really know, but it makes for exciting discussions.

Every village keeps a shrine to the twelve Passions, usually in the oldest foundation dome. The village always keeps a small offering of food and drink on a table in the shrine in case the Passion should choose to visit, although I suspect the Passions require little in the way of sustenance. It is, I suppose, the intention that counts. Also within these shrines the t'skrang will place the most beautiful works of art they can find. As I have mentioned before, we believe that the feelings evoked by certain works of art originate with the Passions, so that collecting these works in shrines is only logical.

A village shrine is open at all times to all people, and even the smallest shrines enjoy considerable traffic. They are places for quiet introspection, and in the close confines of the village, a rarity indeed. Traditional ceremonies such as marriage, Naming, and the blessing of the annual riverboat journey are celebrated in the shrines, as well as the customary Barsaivian festival days dedicated to each of the twelve Passions. It is quite true that most t'skrang shrines still dedicate altars to the three mad Passions of Dis, Raggok, and Vestrial. The icons to these Passions we keep covered in black cloth, but we still remember them by their old names: Erendis, Rashomon, and Vestrial. Their holy days are no longer celebrated, but on Midwinter's day, we gather to mourn their passage into madness.

The Passions upon whom the t'skrang most often call are Thystonius, Chorrolis, and Upandal. We name Thystonius the Guardian of *Jik'harra*. He fills the heart with valor and lends his strength to the battle-ready. Chorrolis, of course, is the Father of Trade, and before any riverboat leaves the dock, we ask for his blessing. Upandal aids all our efforts in building and repairing everything from crafts to fire cannons.

Very few t'skrang questors roam the world, probably because our stories and traditions portray the questor's single-minded dedication to a single Passion as an invitation to madness. Do not misunderstand; we share the Barsaivian reverence for questors, and no one dedicated to the Passions (saving of course the Mad Ones) is ever refused village hospitality. We simply do not encourage our hatchlings to become questors. Those t'skrang who do take up the questor's vestments nearly always choose Upandal, the Maker. The reason is quite simple; it was Upandal who gave the t'skrang the fire engine that drives our riverboats.

ON THE T'SKRANG REVERENCE FOR THE OLD WAYS

The concept of *haropas* gives a special quality to the t'skrang relationship with the Passions. But underneath this abiding respect for the powers of the heart, t'skrang have also kept alive an ancient mythology and iconography based on the five elements. Though t'skrang acknowledge the worship of the Passions as a superior and more meaningful path, the old ways continue to surface from time to time, in oaths and superstitions, and in strange tales told late in the night.

The t'skrang think of themselves as one of the elder races, along with the obsidimen, windlings, and dragonkind. They hold the other three elder races in the greatest esteem, especially the dragonkind. As proof of their great and old regard for the windling race, t'skrang will sometimes build their dwellings with windlings in a forest near the river's edge. Their respect for the other eldest race shines through in the fact that the lore of every t'skrang *niall* advises that there is no truer companion in adventure than an obsidiman.

Some of the older villages along the river keep small shrines along the shore that protect huge footprints embedded in the mud of the Serpent. We call these places Founder's shrines, and maintain a traditional pilgrimage route from Lake Ban to Syrtis Aropagoi that follows twenty such shrines. Those who complete this pilgrimage are granted an immediate audience with the Shivalahala Syrtis, although very few take up the challenge any longer, much less succeed. I have always intended to make the journey in my old age, for there are some questions I have saved to ask the prophetess before I travel down river to the sea.

In the woodlands where Shivoam's streams and tributaries run wild and ragged, travelers can still find an occasional shrine or cairn marked with the ancient t'skrang language near waterfalls and rapids. These ancient testimonials to the power of the river's song to bring forth new life attract primitive t'skrang in the jungle lands, where they lay offerings and pray for fertility at planting time or for a successful egg-brood. The ancient t'skrang mythologies prompt even modern, civilized t'skrang to sing river songs to the eggs in the hatcheries from time to time.

A TALE OF WINDLINGS

A great number of the writings we have collected concerning windlings, including the following text that begins Volume VIII of this work on the denizens of Barsaive, were written by members of other races. Many windlings view the written word as merely a means for keeping trade records and other dry but necessary documents, and therefore not a fit medium for the story of a race. For such a lofty subject as what it means to be a windling, our small, winged brethren would prefer to compose an epic song or create a wondrously complex dance rather than reduce the tale to a written history. To begin this volume on windlings, we have instead chosen the writings of a troll troubadour who has given us a surprisingly complete and perceptive portrait of the windling race.
—Presented for the edification of the reader by Thom Edrull, Archivist and Scribe of the Hall of Records, 1506 TH

My name is Chag Skat, troubadour of the village of Donok, near the foothills of the Caucavic Mountains. I tell stories and sing songs for meat, bread, and sometimes coin—when folk can afford it. Being a troll, I tend to draw a crowd; most people can't quite believe that a troll musician exists, let alone a troll musician who's good at his craft.

But I am good at it, friend, and I'll tell you why—because I love it. I love wandering all over Barsaive, which is my own beautiful land as much as any other Name-giver's, and seeing all the wonders there are to see. Folk in Donok laughed at me or called me soft in the skull, but I wanted to see more than high mountains and hear more than deep, troll voices all my life. Don't misunderstand me—I love my own folk as dear as I love my life. But I love the world too, and everything in it. The Universe gave us a place full of variety to live in, and I say why waste it by staying home?

There is a point to all this blather about myself, in case you wondered. A good troubadour always gives folk a little background to a story when they need it, and I thought plenty of folk might want to know why in the name of the Universe a troll troubadour would spend the greater part of a year living among windlings. I'll tell you why, friend. Because they're different, and I wanted to know about them. And now I do. And the Great Library of Throal even paid me a pretty sum to include my work in their great book about all the peoples of Barsaive! Me, a troll, whom too many ignorant folk might think has no more learning than a thornbush. I owe that to my friends in clan Lisvara. They're good folk, windlings. I like them. But I tell you, friend, I've never seen any folk so small in my life!

ON THE NATURE OF WINDLINGS

In my travels, I've met folk of every Name-giver race. Of us all, windlings are the smallest: tiny, winged, humanlike creatures with small, nimble fingers and sweet voices. The beauty of sunlight shining through their wings is truly a wonder to behold. Of course, being so small in a world made for larger folk (though not made *quite* large enough, if you ask me) turns everyday life into a challenge for these little ones in a way most other folk couldn't begin to understand. I understand a bit, from the opposite side of the coin, because a troll like me has to cope with beds and chairs too flimsy to hold us up, doorways so small that we bruise our shoulders and crack our heads, and so on. But even I find life easier than a windling might.

Go on, friend, imagine it just for a moment. See yourself reading my words in the Great Library of Throal, and wanting to

read the next page. Imagine having to get up, fly over to the edge of the book (which is almost as big as you are), grab the edge of the parchment, and heave it up and over. Or imagine walking into a tavern at the end of a long, hard day on the road, desperate for a drink, and finding out that the tavernkeeper's smallest cup is so big that you can only heft it using both hands, and even then you're likely to bathe in your ale while trying to get some down your parched throat, eh, friend? That's the kind of challenge a windling faces every day, unless he stays home where things are his size. And that's why a windling likes nothing so much as a challenge. Some people might sulk and whine that the world wasn't made exactly to suit them—not windlings. A windling takes it in stride, and even prides himself on coming up with the cleverest or most amusing way to get around his difficulties.

To give you a bit of an idea of who windlings are and how they think, I give you the words of Woohrt, a windling thief who stood me to several rounds of good, stout ale in a Kratas tavern. (Drank me under the table, as it happens. Never judge a windling by his size. . .)

"You amaze me, friend Chag. A grounder like you, taking such an interest in the ways of my people? Such curiosity—you might almost be a windling yourself! With wings as big as riverboat sails, of course. . .there now, don't scowl. I meant no harm. You know how my windling tongue likes to run away with me. If you will permit me, I shall salve your wounded feelings with another mug of ale. Wench! Another for my oversized friend. . .and a small glass of keesris for me.

"So you wish to know of windlings, eh? I will tell you the most important difference between a windling and any other Name-giver. We, my grounder friend, can fly.

"I know perfectly well that I have stated the obvious. I said it because most people never think what it means. A windling can fly—four little words that mean so infinitely much to our ways, our joys, our very existence as a people. Do you know why I call you grounder? In the windling tongue, the word is "kooweesh," and it means a prisoner of the earth—a slave to the kiss of the ground. You grounders cannot soar above the ground, as we can. We windlings can escape the bonds of earth. We can become a part of the air, seeing the world in a way that no one else can. Because we can fly, we have a kind of freedom that wingless folk can only dream of.

"When you fly, the earth beneath you and the sky above you change from moment to moment. Imagine the glory of flight, friend Chag–feel the wind rushing past your ears, playing gently with your hair like a lover's fingers, caressing every inch of your skin like a cool bath on a warm morning. Imagine the sky turning above you like a vast, blue wheel shot through with white clouds, as you spin and dip and soar and even turn somersaults to express your joy at the sheer beauty of the day. Imagine the land of Barsaive, stretched out below you like a tapestry—the emerald forests giving way to the tawny gold of the plains; the folds of the hills like patterns woven into rich, padded silk; the mountains rising like beads of jet or smoky topaz from out of the fabric of the whole. Imagine all that beauty, each picture changing by the moment into something even more beautiful and wonderful. Such is the life of a windling, my curious friend. Every moment brings its own beauty, and everything new is a wonder.

"We love anything new or interesting, even if it is also dangerous. Indeed, a little danger adds spice to life. Many windlings wander the world in search of the new and different, much as you are doing. (By the Universe, friend Chag, you *could* almost be a windling!) I have known windling wanderers who happened upon some other race's quaint custom which so impressed their kin in the telling that the entire clan adopted the custom. Until, of course, a new and more interesting one came along to replace it!

"A windling will try absolutely anything at least once, and count it worth the doing even if it hurts him. Many of our fellow Name-givers think us addle-brained for behaving so, but we are the gainers by it. You see, a windling learns more of the world by seeking new experiences and meeting new people—and the more we know of the world, the easier it is for us to survive its challenges. This world of ours, alas, was not made with the needs of small beings in mind. But you are a troll, and so you know whereof I speak. This world was not made for your folk, either.

"Friend Chag, you and I really do have an extraordinary amount in common."

ON WINDLING APPEARANCE AND ANATOMY

Anybody who's seen a windling knows what they look like, of course. Little folk they are, about the size of my forearm, with wings as delicate and fine as gossamer. Ever seen a leaf after a beetle's chewed through it and left only the veins of the leaf behind? Windling wings look a little like that. Like the veins of a leaf, but shimmering as if overlaid with spun glass. With their slender bodies and pointed ears, windlings look a little like elves. In fact, I've heard tell that some sages and scholars think windlings and elves are distant kin. I even heard some poor ork in a village marketplace sneer at a flock of departing windlings as "bitty elves with wings," at which point the windlings swarmed around the ork's head and thumped him soundly with small cudgels. Not that windlings have anything against elves, mind—they're just proud to be windlings and take offense at being called anything else.

Windlings can fly, of course, and they also have a keen sense of smell. I've seen windlings who could tell you what's in someone's pocket just from getting a good snootful of the air nearby. I watched them for a full year, and I think they use that sense of smell to navigate through the air. Almost as if they smell what's in the way before they see it. (I'd like to see what happens if a windling with a head cold tries to fly!)

ON THE UNIQUE NATURE OF WINDLING SIGHT

They can see perfectly well, of course. No trouble at all with a windling's vision. Matter of fact, they can see one thing that other folk can't—magic. Most Name-givers who want to see magic have to be wizards or follow some Discipline much like wizardry to do it. They've got to work hard, learning the right spells and all. But a windling's *born* seeing magic. They can see it as easily as I can see in the dark, or a human can see the nose on his face in a mirror. They see magic so easily because they're closer to it, more a part of it than any other folk. Of course, the magic of the world is in all of us—no one knows that better than me, who's been so many places and seen so many different sights. But the magic seems stronger in windlings, somehow. Maybe it's because they alone can touch the sky as well as the earth, and so they have two elements belonging to them, instead of just the one that most of us have.

OF BIRTH AND GROWTH

A baby windling's a rare and wondrous thing. Small enough to fit in the palm of my hand, wings and all. They learn to fly at about ten days old, and by the time they've lived a year they're as clever as a three-year-old troll child or a five-year-old human. And can they get into mischief! Take the normal curiosity of the adult windling, then imagine it as three or four times as much. That's how curious windling children are. They can't keep their little hands out of anything, and the only thing that slows them down is the sheer fatigue of flying. Their parents don't say a word against them, no matter what they do. To their way of thinking, a curious and mischievous child is more likely to meet the world's challenges well, so windling parents encourage such behavior. Windlings also love children all the more because they have so few.

A windling comes of age at about his thirtieth year and usually chooses a mate before turning forty. Most windling couples have only one child during their entire lives, which can last as long as 170 years. Some have two children, but it's the rare windling pair lucky enough to have three. No one knows why. More males are born than females, and that too is still a mystery. Of course, most windlings don't bother their heads with the whys and wherefores of such things. They simply see these facts of windling life, like everything else, as a challenge to be met. They cope with their small numbers of offspring by caring for each one as though it belonged to them. As for all the extra windling males, the little folk have come up with an interesting mating custom that keeps down the number of mateless males. I'll tell more of that custom later on.

Female windlings can only conceive children for 20 days during the fall of the year, and they carry the babe for six months. All windlings are therefore born in the spring, within 20 days of each other. A carrying mother can fly as easily as

any other windling until her fifth month or so. For the final month she stays home, lying in bed and reveling in being waited on hand and foot until the babe is born. Not just her mate waits on her, either. The whole clan plays along, as excited and happy about the coming birth as a t'skrang merchant who's just made his first profitable trade.

ON HOW FLIGHT MAKES A WINDLING

As the thief Woorht told me, flying is a windling's heart and soul. A windling unable to fly is a cripple, like a troll both blinded and lamed. In my year with clan Lisvara, I learned that flying makes windlings different from the rest of us in more ways than one. When a windling flies, he has to see in a special way. It's not enough to see the path ahead of him and the road behind; he also has to see what's above him, below him, and all around him. This way of seeing spills over into the way a windling thinks—instead of seeing only one or two sides to a question or problem, he sees three or four or even five. Some folk call windlings soft in the skull because they flit from idea to idea as fast as they fly from place to place. I tell you otherwise, friend. A windling sees much more, in more different ways, than any other Name-giver race. If you ask me, the rest of us could learn a thing or two from them.

Though most windlings hide it well, flying tires them out as much as running or swimming might tire a human or an elf. Most windlings can fly easily for a quarter of an hour or so, but then must rest awhile before soaring away from the earth again. They like best to rest on the shoulders of larger Name-givers, getting comfort and company at the same time. Windlings who serve in local militias often use war dogs or large lizards as mounts, to keep from having to fly throughout a battle.

A windling's wings look more fragile than they are, which ought to surprise no one. Anything meant to carry a twelve or thirteen-pound body through an element as light as air needs to be tough. The one thing a windling wing can't stand up to is water. A wet windling wing gets heavy, making it harder to fly. Worse yet, the water softens the wing to the point where it might tear—and if that happens, the windling might as well forget about flying out of danger.

I saw what happened once to a windling whose wings got wet. He was flying too near a human village in a light drizzle that suddenly turned to a blinding downpour. A farmer's dog got the scent of him and started barking and snapping and slipped his rope just as the heavy rain started falling. The windling didn't have a chance. I shouted and threw stones, but the dog was on him in a heartbeat. The beast shredded the windling's wings to ribbons, then lost interest and left the poor creature lying in a twitching heap. I went to him, but all I could do was wrap him in my cloak so that he could at least die in a little comfort. I've seen some dreadful sights in my time, but that's the one that still gives me nightmares.

ON THE IDEALS DEAREST TO WINDLINGS

Those who know little of windlings often think them foolish, or even get angry because they do not understand them. Why can't windlings take life calmly and let things be, they ask. Why can't they act one way all the time, like other decent folk? Why can't they understand that life is a serious business? Why can't they ever keep still?

Well, friend, they have their reasons for being as they are, just as any other Name-giver does. A windling loves change, freedom, and feeling above all else. What's more, he sees these three ideals as different parts of the same thing. Change is freedom made real, and freedom makes change possible. And feeling—love and joy and anger and pride as deep and rich as the blue of the sky—makes a windling's freedom sweet and gives each change meaning.

OF THE VALUE OF CHANGE

The windlings of clan Lisvara have a saying that any windling anywhere would agree with: "Any day without a new experience is a day not lived." In a windling's view, just as nature grows and changes, so must they. Windlings show their love of change by borrowing customs from other Name-givers, the more often the better. When I told clan Lisvara that my

people build snug homes by digging them out of the hill-sides, the whole clan spent the next month lining the insides of all their hollow-tree dwellings with earth (grass side up, of course). Another time, my friend Keerht came back from a day at a nearby village fair, and told his clan he'd seen a human male bowing to a human female. For weeks after that, all the clan males went around bowing elaborately every time they met a windling female. (Then Keerht spent an evening in the village tavern, and saw a human male grab a tavern wench by the waist and sit her on his lap. The male windlings tried to adopt that little custom, but the females were having none of it. They got the males back to bowing right quick.)

Scholars talk of change meaning freedom to windlings, and of course that's true. For myself, I think windlings also love change so much because they love nature. So many different sights and smells and sounds, so many different beauties and dangers and wonders, exist in nature for any wishing to seek them out. The windlings see themselves as nature's most beloved children and want to be as much a part of their Mother as they can.

OF THE WINDLING LOVE OF FREEDOM

Love of nature also explains why windlings love freedom. For a race born and raised in the woods and wild lands, to be held captive is worse than dying. Many windlings so dislike any feeling of captivity that they avoid living in Barsaive's cities and towns. To them, walls and ceilings made by any hand but nature's feel like a prison. Even the ones who do live in so-called "civilized" towns alongside other Name-givers try to keep their sense of freedom by moving from place to place, rarely staying in one town or village for very long. Most windlings live like clan Lisvara, in settlements deep within Barsaive's forests and jungles.

ON LIVING A LIFE OF FEELING

Along with the love of change and freedom, windlings teach their children to love life and live it fully. Why live free, they say, unless you use that freedom to experience and revel in everything? A life without feeling is unknown to a windling. Everything they do, they do with a fervor that might make a Passion dizzy. If a clansman dies, they mourn his loss as if the world had ended. Where other races make merry for one day at a fair or festival, a windling celebration lasts for many days, over something as ordinary (at least to other folk) as a good pressing of wine or a successful hunt. A windling becomes enraged over a slight that would make another Name-giver feel only a moment's anger. Despite their miniature size, these folk do nothing in small measure. Other folk seek change, but windlings embrace it. Other folk enjoy freedom, but windlings revel in it.

OF DIVERSE WINDLING CUSTOMS

I have told of some of the windlings' ways and will now speak more of them. It should come as no surprise that windling ways differ greatly from the ways of trolls! Windlings live by hunting and gathering the fruits of the land, which they believe nature creates especially for them. When I have tried to explain to windling friends what farming is, they broke out into hoots and shouts of laughter—they kept asking me why anyone would bother with all that work. Races used to toiling for their bread may think the windlings downright careless about the getting of food, but windlings are never wasteful. They hunt or gather what the clan needs for each day, using every scrap of what they find or kill. When planning for a feast, they gather twice or three times as much and store some, but otherwise they make little provision beyond each day's needs. (A windling feast is a marvel—I will tell of those later.)

ON COMING OF AGE

A windling comes of age in his thirtieth year. For the coming-of-age ceremony of the Lisvarans and most other windling clans in Barsaive, the windling must fly to some perilous place and return with a token that proves he has faced and mastered danger. Most windlings, though not all, use their flying skills in the coming-of-age ritual.

Once the windling returns with proof of his or her courage, the clan tattoo master designs a tattoo for the clan's new adult. The new adult windling may now take a mate, start a family, and practice a trade.

OF MATING AND FAMILY LIFE

Windlings mate for life and raise their children in common. Every member of the clan teaches each child what they know of the world. A female windling warrior may teach her son how to fight, a male windling artist may teach the child how to create tattoos, and so on. (I will speak more of windling clans further on.)

Windlings go courting in the spring, the same season in which every windling child is born. If a windling male and female strike each other's fancy and the male has no rivals, the pair take betrothal vows for a year and marry in the following spring. If more than one male wants to wed a female, the clan holds a contest that they call a sleerah. I saw one such contest myself, when my friend Keerht courted a little lass named Shelah. (Such rivalry is common, because there are so many more male windlings than females. The windlings invented the sleerah to solve the problem of too many males wanting mates they can't have—it's ingenious, but brutal.)

In the sleerah, the males attempt tasks of great difficulty and danger, witnessed by fellow clansmen who watch from a safe distance. Often, the stunts become so dangerous that unlucky male windlings die during the contest. As it happens, one of the four rivals for Shelah died trying to capture and ride a wild eagle; it threw him off suddenly, not a fingerspan from the top of a bramble thicket. The poor fellow had no time to right himself and died impaled on the thorns. Of course, the clan stopped the sleerah long enough to hold a mourning feast. They did the poor lad proud—bewailing his loss, praising his daring, and eating and drinking to his departed spirit for close on three days. Then they started right up with the sleerah again, each of the remaining three rivals still just as mad to win the hand of pretty Shelah. Much as I like windlings, sometimes they bewilder me.

Once every rival has completed the contest (in one way or another, if you take my meaning), the female chooses her mate from among the surviving males. She needn't choose the one who succeeded at the most tasks, either. The tasks of the sleerah show the female how each male stands up to danger and frustration and also let her know how well he solves problems. An arrogant male who fancies himself the winner often loses out, because the female finds a humbler "loser" more appealing as a mate. That's how Keerht won Shelah—he'd managed to snag his eagle and was just climbing up its leg to swing up onto its back when he saw his friend Tesarh fall past *his* eagle's talon and tear a wing. They'd had hard words over both wanting Shelah, but old friendship won out. Off the eagle's leg went Keerht, diving down to catch Tesarh and carry him to safety. That act cost Keerht success at eagle-riding, but it impressed Shelah more than any feat of daring could have done.

A windling can marry within his or her own clan, but because the clan is so small, he often finds few partners to choose from. Many windlings, especially the extra males, choose to mate outside their birth-clan. When such a mating takes place, the new couple join the male's clan, and the female windling is formally adopted into it. Being windlings, they naturally

throw a welcoming feast, which lasts for five to seven days. Needless to say, the custom of marrying out of the clan is well regarded in windling society! Both clans get a feast out of it—the one to see the couple off, the other to welcome them home—and most times, the male's clan gets a new female member who may bear children. The female's clan loses a woman, of course, but they also have one less extra (and possibly discontented) male. Both clans claim the children of such mates as kin, and very often foster them back and forth during their childhood years.

Though all windling adults help to raise the clan's children, each child's kin-parents (mother and father by blood) choose another mated couple soon after the child's Naming to join with them in acting as the infant's closest care-givers. To put it in terms that other races might more easily understand, each baby windling has four parents and a vast number of loving uncles and aunts!

On the Ritual of Naming

The birth of a windling child is a rare and therefore precious event. Windlings celebrate a birth for ten days, ending the feasting with a naming ritual. The nobles of clan Lisvara let me watch one, and I have written the words of the ritual as I remember them.

By the time a newborn windling reaches his tenth day, he has learned to fly, though not with an adult's skill. The child's kin-parents, the clan noble (the leader), and the rest of the clan gather near the clan's central dwelling—often a hollow tree—at dusk and catch a horde of fireflies, then set them loose within the leafy tree branches. His way lit only by the glow of the fireflies, the young windling must weave through an obstacle course of leaves, branches, and barriers woven of leaves and vines. The course always has four sharp turns in it: one for the north, the South, the East, and the West.

When the child clears the north turn, his kin-father says: "From the North comes cold wind and driving rain. May the sun always warm your flight, and may your wings always be dry."

When the child clears the south turn, his kin-mother says: "From the South come warm and gentle breezes. May the air always fill your wings and lift you to new heights."

When the child clears the western turn, the clan noble says: "The West brings the end of day and the coming of night. May you see many sunsets."

When the child clears the eastern and final turn, all three adults say: "As the new day starts in the East, so a new dawn begins for you. From henceforth, you are Named (name). Though you may earn other names, this name is your beginning. You need not live up to this name, for it is yours by birthright. May your heart ever be as light as your wings. Always remember that the two things no one can ever take from you are your wings and your name."

Once the child completes the ritual, he and the clan adults recapture all the fireflies. At the evening's feast in the child's honor, the newly Named windling must eat all of the fireflies; by this, he shows that he is light of heart.

OF LANGUAGE AND WINDLING HUMOR

Windlings are famous—or infamous, depending on whom you speak to—for their sense of humor. These lighthearted folk love to tease, and the more serious the target of their joking, the better they like it. They mean no harm by it, mind—but they see it as part of a windling's place in life to show others the humor in it. If a windling can make you smile with his teasing, he's happy—and if he provokes anger, that also makes him laugh because he finds the seriousness of other races so foolish.

I admit that sometimes my windling friends laughed at things that might well shock right-thinking folk. They shocked me, once or twice. Once, me and some of the windling lads went to a tavern in a nearby village, and saw a drunken ork die in a silly accident. A scorcher, he was, boasting about the gold and gems he'd stolen from a rich merchant. He bobbled around in his hobnailed boots, showing us all his brilliant swordsmanship (which was anything *but*, mind). A too-vigorous swing of his sword sent him pitching heels over head into an oak table. Knocked the table over, he did, and the pitcher of

ale on it crashed down on top of his head. He lay there for several heartbeats, the ale dribbling into his slack mouth, and the windlings laughed until tears ran down their cheeks. Only after he'd lain there for several minutes without moving did anyone realize he'd broken his silly neck. At that, of course, my windling friends wept from sadness—and a little shame, I think, that they'd been laughing at a dead man.

Most of the misunderstanding about windling humor comes from the simple fact that windlings think differently about what to take seriously and when. Small-minded, easily angered folk call windling humor malicious, but they know nothing about it. Windlings find almost everything funny, and that simple fact has kept them a joyful, lively folk instead of a whining, poor, and miserable one. Windlings laugh at each other all the time, and most of them can't quite believe that anyone might truly feel angry over "a bit of harmless joking." A windling sees teasing and joking not as a hurtful thing, but as a sign of affection. He'll laugh at his own foolishness as much as at any other's and sees no harm in either.

On the Curious Custom of Insult Contests

Windlings often hold insult contests just so that they can poke fun at each other. In an insult contest, two windlings insult each other's looks, manners, clothing, achievements, and anything else they can think of, dreaming up the funniest and most accurate insults under the watchful eye of a moderator. The moderator judges the appropriateness of each insult, and the windling who delivers the cleverest insults that are also on the mark wins the contest. Though outsiders might find such teasing cruel, the windlings themselves think otherwise. No windling would dream of taking offense at an insult made during one of these contests. (One interesting thing I noticed; not a single windling ever called another one short. I guess they just might take offense at that!)

On the Pleasant Diversion of Joke Contests

Windlings also hold joke and pun contests, in which two windlings trade inventive turns of phrase or outrageous jokes about a single topic, chosen by a third windling who judges each pun. The first windling who can't come up with a good joke or pun loses, and often must stand the winner to a round of drinks. Windlings love any kind of play, especially word-play, and the combination of clever words and quick thinking make joke contests one of the most popular windling customs. The average windling, by the by, makes twice the troubadour that many another Name-giver might hope to be. As a troubadour myself, I know of what I speak.

On the Wonderful Amusements of Tall Tale Competitions

Even more beloved than joke contests is the telling of tall tales. A windling proverb says, "If your stature is small, let your words be big," and every windling I've ever met believes in every word of that old saying. In the tall tale competitions, windling humor and love of storytelling reach their greatest heights.

Two windlings each have a set time in which to tell an outlandish tale, but one with a grain of truth just large enough to make the listeners wonder if it truly happened. If anyone doubts that windlings can lie with the skill of a master craftsman, come and hear one of these contests. They weave together truth and falsehood, reality and exaggeration as a master basketmaker weaves his reeds. I tell you honestly, I envy this windling skill; would that I could spin such outrageous stories from only a seed of truth.

ON OTHER WINDLING REVELS

In addition to insult, joke, and tall tale contests, windlings hold revels at the slightest excuse. They may hold a feast for such important occasions as a naming ritual or a wedding, or for such minor (to other folk) occasions as the building of a new shelter or even a lovely morning. The harvesting of keesryps is a favorite occasion for a week-long revel; I will speak more of that when I tell of windling wine, further on. Most windling revels begin at sundown and last for three days, and feature all manner of eating, drinking, tale-telling and music. An openhearted and curious folk, windlings who live near towns or villages where other Name-givers dwell often invite their neighbors to these revels. They take special delight in making the strangers tell tales of their own people.

ON THE CUSTOM OF WINDLING VENGEANCE

Folk who think of windlings as frivolous, fun-loving, and harmless might be more than a bit surprised to learn that windlings are quick to anger. Windlings not only get angry, friend, they stay angry. Not a Name-giver race in Barsaive

holds a grudge as long or as well as a windling. It makes no matter whether you offend them on purpose or by misadventure— you'd best apologize right quick, or you've trouble on your doorstep.

Windlings rarely, if ever, offend each other. Certainly I never saw any member of clan Lisvara raise a hand to another in anger. But if another Name-giver gives offense or injury to a windling and speaks no word of apology, the offended windling gathers his kin and close friends to help him avenge the slight. I've heard angry windlings talk of the punishments they meant to inflict, and I'd not face them for all the coin in Barsaive. For a mild offense, the avengers confine their punishments to embarrassing practical jokes; anyone foolish enough to seriously cross a windling may well be dead within days. I once heard a band of windling avengers plotting to send some poor dwarf over a cliff by flying around his head like angry wasps until they herded him to his death (though Keerht later told me that few windlings go quite that far).

Luckily, making peace with a windling is easy. They are quick to see the funny side of even the deadliest insult, and they swiftly forgive anyone who honestly admits his fault. A public apology or a gift of food or wine easily wins them over.

NEVER THREATEN A WINDLING UNLESS YOU WANT A LIFE-TIME OF HARASS-MENT. I TRIED IT ONCE. STUPID. THREATS JUST MAKE THEM ANGRIER.
—KAROK, TROLL WARRIOR OF KRATAS

OF WINDLING CLANS AND NOBLES

The troubadour Telourian once said, "Windling society is like troll glassware. No one can imagine them creating any, and no one has ever seen it." I pity Telourian, I really do. He's an elf, and sad to say, he's saddled himself with the sense of superiority that keeps plenty of elves in Barsaive from ever learning anything. Not all elves are like that, mind, but too many are. Well, I hate to break it to poor Telourian, but windlings do have a society. (And trolls make fine glass, by the by. It's so fine, we'd rather keep it than give it to anyone else.) Too many folk think that because windlings borrow customs from others whenever they like that they don't have their own way of doing things. But they do, friend, and it's just as good a way for them as any of ours are for us. Where we live in villages or moots, they live in clans. And where we have headmen or chiefs or even kings, they have nobles.

As a small people, the windlings prefer to keep their living arrangements at a size they can easily manage. A windling clan numbers six or seven families, usually 30 or so individual windlings, of which at most seven or so are children. The clans build dwellings about 15 feet off the ground in clusters of trees, well out of reach of dangerous animals. Each member is fiercely loyal to his own clan, even more so than windlings across Barsaive are to each other, and because the clan adults care equally for all the children, they all regard each other as closely as we regard our blood kin. Though each windling child knows which clan members are his own blood, known to him as kin-mother and kin-father, he feels the same closeness and love for all of his elders.

Each clan has a clansong, which names each member of the clan, tells a little of him, and names his kin-parents, mate, and kin-children. With the birth of each new windling child, the clan adds a new line to the song. The noble of clan Lisvara allowed me to write down a fragment of their clansong, which follows.

Clan Lisvara, clan Lisavara, we sing of clan Lisvara
　　unto all generations.
Great Shurah, our foremother, kin-sister to Relft the thief,
　　kin-mother to us all.
Swift and silent Relft, the thief, kin-brother to Laarh the archer,
　　kin-father to Keerht and Mhari.
Laarh the archer and wind-master, mate to healer Gheeria,
　　kin-father to Shelah.
Keerht, wind-dancer and troubadour, kin-brother to Mhari,
　　new-mated to Shelah.
Mhari the beastmaster of great and surpassing skill,
　　kin-child to Gheeria.
Gheeria, Garlen's beloved, mother of two children,
　　kin-daughter to Sheorh. . .

(Since leaving the windlings, I've tried to perform a clansong in a few taverns—even, once for King Varulus himself, can you believe it!—but a troll's deep voice can't match the sound of a windling's trill.)

Whenever a dispute arises among clansmen or between clans, the windlings look to their clan's noble for guidance. These clan rulers (of a sort) earn their positions as leaders not through age or might or riches, as is true of many Name-givers, but by persuasion. A windling who can convince the greatest number of his clansmen that he will lead them well and do right by them all without thought for his own gain becomes a noble. Most windlings prefer a leader who has a mate and children, but any member of the clan can hope to become its leader.

The clan leader keeps his or her power until he loses the support of the clan, and even then may hold it for a time until a better candidate appears. If a leader loses the support of his followers, they still obey him, but grudgingly. Often, they refuse to finish any task the noble assigns them. When another candidate appears, the clan switches its allegiance, and the new noble takes power without much fuss.

On the Curious Rite of Listening

When a noble speaks, he or she can invoke the Rite of Listening, a strange custom whereby all windlings in the clan must stop what they are doing to listen to the noble until he or she has finished speaking. I call this custom strange because, though all must listen, they may cease listening (or even choose a new noble) if the noble who invokes the rite has nothing of interest to say. The noble can command attention, and yet he does not command attention. Truly, it is a most curious custom, and I have yet to understand it!

Of Other Honorable Posts Within Windling Clans

In addition to the nobles, most windling communities have windscouts, windmasters, and wind-dancers. Windscouts safeguard the clan against airborne perils, patroling the skies and alerting their fellow windlings to any threat they see. Windmasters serve along with other warriors as the clan's soldiers, both in the air and on the ground; the wind-masters receive special training in the use of flight in battle.

Certain windling warriors, called the *harresa-tis,* or "hardy ones," serve as land and air cavalry. The *harresa-tis* alone among warriors wear windling-sized ring mail, crystal plate mail, or metal armor, and use shields the size of a human's buckler. The *harresa-tis* wield spears, which they use as lances, windling bows, and windling broadswords, and they wear helms made from the skulls of wild beasts. The ground cavalry ride beasts known as *kues,* that look as if they were moth-ered by a wildcat and fathered by a lizard. Airborne cavalry ride *zoaks,* furred creatures that resemble bats. Despite their small size, they make dangerous enemies. The sight of the *harresa-tis* arrayed for battle can make even the biggest opponent think better of attacking, assuming he's got any sense.

Wind-dancers are much like troubadours and have a special gift for becoming one with nature. They preserve windling culture and history, creating elaborate songs and dances to tell tales of momentous events. (I can hear some of my fellow Name-givers laughing at the very thought of windling culture, but even the ever-changing windlings have certain ways that are all their own. Were I as ignorant of windlings as some folk are, I should not laugh too hard.)

According to windling legend, a queen rules over the nobles and all the clans. My friends in clan Lisvara tell me that most windlings don't truly believe in the queen; they even hinted that the Windling Queen is a joke, started by the windlings themselves. One wind-dancer (whom I'll not name for his own safety) told me that the Windling Queen is a satire of the Elven Queen, Alachia, who has the cheek to demand the loyalty of all faerie creatures. (Then again, the wind-dancer might have been pulling my leg. Windlings love to do that. I could understand if his tale were true; in my opinion, high-and-mighty Alachia expects more than any decent person can stomach.) Nobody has ever seen the Windling Queen, let alone had an audience with her.

ON DIVERSE WINDLING ARTS AND CRAFTS

Too many folk believe that the windlings' changeable nature means that they have no true arts or crafts. I've even heard folk claim that windlings can't possibly build or make anything because of their small size, though why small people shouldn't be able to build houses, work metal, and suchlike just as well as larger folk is a mystery to me. Of course, the ignorant will believe anything. Some point to the many weaponsmiths and armorers of other Name-giver races that make windling-sized battle gear as "proof" that windlings make nothing of their own. I can tell you otherwise. Windlings are builders and smiths, craftsmen and poets, and every other kind of artisan that exists in Barsaive.

Many of the best shops and merchant stalls in Bartertown and other cities sell windling-sized goods, though at high prices. Of course, the workmanship is perfect, and the high price comes from the sheer labor needed to make small weapons and decorative items. Blessed with nimble fingers, sharp eyes, and quick minds, windlings make decorative goods that are prized throughout all Barsaive. Most windlings use the bounty of nature to create their goods: a bird feather, a piece of quartz, a bit of amber, a rosebud, and so on. An inspired windling craftsman can create a thing of such beauty that it hurts your heart to see it. Clan Lisvara's finest craftswoman, old Lharial, made me a wind chime as a parting gift, and is it a beautiful thing! The pieces look like spun glass, etched with spiraling leaves and vines, and they ring with a sound like silver bells. I've never seen anything so lovely in all my life. When I told Lharial so, she told me tales of windling artisans whose works would make her wind chime look like a mud sculpture.

OF WINDLING DWELLINGS

An old windling proverb says, "Live with nature, not against it." Taking this old saying to heart, windlings build little. Most often, they live in the highest and leafiest branches of trees, using leaves as roofs and walls to shelter them from bad weather. Sometimes, they build lean-tos of small branches and leaves against thicker branches or tree trunks. Windling clans such as clan Lisvara, which have chosen to settle in one place, dwell in the trunks of wide, tall trees, using natural hol-

lows where they find them and carving out more when they need to. These tree-homes are the heart of the clans; the windlings practice their many crafts and hold important ceremonies there.

A few windling clans build tall towers of thin ceramic, which hardens to be almost as strong as wood. Often as tall as five trolls, these towers look like windling kaers. City-dwelling windlings often build shelters in the second-story eaves of various buildings. All windlings prefer simple furnishings; a few hammocks for sleeping and a table or two for holding food and drink at mealtimes is all that most of them need or want. A windling wizard may build a shelf or a case to hold his books, or a merchant may need shelves for his records, but most windlings prefer to live unencumbered by objects.

A Brief Discourse On Windling Kaers

The windlings built only a few kaers, often preferring to wait out the long centuries of the Scourge in the company of the other Name-givers whose ways they found so entertaining. A windling kaer, of course, is a nightmare for an explorer of another race. Few walkways or doors in those tall towers are large enough to allow any other Name-giver to pass, and all the rooms within are built for a windling's small size. Also, because windlings are most accustomed to flying, the many levels of their towers have doors in ceilings and floors. Makes perfect sense for a race that moves about by flitting through the air—but for a grounder, limited to the use of his feet, getting through every door means a tiring climb.

OF THE CRAFTING OF
WEAPONS AND ARMOR

Of course, windling weapons and armor are the most famed of all windling creations. More than a few Name-givers who know nothing else about windlings have heard the famous words of the windling weapon-smith, Galassa: "Even a dragon screams if someone pokes a needle in its eye." The two most common windling weapons are the bow and spear, which resemble the larger versions that other Name-givers use. Windlings also carry swords and daggers, made especially for their small hands to wield.

Nets and blowguns are weapons much favored by the hunters of clan Lisvara, who use them with great skill. The nets are made of many closely woven strands of a thin, tough fiber that the windlings call *sadoor*. Folded into small squares for carrying, when released, the nets expand to nearly half my height (and I'm close to nine feet tall). The nets can trap anything the size of a human or smaller, but won't hold any creature the size or strength of a troll or an obsidiman. The blowgun, prized for its silence and simple construction, allows the windling hunter or warrior to attack from out of harm's reach.

Windlings most often use both nets and blowguns with poisons. They soak *sadoor* nets in a liquid that can paralyze at a touch, and dip blowgun darts in either the same poison or a stronger, lethal one. This use of poison is another thing about windlings that some other Name-givers don't like; they call it dishonorable, a foul tactic that no one can fight. The windlings, for their part, claim that poison helps them bring down large animals or evens the odds for them in battles with larger enemies.

Windlings rarely wear heavy armor, preferring to fly light so that they can move swiftly. They also prefer armor made of leather, which they often buy in bulk from merchants and tailor to fit their small frames. Save for the *harresa-tis*, I have never seen a windling use a shield; most windling warriors keep their hands free to make maneuvering in flight easier.

OF THE WORKING OF METAL INTO JEWELRY

Though they favor using natural items like feathers, flowers, and such, windlings also work precious metals and gems into beautifully wrought jewelry. My windling friends like to claim that Queen Alachia demands from them a monthly tribute of windling jewelry, and after seeing theirs, I believe that tale. Windlings use their small fingers to shape the metal into finer detail than Name-givers with larger hands can make.

Above all, most folk desire windling brooches, which are most often a single gem mounted in copper, silver, or gold. Windling craftsmen carve delicate patterns on the facets of the gem and shape the mounting into graceful spirals, knotwork, and other designs made to resemble woodland plants. Wizards especially prize these brooches, often using them to create blood charms, cloaksense brooches, and other magical items. Like everything else of windling make, such jewelry costs a quarter again as much as adornments made by other craftsmen.

OF THE ART OF TATTOOING

My friend Shehwar, clan Lisvara's tattoo master, is fond of asking what canvas for art could possibly be better than living skin. Many of Barsaive's Name-givers tattoo their bodies, and windlings are no exception. Because of their nimble fingers and eye for fine detail, windling tattoo masters are among the best in Barsaive. Of course, the customer of a windling tattoo master had best make a good first impression. The demands of their difficult work make many windling tattoo masters touchy and easily annoyed, and they can take spectacular revenge on those who slight them. Shehwar told me the tale of Doolsek, a bad-tempered ork who forced a windling tattoo master to make a design on his back and then refused to pay for it. Knowing that the offended artisan might well tattoo something other than what Doolsek had demanded, the ork inspected the work in a mirror. To his relief, he saw exactly the tattoo he wanted. Of course, Doolsek didn't know that he had bullied an illusionist. As soon as Doolsek left the tattoo master, the illusion faded, leaving behind a filthy insult against the elven race. A few days later, while bartering with elven warriors for passage across a road, Doolsek felt warm and took off his shirt off to cool himself. The elves, seeing the tattooed insult on Doolsek's back, used the ork as target practice for their arrows.

OF WINDLING GARB

Windlings wear simple, lightweight clothing, often stitched with cured leather. As flyers, windlings prefer to travel light and refuse to wear any clothing (such as fashionable hats) that serves no real purpose except as decoration for the body. On their feet, windlings most often wear sandals or soft, light, ankle-high boots. Not a windling alive would ever wear boiled-leather boots like mine; indeed, my friend Keerht once asked me if I wore such heavy boots to keep from floating off the earth. "For you have no wings," he said earnestly, "and therefore could not make yourself go in any direction you might wish. I can see where such a fate might frighten you, friend Chag." (After a time, I stopped wearing the boots except to go on long tramps, and Keerht took to sleeping in them. Once I nearly put them on with him still inside, but that's another tale.)

The few windlings desperate enough to fly in foul weather wear huge, hooded cloaks large enough to cover their wings. Because water is such a danger to a windling's wings, these little folk take every possible precaution against getting them wet in rain or snow.

OF THE ART OF WINDLING DANCE

When asked whether music or dance means more to a windling, the troubadour Windsong, about whom windlings still tell legends, is supposed to have said, "Why not ask which wing does a bird need most to fly, its left or its right?" Windling dance is a marvel above all marvels, blending intricate movements of arms, legs, and wings into breathtaking beauty. In some of the movements, their wings catch the sunlight, creating brilliant colors that blend with the dance. Many of their dances are old and established, but windlings also enjoy improvising ones from the steps of the old. Windlings love dancing so much that they do it on any occasion—weddings, funerals, victory celebrations, or even to celebrate a fine mug of ale.

ON THE UNIQUE BEAUTIES OF WINDLING MUSIC

Windlings love music as much as they love dancing and see the two arts as sides of the same coin. They create melodies without words and also epic ballads; indeed, they love songs, and often quote the troubadour Windsong's famous words that "Poetry is but good music with the melody left out." Windlings have created many wind instruments, but they love pipes and flutes above all because these delicate instruments let them play a jolly jig one minute and a dirge the next.

Rather than tell stories of their past as other races do, windlings sing and dance them. Poetry, epic tales, and all their history are performed with musical accompaniment. To windlings, the only true way to tell their people's history is to sing the ancient songs and dance the ancient steps.

I was lucky enough to watch Keerht and his friends dance and sing a story of the regiment of dwarfs that saved clan Lisvara from a horde of advancing ogres. Three windlings played different tunes that fit together like well-woven reeds in a basket: one for the dwarfs, one for the ogres, and one for the beleaguered windlings. As they played, the rest of the performers danced the parts of the dwarfs and ogres. When the tale reached the battle, I saw with delighted surprise that the dance steps mimicked the troop movements of both sides.

On the Telling of Windling History

According to a windling proverb, "If it cannot be sung about, it is not worth remembering." Windlings keep few written records of their history, preferring to remember their people's stories through song. Though most windlings know how to read and write, they consider writing a dull activity, suited for trade and such, but not for anything so meaningful as the history of the windling race. When I asked for writings on the history of clan Lisvara, the clan noble first greeted such a suggestion with hoots of laughter, and then asked me, "How should we remember the old stories for our children, unless we sing them around the fire for each new generation?"

Most other Name-givers cannot sing windling songs properly, having not the light, trilling voices that the little people have. Elven voices, with their light, clear tones, come closest to sounding like windlings, though even the greatest of the elven troubadours has yet to devise a way to mimic the hum of a windling's wings. One troubadour I know has made a stringed instrument she calls a *kahevar* that sounds a bit like the windling hum, but even it misses the mark by a fair length.

As far as I can tell, windlings do not have a legend of their creation, though some songs tell of the windlings' home in a magical woodland on the far side of Blood Wood, away from the Kingdom of Throal. Thus far, no windling explorer has found such place, or at least, no windling has lived to bring the tale back to his folk. The windlings do have a few tales of the Scourge, most concerned with the warning signs of its coming and the anguish of living below the ground or in sealed citadels, shut away from the glories of nature. Many windlings spent the Scourge in kaers built by other Name-givers, taking shelter in eaves and ceiling beams. The natural exuberance and humor of windlings dwindled during that dark time, as the windlings felt themselves dependent on the good will of their fellow Name-givers. Not surprisingly, they wished to avoid the slightest risk of offending their larger brethren and so often had to hide their true nature. Though some might wish they had stayed subdued, I say thank the Passions that the windlings have become themselves again since the retreat of the Horrors. Barsaive would be a colder, lonelier place without their warmth and laughter.

ON THE MAKING OF WINDLING WINE

The windling race sees the making of liquor as an art. Windling clans from Barsaive's lowlands, including clan Lisvara, brew a potent wine from a berry that grows in their lands, called *keesryp* in the windling tongue. These tiny, bright blue fruits grow in shrubs at the base of large trees and contain a sweet, refreshing juice. The sky-blue wine brewed from

keesryps is known as *keesris,* and is much sought after among elves, humans, and t'skrang. Most orks, obsidimen, and trolls find it too weak for getting properly drunk, though I began to acquire a taste for it after living among windlings for so many months. Still doesn't get me drunk, mind, but it does make me cheerful. Most dwarfs, of course, would as soon drink water as *keesris*—but then, they've got ale strong enough to kick a thundra beast's teeth in by comparison, so it's no wonder. Windlings, of course, can get as merry as a jester on a mere thimbleful of the stuff, and they drink it at the slightest excuse.

The *keesryp* ripens in the tenth month of the year, and the windlings make a great occasion of gathering the berries. Many a lowland clan gathers in the same stretch of woodland for the berry harvest, and they spend days on end picking *keesryps,* feasting, drinking, and sharing tales by the night-time fires.

ON THE NATURE OF WINDLING TRADE

Though a few windling clans have observed other folk in the pursuit of wealth and have chosen to follow their ways, most windlings have little use for making money except as a means to survival. It's the rare windling who piles up riches as an end in itself. Most windling clans barter for anything they need from the caravans that pass by their settlements. In Barsaivian cities, of course, windlings have merchant establishments just as any other Name-giver might.

A few windlings own thriving businesses in cities and trading posts across Barsaive, some to meet different kinds of folk and learn their ways, and some to give comfort to other windlings who may be passing through. These latter like nothing better than to offer their own a friendly face and a little bit of home. A windling innkeeper has rooms for larger folk, of course, but almost always has plenty of rooms built for windlings. Most of these have windling hammock-beds, and some even have small lean-tos along the eaves of the inn where the innkeeper's fellow windlings can stay in comfort.

Having stayed in such establishments, I find them just as good as any other. In fact, windling innkeepers are among the most hospitable folk in Barsaive. To those who think of windlings as folk who live to insult other races, try staying in a windling-run inn. Oh, and don't start off by insulting the innkeeper. He'll take that from a fellow windling, but not from anyone else unless he's already decided to call you friend.

As for windling thieves, they ply their trade not for coin, but for the thrill of living a thief's life. (Cold comfort, of course, for the victim whose pockets the thief has lightened)

ON WINDLING SPIRITUAL BELIEFS

Most windlings have little to do with the kind of worship of the Passions common to other Name-giver races. A human or an elf or a dwarf might go to a temple of Garlen, say, or Floranuus, on a certain day and swear to perform certain acts of devotion in return for the Passion's interest in his or her affairs. Not so a windling. For them, the Passions are not to be found in a building or in any one place, but in every place. To feel the Passions' presence and be with them does not require any other act of worship than to listen with a quiet heart. Windlings see the Passions as the source of all that they are and believe that they can touch the Passions at any time. They see no need to set aside holy days or feasts for worship, as others do, but believe that the Passions exist to be called upon in time of need.

Many windlings, however, hold a special place in their hearts for Floranuus, the Passion of revelry, energy, motion, and victory, and for Lochost, Passion of rebellion, change, and freedom. These two Passions between them embody the ideals that windlings hold most dear, and the qualities that they most prize. I have heard tell of a few windling questors of Floranuus, though they are extremely rare.

OF WINDLING BELIEFS ABOUT DEATH

Though no sane Name-giver looks forward to death, windlings possess the strongest will to live of any Name-giver race in Barsaive. A windling sees death as a state without change and fears it beyond almost any other fate. Other races may find comfort in the thought of an afterlife, but promises of "a life to come" mean little to windlings. They love life so much that they cannot conceive of anything better. The troubadour Windsong said it best: "A windling always moves, always changes, always laughs. Death is final. In it there is no change, no laughter, no movement. Death we do not speak of. Let us set our minds instead on the present and celebrate our lives." Indeed, windlings rarely use the word "death," instead speaking of the "final change," "flight's end," "riding the astral wind," and "becoming one with the sky."

This fear of death might seem odd, given the windlings' love of risks, but in truth it only adds spice to life's hazards. When a windling takes a risk that others deem foolish, he is living his life at its fullest; in windling belief, one never values a thing so much as when one may lose it. Some folk, of course, claim that windlings take such risks because they are too weak-minded to recognize the consequences. They say that windlings get away with defying death as often as they do because the possibility of dying never crosses their tiny minds. Well, if those ignoramuses can tell me how a people who think so little of the future can possibly raise children as carefully as they do, or even why they care so much about the coming generations, then maybe I'll think about agreeing with them.

Let me point out that for all their love of risk, no windling ever does anything truly soft-headed, such as diving into the open maw of a dragon or flying unarmed and naked into a horde of axe-wielding ogres. Windlings simply deem different things risky than do most of the rest of us.

When a windling dies, his clan members and close friends gather together, acknowledge the passing of the loved one, then burn the body and scatter the ashes to the wind. After this brief death ritual, the clan throws a feast to remember their fallen brother by telling stories of his life and drinking huge amounts of *keesris.* As a windling sees it, the only way to escape the awfulness of death is to make a funeral a merry occasion. The clan includes the death of their fellow in the clansong, but makes no other record. This lack of records drives many a scholar to distraction, should he try to determine a windling's lifespan or the year in which a notable windling lived. Not surprisingly, windlings find undead beings particularly repugnant. Not only do such awful beings remind windlings of their own mortality, but they are an abomination of nature and thus doubly offensive to beings who so revere nature as do the windlings.

ON THE MANNER OF WINDLINGS TOWARD OTHER NAME-GIVER RACES

I have touched on this subject earlier in my tale, with regard to windling humor and the many ways in which folk who know little of windlings misinterpret it. Sad to say, too many folk in Barsaive misunderstand not only windling humor, but many windling ways of thinking and acting. I can only hope that my small work does its part to broaden narrow minds by explaining some of the reasons why windlings behave as they do. After all, haven't they a right to their ways, just as any of us have to ours?

To give you an idea of just how small-minded some folk are, I give you the following journal entry. I'm ashamed to say it was written by one of my own race, who hates windlings for the same silly reasons that too many of my folk do. (Which is to say, no reason at all—but I'll say more of that soon enough.) You have to feel sorry for someone who thinks as this poor fool does, getting angry and hateful because not every Name-giver behaves as *he* thinks is proper. Not all trolls are like this one, believe me.

—*From the journal of Targ Boneslicer*

Windlings? You want to know what I think about windlings? By the Passions, I can't stand the little gnats!

'Tisn't a matter of size, not at all. Not a bit of it. Live and let live, I always say. Trouble is, those little flying pests won't let me alone. They're the ones who judge others by size. I'm too big and clumsy for them, and the little insects never give me any peace because of it!

Me, I think those little gnats secretly hate being so small. So they try to make up for it by playing the fool, laughing at everything, but especially at bigger folk. Guess who they like to pick on most? The biggest Name-givers, that's who. 'Course, they don't tease obsidimen much, because it takes an earthquake, a fire, and a flood all at the same time to rouse the rock-men. No fun teasing a stone, is it? So which very tall, very large race is left to tease?

That's right, friend. Trolls. Like me.

Before anyone calls me ignorant, let me say that I've traveled a bit. I've met so many windlings in so many places that I've lost count, and every single one of them has made jests about my size. Oh, we start off civil enough, but sooner or later some little winged rat makes a joke at my expense. Naturally, I get annoyed. Wouldn't anyone? 'Course, that really sets the little beasts off. They laugh and snigger and joke, each mean jest more hurtful than the last, until even a patient fellow like myself can't stand anymore. I tell you, I'd like nothing better than to grab the little beasts and squeeze them until their little heads pop off!

So now that you've read the words of friend Targ, you tell me. Who judges who by size, eh?

Of course, there's a grain of truth to some folks' dislike of windlings. Their joking can get under the skin and they have other ways that to them are just ordinary, but that others may take offense at. Windlings place little value on privacy, to give one example, and often ask blunt questions about things that most others would call none of their affair. They also tell you exactly what they think, sometimes even if no one asks them. A windling sees no sense in hemming and hawing; if he has a thing to say, he says it. If he hurts someone's feelings, no matter. A simple apology makes things right again, so why waste time sparing folk hard truths? Of course, in thinking this way, the windlings make the mistake of believing that other folk accept apologies as easily as they do. Not all races are as quick to forgive.

Windlings also have little of what other folk call manners. They adopt what customs amuse them and drop them if something new catches their fancy. Except for the ideals that shape a windling's soul, little about them remains unchanging. What use do such changeable folk have for the kind of grand manners beloved by elves, say, or for the tangled web of trade manners common to dwarfs and t'skrang? A windling has those kinds of manners for as long as he enjoys having them, and no longer. This drives some folk wild, because they persist in believing that a windling who doesn't respect their customs of politeness means to insult them. Of course, no such thing is true—windlings are just behaving like windlings, just as trolls behave like trolls and dwarfs behave like dwarfs and so on. If a windling really means to insult you, he won't just act with what you'd call bad manners. He'll call you "dirt-kicker" or "mudclod" to your face, and more than once.

One good point about windlings that too many overly judgemental folk overlook is their interest in making friends with folk from all the Name-giver races. I'd rather be with friendly folk like that than with races like elves, who look at you as if you're dirt underfoot unless you've got pointed ears!

ON THE WINDLING VIEW OF DWARFS

A dwarf is a creature of serious mind, which most windlings don't understand. Oh, they can be serious about the things they consider truly important, like change and freedom, but to be serious about everything? Such a way of thinking and living would drive a windling mad within a day. Dwarfs interest windlings precisely because of their relentless seriousness and love of complexity. But these qualities also make them the ready target of a windling's teasing. "Plodders," the windlings call them sometimes, or stoneheads, because of the dwarfs' love of rock and earth. Many windlings see a kinship

between windlings and dwarfs, because dwarfs are the nearest to windlings in size. Believing that the dwarfs understand the difficulties of living in a too-large world in a way that no other folk do, most windlings regard every dwarf as a friend.

ON THE WINDLING VIEW OF ELVES

Windlings delight in the company of elves, cherishing their beauty and the closeness to nature that both races share. Of course, elves come in for their share of teasing, mostly because of their insistence on a manner so grand that it makes a king seem like a gutter thief. (A ripe target for jokes, eh, friend?) The elves of Blood Wood, however, windlings loathe. A windling regards the blood elves as a crime against nature, because they have taken the gift of life and turned it to constant torture. No self-respecting windling gives a moment's credence to Queen Alachia's claim of sovereignty over them; in fact, many a windling troubadour earns a living telling wickedly funny stories that poke fun at "Her High and Mightiness."

ON THE WINDLING VIEW OF HUMANS

Humans come in more shapes and sizes than any other Name-giver race, and this dazzling variety delights the windling mind. Loving the new and different as they do, windlings find humans in all their many guises the most fascinating race in Barsaive. Of course, a fair number of windlings mistakenly assume that such diverse people have a free spirit to match and tend to find out otherwise the hard way.

Many windlings seek out human traveling companions, taking up with the first one who strikes their fancy. The windling watches his human friend closely, mimicking actions that interest him and will stay with his companion until he no longer finds anything new or diverting in the company. If the windling loses interest, he abandons the human with no more than a simple farewell. This casualness irks many humans, who mistakenly see it as a sign that windlings do not value human friendship. In truth, a windling always remembers his traveling companions. If any human with whom a windling has wandered should turn up at the windling's settlement, the windling goes out of his way to show his friend the best of the clan's hospitality. A windling's abrupt departure from a companion does not mean that he feels no friendship, but simply that windlings dislike elaborate goodbyes.

ON THE WINDLING VIEW OF OBSIDIMEN

An obsidiman's rocklike slowness and calm fascinates the swift-moving, emotional windlings. Indeed, there are probably no two races in Barsaive so different from each other as windlings and obsidimen. Plenty of folk from other races might find such great differences good cause to be wary, but not so windlings. For them, differences are a thing to celebrate, the greater the better. (I ask you, how can anyone dislike folk with that kind of courage?) Everything about an obsidman—his slowness, his great height, the fact that he is made of living rock—interests a windling. Many windlings find their interest returned, which truly delights them—they find it funny that such a solemn, incurious folk as the obsidimen find *them* fascinating. (After all, a windling takes his own ways for granted just as much as anyone else does.) This interest in each other binds windlings and obsidimen together in a curious way and often leads to firm friendships between members of both races. In fact, the only obsidiman that won't draw a small crowd of interested windlings is a drunken one. Being no fools, windlings stay good and far from a reeling rock-man. No sense getting crushed underfoot by an obsidiman gotten happy on strong dwarf stout, is there?

The one thing about obsidimen that truly puzzles windlings is the rock-people's refusal to either tease back or get angry at windling jests. Accustomed as they are to other Name-givers getting upset and going off for a good sulk, they expect the same reaction from obsidimen. They don't get it, of course. Nothing much gets to a rock-man. An obsidiman stays as calm as a glass ocean, no matter what jests a windling makes at his expense. Most windlings find that calmness the most fascinating thing of all.

ON THE WINDLING VIEW OF ORKS

Windlings have a funny view of orks, most often dependent on the ork in question. Long ago, Barsaive's other Name-giver races enslaved the orks, all save the windlings (who'd rather die than enslave anything). Windlings have an especial sympathy for orks because they suffered through a windling's worst nightmare—or at least, windlings *want* to sympathize. Trouble is, plenty of orks want nothing to do with windlings. Quite a few orks forget that the windlings ever treated them different than everyone else, and those who remember that the windlings alone did not make them slaves often blame the windlings for not forcing the other Name-givers to stop the horrid practice. Many orks have foul tempers and take offense

Windlings

TREVLIA TROLLSLAYER, LEGENDARY WINDLING WARRIOR.

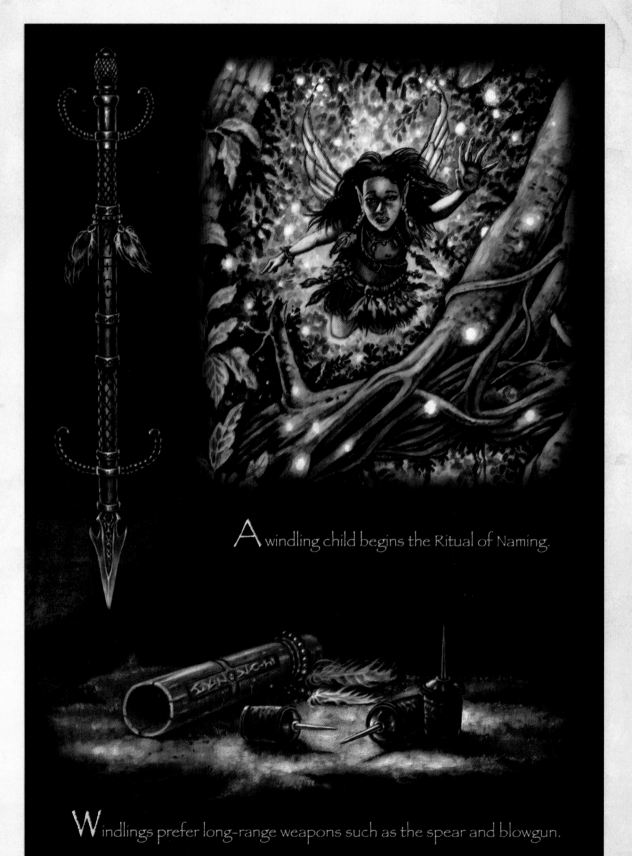

A windling child begins the Ritual of Naming.

Windlings prefer long-range weapons such as the spear and blowgun.

The windling thief P'kris guards his hoard of stolen treasure.

The windling weaponsmith Ixia crafted this dagger in her own image for Varulus III, King of Throal.

Windlings craft cunning jewelry from materials found in nature. Their exquisite designs are favored by the other Name-giver races.

The floral belt of Garlen, worn by questors of the Lisvara clan.

Gnarled branches obscure the entrance to the abandoned kaer of clan Lisvara.

at windling jokes more easily than any other folk. Well, there's only so long a windling can take being shouted at before he stops teasing for friendship's sake and starts teasing to hurt. Too many orks make windlings angry, and too many windlings vent their anger without thinking. No wonder, is it, that these two races get along about as well as a dragon and an elf. Though I've known windlings and orks to be friends (a windling can make friends with anyone if he's a mind to), the ork always has uncommon patience and the windling, uncommon restraint.

ON THE WINDLING VIEW OF TROLLS

Well, here's a sensitive subject and no mistake. Ask anyone in Barsaive what they think windlings think about trolls (and vice versa), and they'll tell you that trolls and windlings loathe each other. What they can't tell you is the reason why. In truth, and I hate to say this, we trolls have brought the windlings' dislike upon ourselves. My own folk'll likely call me a traitor to my kin for saying so, but it's true. From my year with clan Lisvara, I've learned that windlings in general are interested in everything and want to make friends with everyone. Ask yourself for a moment why a friendly, curious, openhearted people like windlings would dislike, even hate, an entire race. Because we're bigger than they are, as Targ Boneslicer thinks? Hardly. Windlings love obsidimen, and the rock people are almost as big as us trolls. Because we're different from them? Wrong again, friend. Windlings love differences—there's nothing they like so much as the unfamiliar. No, the enmity between trolls and windlings stems from the simple fact that trolls as a race have never had any use for windlings and had the poor manners to let them know it. Little, we call them, as if smallness were an offense. Flighty, foolish, soft in the skull, puny, cowardly, no use in a pinch—trolls call windlings all of these things and worse. Well, a windling won't take being insulted, and it would never occur to the average troll that he might owe a windling an apology for insulting him. We trolls have given windlings reason to hold a whopping grudge against our folk, and that's exactly what they do.

As proof of my point, I offer my own experience with clan Lisvara. The windlings accepted me, opening their hearts and hearths in spite of their grudge, because the simple fact that I wanted to learn their ways meant (to their way of thinking) that I had "apologized" for my folk's longstanding insults to the windling race. Like the generous folk they are, they accepted my "apology" at once, forgave me any wrong any troll had ever done them and treated me like a sworn brother for as long as I stayed with them. And if I ever go back, as I hope to, they'll welcome me home as if I were kin to them.

On the Legend of Mraga and Its Meaning

When I asked my windling friends why they so disliked most trolls, the wind-dancer Sheorh told me the legend of the troll king Mraga. I give you her own words, as I remember them.

"Long ago, in a time so distant that the Scourge was yet unheard of, Mraga ruled over the troll kingdom of Ustrect. Now in those days, the great windling artisan Windeyes of clan Deosylh lived near to Ustrect, and she crafted jewels and swords of great beauty and cunning. Word of Windeyes' wonderful works reached the ears of King Mraga, and he determined to see her creations for himself. But all he knew of Windeyes was her name—that she was a windling, he knew not.

"So Mraga issued a proclamation, that all traders and merchants in Ustrect who sold jewelry, weapons, and any other metalwork should come to his court. And of each of them, he asked, 'Are you Windeyes?' And each of them said, 'No, my lord, I am not.' And when he asked, 'What can you tell me of Windeyes?' each of them said, 'Only that she is the greatest worker of metal in all the world.'

"Mraga extended his royal command to all merchants, traders, and artisans who passed through Ustrect. Of them, he asked the same questions, and they all gave him the same answers. He wrote letters and sent embassies to all the other peoples of nearby realms—the dwarfs, the elves, the obsidimen, the orks, the humans, the t'skrang. To all he wrote, save for the windlings, seeking Windeyes. All gave him the same answer—Windeyes, the greatest worker of metal in all the world, dwelled not among their folk.

"At length, Windeyes herself heard of King Mraga's search and took pity on the troll king. 'I will go to Ustrect and show him my finest work. I will make him a gift of it, in return for his having so honored me that he would seek me the length and breadth of the world.' So saying, Windeyes packed a bag full of her finest creations, brooches and bracelets and daggers and swords of surpassing beauty, and went to Ustrect.

"When King Mraga saw her in his great audience chamber, he scowled at her and demanded to know her business with him. 'I am Windeyes,' she told him. 'I have heard that you wish to see my work—therefore, see what I have brought you.' And she opened her bag and presented to King Mraga her most beautiful creations. 'Choose one, great king. You have

honored me by seeking me so earnestly, and I would make you a gift of equal worth.'

"But Mraga laughed until the ceiling echoed with the sound. 'Take a gift from a windling?' he said. 'I will take no gift from a liar like you. You are not Windeyes. You cannot be the greatest worker of metal in all the world—no mere windling could accomplish so much! Do you truly expect me to believe that your foolish, flighty race knows enough of any craft to create the simplest object?' And his eyes were darkened by scorn, for he looked at Windeyes' creations and saw not their beauty. He swept them aside with his booted foot, saying, 'Take these stable-sweepings out of my sight, before I have you killed for your presumption! Windeyes, indeed!'

"So Windeyes gathered her treasures and left Ustrect. But she left one treasure behind, just as she said she would—a jeweled dagger, buried in King Mraga's throat."

I had never heard this tale, until Sheorh told it. No troll of my acquaintance has ever heard it, or any of the countless others like it known to each windling clan. Sheorh spent many a year traveling around Barsaive, collecting the troll legends of other windling clans, and she tells me that every clan has its own version of a tale in which a troll grievously insults an honored windling for no good reason. She thinks, and I agree, that the tale springs not from a real event, but simply from the trolls' longstanding disdain for the windling people.

ON THE WINDLING VIEW OF T'SKRANG

T'skrang share with windlings a flair for drama and a zest for life, and so windlings regard the t'skrang as brothers of the soul. Despite the fact that most t'skrang dwell near and in water, an element hazardous to windlings, the little flyers often make companions of the most flamboyant t'skrang they can find. T'skrang also share the windlings' sense of fun and often answer windling jests with jokes and friendly insults of their own. Of all the Name-giver races, the t'skrang come closest to understanding the affection that underlies a windling's incessant teasing and therefore will play along with their windling companions. In their joy at finding a race as playful as themselves, windlings often treat t'skrang with special courtesy.

HOW WINDLINGS SEE THE THERAN EMPIRE

Though almost everyone in Barsaive hates the Therans, the freedom-loving windlings especially despise the Theran Empire. Resting as it does on a foundation of slavery, the Theran Empire strikes most windlings as an offense against life, the Passions, and every moral value that decent folk hold dear.

Theran slavers, especially, rouse windlings to a kind of hate and fear that they feel for no one and nothing else in this world. The little folk's longstanding dislike of trolls is a mere moment's tiff compared to their loathing of the Theran slave trader. Windlings fear slavery as they fear nothing else, save for the Horrors. Whether the slavers hunt windlings or other Name-givers makes no difference; a windling will fight just as hard to save another Name-giver from capture by a slave driver as he would fight for a fellow windling.

Lucky for the windlings, few Therans want windling slaves. Every so often, possession of windlings becomes a fashion, but it rarely lasts more than a few months. Rich Therans with visions of windling artisans forced to craft jewelry for them, or flocks of windling messengers carrying their express commands all over the streets of Vivane or Sky Point soon find their newly bought windlings sickening and dying from the misery of living in chains. Some say that a captive windling simply wills himself to die, and indeed, it's the rare windling who survives the Theran slave life for more than ten or fifteen days.

The Theran Empire's airship fleet offends most windlings almost beyond reason. As children of the air, Barsaivian windlings find the Therans' presence in their best-beloved element a revolting intrusion. They react with the kind of disgust that a troll or a human might at finding maggots in his drinking water. Often, windlings relieve their outraged feelings by sabotaging Theran airships. Such acts are a popular test of courage during mating season.

On the Curious Nature of Theran Windlings

Theran windlings do exist, of course, however much our windling brethren in Barsaive would like to think otherwise. Every Barsaivian windling I've ever met finds the very thought of Theran windlings deeply shaming, and few will own them as kin. This reaction, from a people whose loyalty to all windlings everywhere is only exceeded by their fierce love for their own clansmen, shows just how much the little folk despise the few of their number who take on Theran ways.

The windlings of Barsaive despise their Theran kin for a single, overwhelming reason. Theran windlings accept slavery, thereby throwing away one of the highest ideals of windling culture as if it had no more worth than a clod of mud. Theran windlings think of themselves as Therans first and windlings second, and so manage to tell themselves comforting lies about the slavery and misery that prop up the Theran Empire. Believing that Therans are naturally better than any other folk on the earth, they say that Barsaivians and others are not worthy of the freedom that all windlings love, and so it is right to enslave them.

As it happens, I had an interesting encounter with a Theran windling during a stay at an inn near Vivane. (Not in Vivane, of course—I've not much love for the Therans, myself, no matter how much coin they pay.) In the course of our conversation (which was brief enough—I was nought but benighted, Barsaivian scum to him!), I asked him if he'd ever seen a windling slave, and how that made him feel. He answered that any windling of Barsaive foolish enough to get caught by the slavers clearly didn't deserve freedom, and that it was better such a windling should die than live to breed more fools. (He would have warmed to his subject, but I shut him up by pouring his ale pot over his head and gorgeous suit of clothes. If I ever see him again, I just might pop his little head off.)

DENIZENS
OF EARTHDAWN VOLUME ONE

GAME INFORMATION

GAME INFORMATION

Rules and rubrics may tax the brain, but without such things we'd have no game.
Rafkallon of Elliv Skralc

Denizens of Earthdawn, Volume I, provides gamemasters and players with a wealth of detail regarding four of Barsaive's Name-giver races. The information on each race appears as an excerpt from one volume of an eight-volume set, originated by the Library of Throal, each volume dedicated to exploring all aspects of one race. This first book describes elves, humans, t'skrang, and windlings. A second book will describe the dwarfs, obsidimen, orks, and trolls.

The **Earthdawn** rulebook is required to use this book, and the **Earthdawn Gamemaster's Pack** and the **Earthdawn Companion** are recommended. Though the information in **Denizens, Volume I,** creates a rich and diverse background for each of the races discussed, the general information provided in the **Barsaive Campaign Set** further fills out the **Earthdawn** universe, and so players and gamemasters will find that set useful when reading this book.

The fictional descriptions in this book describe how the elves, humans, t'skrang, and windlings of Earthdawn interact with their world, where and how they live, their cultural traditions and biases, their relationships with other races, and so on. Our goal in providing this information is to help players roleplay characters of these races by describing each through the eyes of the people of Barsaive.

The **Game Information** section provides new game rules for these four races, including new Disciplines and talents, race-specific skills, new equipment, and rules for gaming certain racial characteristics. In some cases, these rules expand on those described in the **Earthdawn** rulebook (**ED**) and the **Earthdawn Companion** (**Companion**). This section also offers suggestions for roleplaying characters of each of these races, drawing on the broadest characteristics of each race as described in the fiction.

ROLEPLAYING HINTS

The stories of the elves, humans, t'skrang, and windlings were written to create a more fully realized game universe for the world of Barsaive and give players more to work with when roleplaying characters of a fictional race. The roleplaying hints summarize the broadest features of each race, providing a sketch on which to base the beginnings of a character. Because they represent the stereotypical and underlying qualities of each race and their important sub-groups, players should keep these ideas and concepts in mind when roleplaying characters of these races.

It is also true, however, that not all members of a race will act the same. Not all t'skrang, for example, seek *haropas*. Likewise, some windlings desire a comfortable, routine life, rejecting the constant search for change and passion common to their race. A few bored, dispassionate windlings surely exist somewhere in Barsaive!

In general, one of the easiest ways to express the ideals and attitudes of a race is to choose specific personality traits to represent those ideals and attitudes. We suggest in the rulebook (pp. 59–61, **ED**) that players choose personality traits for their characters to reflect the character's Discipline. This same tactic can be used to explore the unique aspects of a character's race. For example, a player creating a t'skrang character may choose the personality traits of flamboyant and energetic to represent *jik'harro*, while an elf character may display the traits of private and pensive, to represent their quiet confidence in their heritage.

ELVES

More than other races, the elven people attempt to live their lives in such a way that they integrate all aspects of their culture and personalities into a seamless whole. Players creating elf characters should consider how to combine the racially specific aspects of their character, like pride in their culture and sorrow for Blood Wood, with all other elements of the character's life.

For most elves, the most basic part of their being lies in their connection to nature and the world around them. The elven people consider themselves defenders of nature; its destruction always destroys a bit of the elven people, too. Elves design all their rituals to preserve harmony with nature, try to capture nature's beauty in art and craftsmanship, and keep alive those traditions that honor and revere nature.

Artistic endeavor offers the elves a way to express their love for and reliance upon nature. All elves learn many different forms of artistic expression beginning

soon after they are born, and most continue to practice at least one art form throughout their lives. Many elven adepts choose a racial art form as their artisan skill. For example, elven troubadours often hone their traditional music and dance skills to prove they remain untouched by the Horrors, and elven magicians commonly embellish the embroidery on their robes with the unique threads created by elven textilers. Traditions inspire every part of elven life, and the traditions of his culture are an integral part of an elf's upbringing. Beyond the traditions they maintain through their rituals of nature, and more than the traditional art forms, cultural traditions guide and influence elves throughout their lives. The rituals and customs a player gives his elf character can help emphasize this aspect of the elven race. A player might choose, for example, to create specific cultural traditions for a character raised in one of the elven cities that lie deep within the forests of Barsaive or may adapt a forest tradition for an elf family that has lived in a city for generations.

Based on the way literature of the fantasy genre and others usually portray elven nature, players traditionally give their elf characters an attitude of superiority over other races. That attitude can certainly be justified in the context of **Earthdawn**, but the elven population of Barsaive must also constantly struggle with the knowledge of the existence of the blood elves. Rather than regarding elves with awe, the other races often look down on all elves as corrupt because of the choices made by the blood elves. As a race, the elves of **Earthdawn** cannot be characterized as humble, but they tend to keep any feelings of superiority to themselves; it becomes a more subtle aspect of their personality. And because their traditions make up such a fundamental part of their personality, most non-blood elves feel a deep sense of loss at their separation from Wyrm Wood (now Blood Wood). Their lack of contact with the historical seat of their culture and

government causes these elves further anxiety, and the anguish they feel colors all their perceptions and affects every part of their lives.

The nature of elven characters can also rely heavily on the idea of the Journey along the Wheel of Life as represented by the five Paths. Though not all elves embrace this philosophy, those who do feel its influence deeply. Allow the idea that life is not a destination, but a journey, to affect a character's personality and outlook, along with the specific Path a character follows. For example, an elf who follows the Path of Warriors will react differently to a given set of circumstances than one who follows the Path of Travelers. See **Of the Journey and the Wheel**, p. 12, for more information on roleplaying characters who follow one of the five Paths.

HUMANS

The keys to a human character are adaptability and versatility. As much as any other trait, these two represent what it means to be human in Barsaive. Humans are the most ordinary race of all the Name-givers of Barsaive, and while other races think of this as a disadvantage, most humans consider it their greatest advantage. Freed from the necessity of devoting constant effort to reminding other races of how special they are, humans have a way of thinking and acting that allows them to readily adapt to a variety of environments and situations and they feel no need to conform to or deny a stereotype. Their flexibility allows humans to be the only race among the Name-givers able to follow all the Disciplines of **Earthdawn**.

Their ability and willingness to restrain their racial pride makes humans very good at negotiation, especially when dealing with more than one other race. Their unique viewpoint of the world helps them see the larger picture and gives them a wider perspective.

T'SKRANG

Two words from their own language best describe the primary characteristics of the t'skrang: *jik'harro* and *haropas*. *Jik'harro*, or fearlessness, is the attitude most t'skrang embrace as part of their struggle to reach the state represented by *haropas*, or brave passion.

Roleplaying *jik'harro* requires the character to face danger and peril head on, only boasting of their success afterward. Unfortunately, those who find t'skrang lifestyles and attitudes hard to understand usually hear only the tale of the deed and never witness the t'skrang's bravery. Thus, their very real and constant search for *jik'harro* comes across as mere bravado. It is true, howev-

er, that the seriousness of the danger is less important than the act of confronting the danger.

Haropas is a state of communion with the Passions. Players can roleplay this aspect of the t'skrang by keeping in mind and acting on the four pillars of *haropas*: *kiatsu*, *jik'harro*, *p'skarrot*, and *kyaapas*. The first pillar is *kiatsu*, or ritual preparation, which requires t'skrang to confront their fears head-on. Each player may choose the fear their individual character must face. The second pillar is *jik'harro*, described above. The third pillar is *p'skarrot*, which means measure and destiny. To fulfill this aspect of *haropas*, characters must take stock of themselves in comparison to the world around them, and live a life full of rich experience and learning. The last pillar of *haropas* is *kyaapas*, or balance, which asks each t'skrang to balance his life between the demands of self and of society.

The path to fulfilling this guiding principle of the t'skrang can lead in many, unique directions, providing the opportunity for each player character t'skrang to express his racial background differently. Remember, too, that there is nothing wrong with creating and roleplaying a t'skrang who chooses not to strive to achieve the ideals of *haropas*.

While most often players will end up playing t'skrang characters from the Serpent River, some may choose to play characters that are from the other types of t'skrang described in this book. The following are brief guidelines for players choosing to use this option.

Jungle T'skrang

Jungle t'skrang live in a primitive fashion, preferring their life within the jungle to the so-called civilized societies found across Barsaive. Jungle t'skrang find other Name-giver races, with their preference for living inside various structures, difficult to understand and so distrust them to a degree. Their partiality to living in the bosom of nature sometimes leads them to resist their companions' plans to shelter in villages and towns.

Jungle t'skrang rely on relatively primitive weapons and armor, most often choosing spears, slings, or staves, and refuse to wear metal, living crystal, or blood-pebble armor. They also disdain the use of shields. Some tribes of jungle t'skrang use nets and other weapons of entanglement made from vines, equivalent to the nets and bolas described on p. 253, **ED**.

The Pale Ones

The Pale Ones also live a more primitive lifestyle than other Name-givers. Unlike their jungle counterparts, however, the Pale Ones fear open spaces and the outdoors, preferring to remain indoors as much as possible. When traveling outdoors, the Pale Ones become distracted by the unusual, rather frightening sensations of being without shelter and often perform their duties within a group less effectively.

The Pale Ones are most comfortable when using weapons similar to those preferred by the jungle t'skrang, but pick up on the use of swords and knives fairly quickly. Some Pale Ones will wear metal armor.

Winged T'skrang

Most *k'stulaami*, or winged t'skrang, born to the t'skrang society of the Serpent River leave their homes around the time they become adults at age 12. The *k'stulaami* are born with a passion to fly that consumes their nature, even changing their language. The Serpent River t'skrang find these t'skrang difficult to live with and understand, and so it is that most *k'stulaami* find their way to a large community of their kind that lives in the Throal Mountains. These t'skrang rarely choose to travel across Barsaive and live among the other Name-givers, but some do so in order to keep abreast of world events and technological and magical developments.

Most Name-giver races consider the *k'stulaami* to be oddities and freaks, but these attitudes are based on tales and folklore recounted by t'skrang storytellers. Given the opportunity to relate to other races, *k'stulaami* get along well with all but the t'skrang of the Serpent. Many *k'stulaami* resent the Serpent River t'skrang for treating them as mutants rather than kin.

K'stulaami use many types of weapons, often developing unique ways of fighting using weapons taken from adventurers who bother or harass the *k'stulaami* community. They use only the lightest types of armor, so that they can glide unimpeded.

The winged t'skrang can use the *k'stulaa*, the membrane stretching from wrist to hip, to glide by virtue of the Gliding skill that is taught to every *k'stulaami*. K'stulaami characters begin with 1 rank in the Gliding skill. This skill, for use only by *k'stulaami*, appears in **Special Rules**, p. 124. Winged t'skrang may follow the beastmaster Discipline.

WINDLINGS

Above all else, windlings desire new experiences and new sensations. They seek and gain these new experiences and sensations by living passionately and maintaining their freedom. Windlings throw their entire being into the moment. They rarely feel merely "fine," they feel "excellent!" They do not feel "refreshed," they feel "exuberant!" In all things, windlings seek to experience the extreme.

Windlings embrace each day for the opportunity to expand their experience and to change and fiercely protect the freedom that allows them to do so.

DISCIPLINES

Though each of the races described in this book may follow many different Disciplines, if such a thing as statistical analysis existed in **Earthdawn**, it would show that each race tends to follow certain Disciplines more than others. For example, elven characters rarely become cavalryman or weaponsmiths, even though that race may follow both these Disciplines, according to the rules of **Earthdawn**. This section lists the Disciplines most commonly followed by members of each race.

Elves: Elven characters most commonly follow those Disciplines they consider more refined or requiring greater focus. These Disciplines include all four of the magician Disciplines, the archer, beastmaster, scout, swordmaster, and troubadour. Less popular Disciplines for this race include air sailor, thief and warrior. Elves rarely follow the cavalryman and weaponsmith Disciplines. The new woodsman Discipline, p. 112, is available only to elves.

Humans: In accordance with their world view of adaptability and versatility, human characters follow all the Disciplines available in Earthdawn with equal frequency. Humans do not choose to follow certain Disciplines more often than any others.

Human characters do tend to use the Versatility talent to learn talents from other Disciplines, and learn multiple Disciplines more often than other Name-giver races. The new journeyman Discipline, p. 107, is only available to humans.

T'skrang: Most t'skrang characters favor the more flamboyant or active Disciplines, often ignoring the ones they consider dull or passive. They most often follow the Disciplines of elementalist, illusionist, swordmaster, and troubadour, less frequently choosing the Disciplines of archer, cavalryman, nethermancer, warrior, and wizard. The least popular Disciplines for the t'skrang are air sailor, sky raider, thief and weaponsmith.

Many t'skrang characters who serve on a village's riverboat follow the boatman Discipline, p. 106, a new Discipline available only to t'skrang.

Windlings: Windlings prefer to follow the most active and exciting Disciplines. While any Discipline can be made to be exciting, as a rule, windlings find certain Disciplines generally dull. Windlings most commonly follow the Disciplines of beastmaster, elementalist, illusionist, scout, swordmaster, thief, troubadour, and warrior, with fewer of that race attracted toward the Disciplines of archer, cavalryman, and wizard. Few windlings become air sailors or weaponsmiths.

Many windlings become wind-dancers, p. 109, windmasters, p. 110, or windscouts, p. 111, three new Disciplines available only to that race.

NEW DISCIPLINES

This section also describes several new Disciplines unique to characters of certain races. Each of these new Disciplines can only be followed by the race listed under Racial Restrictions.

The new Disciplines appear in the same format as those described in the **Earthdawn** rulebook and the **Earthdawn Companion**. They were designed according to the guidelines for creating new Disciplines on pages 137–51 of the **Companion**, with a few, minor exceptions, mainly that certain Disciplines offer more talents at a given Circle than recommended by the guidelines in the **Companion**.

Though the **Companion** expanded the original 13 **Earthdawn** Disciplines to allow characters to reach Fifteenth Circle, these new Disciplines are limited to Tenth Circle or less. Because these Disciplines have a narrower focus than the original Disciplines, they offer fewer special abilities and, overall, less power.

The asterisk following certain talents indicates new, racially specific talents described in **New Talents**, p. 113.

Durability and Thread Weaving

The bonuses to a character's Death and Unconsciousness Ratings for ranks in the Durability talent appear in parentheses following Durability. For example, Durability (6/5) means that for each rank of Durability, the character adds 6 to his Death Rating and 5 to his Unconsciousness Rating.

Each new Discipline offers the Thread Weaving talent, listed with the appropriate name for the talent in parentheses. For example, the Thread Weaving talent for the windscout Discipline is called Scout Weaving.

BOATMAN

Not every crew member of a t'skrang riverboat follows the boatman Discipline, but those who do make the best officers and captains on the river. The boatman adept must know the river, his crew, and his ship, but most boatmen choose this Discipline out of a fierce desire to know a little bit about everything else, too.

Important Attributes: Dexterity and Charisma

Racial Restrictions: T'skrang only

Karma Ritual: The boatman must be moving somewhere on the surface of a body of water, whether on a boat or swimming under his own power. He must fix his gaze on a point on the shore and remain focused on that point until his movement carries it beyond his view. During this time, he must concentrate and remove all fear from his mind. When the ritual is complete, he says aloud, "I have passed beyond my fear."

Artisan Skills: Craftsman, Music, Storytelling

FIRST CIRCLE

Talents
> Avoid Blow
> Karma Ritual
> Melee Weapon
> Pilot Boat*

Throwing Weapons
Unarmed Combat

SECOND CIRCLE

Talents
> Acrobatic Strike
> Durability (6/5)
> Read River*

THIRD CIRCLE

Talents
> Cast Net*
> Haggle

FOURTH CIRCLE

Karma: The boatman may spend a Karma Point on any action using Dexterity only.

Talents
> Mystic Aim (Thrown weapons)
> Thread Weaving (Net Weaving)

FIFTH CIRCLE

Physical Defense: Increase the boatman's Physical Defense by 1.

Talents
> Engaging Banter
> Evaluate*

SIXTH CIRCLE

Karma: The boatman may spend a Karma Point to increase the damage of any melee weapon attack.

Talents
> Speak Language
> Lizard Leap

SEVENTH CIRCLE

Talents

Recovery Test: The boatman gains an additional Recovery Test per day.
> First Impression
> Great Leap

EIGHTH CIRCLE

Initiative: Increase the boatman's Initiative dice by 1 step.

Talents
> Lion Heart
> Wound Balance

JOURNEYMAN

Journeyman Discipline adepts are rare in Barsaive. Available only to humans, this Discipline takes advantage of that race's versatility and adaptability and enables them to use powerful magic outside the relatively narrow focus of a standard Discipline.

An adept's Discipline functions much like a filter through which the character sees the world. By acting according to this world view, he is able to better use magic. The journeyman views the world as a field of magical possibilities, of which he is able to learn to use a limited variety. Rather than learning new talents from increasingly more advanced members of a single Discipline, the journeyman studies with masters of a variety of Disciplines, learning something specific from each.

Of all Disciplines, the journeyman is the rarest and most difficult to follow. Adepts who choose this path must deal with certain, unique restrictions: they may learn only a certain number of talents and must master each talent before learning more.

Racial Restrictions: Humans only

Karma Ritual: The journeyman sits alone in the most barren area in the vicinity. He imagines seeing the world as viewed by each of the other Disciplines, one at a time, and considers the limited view of the world each perceives. He imagines the world again, this time through the eyes of his own Discipline, and remembers the true diversity of the world. He rises and mimics the common actions of adepts who follow those Disciplines whose talents the journeyman has learned. He may gesture as a swordmaster if he has learned Melee Weapons, for example, or a wizard if he has learned Spellcasting. The ritual ends when the journeyman has mimicked a talent of each Discipline he has studied.

Special Rules

The journeyman Discipline allows each player to tailor the specifics of the Discipline to the type of character desired. Rather than providing specific talents and characteristics bonuses, this Discipline description outlines what the player should consider when designing this Discipline, including the advantages and limitations.

Versatility

The player creating a journeyman begins the game by assigning the Versatility talent to the character twice, each at Rank 2. The sum of the ranks of these two Versatility talents represents the maximum number of other talents the journeyman may have at any one time, up to a maximum of 30.

The Versatility talents do not count toward the required number of talents to advance from Circle to Circle.

FIRST CIRCLE

When creating a beginning journeyman character, the player assigns Rank 2 to each of two Versatility talents, and chooses 4 other talents from all those available to other Disciplines at Circle 1, assigning each of these Rank 1. One of these 4 should be the Karma Ritual talent.

Higher Circles

As the character qualifies for each new Discipline Circle, he can choose new talents from those available to all other Disciplines at each Circle. The journeyman suffers the same limits on talents available at each Circle as adepts of other Disciplines. In other words, he can learn up to 3 new talents at Second Circle, 2 at Circles 5–8, 3 more at Ninth Circle, and so on. He can choose 3 from those available for each Discipline at Second Circle, 2 from those available at each Circle up to Eighth, and so on.

Journeymen may learn talents from their current Circle or any lower Circle. For example, a journeyman character can learn the Durability talent at any Circle higher than Second.

The maximum number of talents a journeyman character can learn is 30.

Because a character may have a maximum number of talents equal to the sum of his Versatility talent ranks, for each new talent beyond the fourth that the character chooses, he must purchase higher ranks in his Versatility talents.

Players must take the following factors into account when advancing their journeyman character through the Discipline Circles.

SECOND CIRCLE
Durability

At Second Circle, the Journeyman may take the Durability talent, which increases his Death Rating by 6 and his Unconsciousness Rating by 5 for each rank in Durability.

NINTH CIRCLE

At Ninth Circle, the journeyman can learn Morphism, a special talent available only to this Discipline. The description of this new talent appears on p. xx. Only another journeyman can train an adept in this talent, and few prove willing to do so. The cost for learning this talent appears in its description.

Thread Weaving

The Thread Weaving talent available to a journeyman character is called Journey Weaving and functions exactly the same as all other types of Thread Weaving.

If the journeyman gains the Spellcasting talent and wishes to cast spells, he must also have the appropriate form of Thread Weaving for the types of spells he wishes to cast (i.e., Elementalism, Wizardry, and so on).

Training

Unlike adepts of other Disciplines, who must receive training only when advancing to a new Circle, adepts of the journeyman Discipline must be trained in each talent. Also, characters using the journeyman need not train to advance to the next Circle; they advance to the next Circle as soon as they satisfy the conditions for advancement (p. 223, **ED**). This makes learning new talents more difficult and expensive than normal. To train in a talent, the journeyman must find an adept of the appropriate Discipline who knows the talent he wishes to learn. For each talent, this training costs 200 silver pieces times the journeyman's current Circle and requires the time and other considerations outlined for advancing to higher Circles on p. 223, **ED**. Once a journeyman learns a talent at Rank 1 through training, he can increase that talent's rank for the normal Legend Point cost.

WIND-DANCER

Wind-dancers specialize in using aerial motion to communicate and entertain. At Fourth Circle, they learn several elementalist spells. Wind-dancers are usually the windlings who discover new cultures and bring traditions belonging to those cultures back to the windling clans. Other races commonly confuse windling troubadours with wind-dancers, because they use many similar talents and skills to create the same results.

Wind-dancer characters always begin with a music skill.

Important Attributes: Dexterity, Charisma and Perception

Karma Ritual: A wind-dancer must "hum" a favorite tune, using only the vibrations of his wings, while flying in an intricate pattern. The song must be at least five minutes long. When the song is finished, the ritual is complete.

Artisan Skills: Acting, Dancing, Music

FIRST CIRCLE
Talents
> Insect Communication*
> Karma Ritual
> Mimic Voice
> Read and Write Language
> Speak Language
> Wind Dance*

SECOND CIRCLE
Talents
> Durability (6/5)
> Item History
> Winning Smile

THIRD CIRCLE
Talents
> Cat's Paw
> Melee Weapons

FOURTH CIRCLE
Spells: The wind-dancer gains the ability to cast elementalist spells. The wind-dancer learns any three elementalist spells from those available at Circles 1–4, except fire-based spells.
Talents
> Spellcasting
> Spell Matrix
> Thread Weaving (Elementalism)

FIFTH CIRCLE
Talents
> Book Memory
> Read and Write Magic

SIXTH CIRCLE
Social Defense: Increase the wind-dancer's Social Defense by 1.
Talents
> Spirit Talk
> Throwing Weapons

SEVENTH CIRCLE
Spell Defense: Increase the wind-dancer's Spell Defense by 1.
Talents
> Endure Cold
> Lasting Impression

EIGHTH CIRCLE
Physical Defense: Increase the wind-dancer's Physical Defense by 1.
Talents
> Dive Attack*
> Graceful Exit

NINTH CIRCLE
Social Defense: Increase the wind-dancer's Social Defense by 2.
Talents
> Air Speaking
> Bardic Voice
> Impressive Shot

TENTH CIRCLE
Recovery Test: The wind-dancer gains an additional Recovery Test per day.
Talents
> Multi-Tongue
> Slough Blame

WINDMASTER

A windmaster possesses special knowledge of how best to use his wings in combat. More than a standard warrior, windmasters fight equally well on land or in the air.

Important Attributes: Dexterity, Strength and Toughness

Karma Ritual: The windmaster must trace a target circle on the ground of no more than one foot in diameter. Then the windmaster makes a flying start from no less than 120 feet away from the target, and no lower than 20 feet off the ground. The windmaster must then swoop down on the target at full speed and drive three windling spears into the circle. When the windmaster accomplishes this feat, the karma ritual is completed.

Artisan Skills: Body Painting, Runic Carving (weapons)

FIRST CIRCLE
Talents
> Avoid Blow
> Dive Attack*
> Karma Ritual
> Melee Weapons
> Throwing Weapons
> Unarmed Combat

SECOND CIRCLE
Talents
> Anticipate Blow
> Durability (9/7)
> Taunt

THIRD CIRCLE
Talents
> Detect Weapon
> Wood Skin

FOURTH CIRCLE
Karma: The windmaster may spend a Karma Point on any action using Strength only.
Talents
> Thread Weaving (Warrior Weaving)
> Wind Dance*

FIFTH CIRCLE
Initiative: Increase the windmaster's Initiative dice by 1 step.
Talents
> Fast Grab*
> Maneuver

SIXTH CIRCLE
Physical Defense: Increase the windmaster's Physical Defense by 1.
Talents
> Armor Bypass*
> Disarm

SEVENTH CIRCLE
Recovery Test: The windmaster gains an additional Recovery Test per day.
Talents
> Air Dance
> Momentum Attack

EIGHTH CIRCLE
Spell Defense: Increase the windmaster's Spell Defense by 1.
Talents
> Down Strike
> Fearsome Charge

NINTH CIRCLE
Karma: The windmaster may use a Karma Point on any action using Dexterity only.
> Critical Hit
> Fireblood
> Sense Magic Weapon

TENTH CIRCLE
Physical Defense: Increase the windmaster's Physical Defense by 1.
Talents
> Impressive Shot
> Whirlwind

WINDSCOUT

A windscout excels at tracking creatures that travel through the air. They also show great skill in exploration and make excellent guards against all kinds of danger.

Important Attributes: Dexterity, Perception

Karma Ritual: Windscouts must fly in a circular pattern at a height of 8 feet off the ground, hovering at the four cardinal compass points (north, south, east, and west). At each point, the windscout must inhale a lungful of air and focus on separating the different scents it carries. When he has identified any scents present, the windscout exhales and flies to the next compass point. The ritual is completed once the windscout reaches the final compass point and exhales.

Artisan Skills: Body Painting, Dancing, Wood Carving

FIRST CIRCLE
Talents
>Air Dance
>Avoid Blow
>Karma Ritual
>Melee Weapons
>Missile Weapons
>Silent Walk

SECOND CIRCLE
Talents
>Air Tracking*
>Anticipate Blow
>Durability (6/5)

THIRD CIRCLE
Talents
>Down Strike
>Maneuver

FOURTH CIRCLE
Karma: The windscout may spend a Karma Point on any action using Perception only.
Talents
>Thread Weaving (Scout Weaving)
>Tracking

FIFTH CIRCLE
Physical Defense: Increase the windscout's Physical Defense by 1.
Talents
>Battle Bellow
>Scent Identifier*

SIXTH CIRCLE
Initiative: Increase the windscout's Initiative dice by 1 step.
Talents
>Dive Attack*
>Bank Shot

SEVENTH CIRCLE
Spell Defense: Increase the windscout's Spell Defense by 1.
Talents
>Sense Poison
>Throwing Weapons

EIGHTH CIRCLE
Recovery Test: The windscout gains an additional Recovery Test per day.
Talents
>Eagle Eye
>Surprise Strike

NINTH CIRCLE
Social Defense: Increase the windscout's Social Defense by 1.
Talents
>Missile Twister
>Safe Path
>Unarmed Combat

TENTH CIRCLE
Initiative: Increase the windscout's Initiative dice by 2 steps.
Talents
>Acrobatic Strike
>Wood Skin

WOODSMAN

The woodsman Discipline combines elements of the beastmaster, thief, and warrior Disciplines. Woodsmen are trained in magic relating to nature and its forms, including animals, plants, and the five true elements.

Woodsman always begin their careers as sentries for elven cities and communities that lie within the forests and jungles of Barsaive. Elves who practice this Discipline live only in and around the wooded areas of the land, and so finding a teacher for training can be costly and difficult. Adepts of this Discipline will only train other elves.

Important Attributes: Dexterity, Perception

Racial Restrictions: Elves only

Karma Ritual: The woodsman must be alone, deep within the forest. He sits with his eyes closed in meditation and imagines walking through the forest toward a specific destination, at least 15 minutes' walk from the spot where the woodsman sits. The woodsman visualizes the path he walks and any landmarks along the way. Once he has reached the destination in his imagination, the woodsman stands and walks to this destination, keeping his eyes closed during the entire journey. When he reaches his destination, the ritual is complete.

Artisan Skills: Body Painting, Runic and Wood Carving

FIRST CIRCLE

Talents

> Avoid Blow
> Karma Ritual
> Melee Weapons
> Missile Weapons
> Silent Walk
> Tracking

SECOND CIRCLE

Talents

> Animal Training
> Climbing
> Durability

THIRD CIRCLE

Talents

> Borrow Sense
> Sprint

FOURTH CIRCLE

Karma: The woodsman may spend a Karma Point on any action using Dexterity only.

Talents

> Thread Weaving (Scout Weaving)
> Throwing Weapons

FIFTH CIRCLE

Initiative: Increase the woodsman's Initiative dice by 1 step.

Talents

> Air Dance
> Claw Shape

SIXTH CIRCLE

Physical Defense: Increase the woodsman's Physical Defense by 1.

Talents

> Endure Cold
> Lizard Leap

SEVENTH CIRCLE

Enhanced Senses: For the cost of 2 Strain Points, the woodsman can enhance one of his natural senses, adding + 2 steps to his Perception when making Perception Tests based on the enhanced sense.

Talents

> Earth Skin
> Second Attack

EIGHTH CIRCLE

Spell Defense: Increase the woodsman's Spell Defense by 1.

Talents

> Poison Resistance
> Wound Balance

NEW TALENTS

The following talents are available only to characters of the races listed with each talent. These talents appear in the same format as those provided in the **Earthdawn** rulebook and the **Earthdawn Companion**, with an additional category of Race Restriction.

AIR TRACKING

Step Number: Rank + Perception **Skill Use**: Yes
Action: Yes **Strain**: No
Requires Karma: No **Race Restriction**:
Discipline Talent Use: Windscout Windlings only

Much like the standard Tracking talent, the Air Tracking talent enables a character to track a flying creature by means of its scent. To track a creature through the air, the character makes an Air Tracking Test against the target's Spell Defense. If the trail is more than 12 hours old, add +3 to the target's Spell Defense. If it has rained in the past hour, add +7. A successful result allows the character to see a trail of what appears to be glowing pollen. The effect lasts for a number of hours equal to the character's rank in Air Tracking.

ARMOR BYPASS

Step Number: Rank + Dexterity **Skill Use**: No
Action: No **Strain**: 2
Requires Karma: Yes **Race Restriction**:
Discipline Talent Use: Windmaster Windlings only

The Armor Bypass talent allows a character to use his combat ability and magic to seek out an exposed portion of a target. The character makes an Armor Bypass Test against the Spell Defense of the target or the armor, whichever is higher. If the test succeeds, the character's attack negates the effect of the target's armor. This talent cannot be used in consecutive rounds.

CAST NET

Step Number: Rank + Dexterity **Skill Use**: No
Action: No **Strain**: Yes
Requires Karma: No **Race Restriction**:
Discipline Talent Use: Boatman T'skrang only

The Cast Net talent allows the adept to use a small, hand-held net as a special parrying weapon. When an opponent makes a successful melee attack against the character, the player may attempt to parry by making a Cast Net Test against the result of his opponent's Attack Test. If the parry fails, the character must take the normal damage. If the parry succeeds, the character takes no damage from the attack. If the Cast Net Test has an Excellent result, the parry entangles the opponent, who suffers a –1 step penalty to all tests and –2 steps to all Attack Tests until he makes a successful Dexterity Test against the character's Cast Net Test result.

The character may only use Cast Net once each Combat Round to parry an attack and may only entangle one opponent at a time with his net. The character may substitute a cloak or other piece of cloth for his net, but by doing so suffers a –2 step penalty to his Cast Net talent.

DIVE ATTACK

Step Number: Rank + Dexterity **Skill Use**: No
Action: Yes **Strain**: 1
Requires Karma: Yes **Race Restriction**:
Discipline Talent Use: Windmaster Windlings only

The Dive Attack talent replaces a normal Melee Weapons attack. The character must have at least 120 feet of clear flight space to the target and be able to reach a starting height of at least 20 feet. To make the Dive Attack, the character plunges into a powerful dive with the express purpose of injuring the target, making a Dive Attack Test against the target's Physical Defense. A successful result adds 4 steps to the attacking character's Damage Test.

EVALUATE

Step Number: Rank + Perception **Skill Use**: Yes
Action: No **Strain**: No
Requires Karma: No **Race Restriction**:
Discipline Talent Use: None T'skrang only

The Evaluate talent gives characters a shrewd sense for the true market value of an object. A character may make an Evaluate Test against the Spell Defense of the item to detect whether an object has hidden value that is not readily apparent to the casual observer. When engaged in haggling or trading, the character may choose to substitute his Evaluate step for his Social Defense. To successfully Evaluate magical items, the character must achieve an Excellent result on the Evaluate Test. In this case, the character learns that the item is magical, but will not be able to assign a reliable cash value to the item or divine the purpose of the item's magic.

FAST GRAB

Step Number: Rank + Dexterity
Action: Yes
Requires Karma: Yes
Discipline Talent Use: None
Skill Use: No
Strain: 1
Race Restriction: Windlings only

The Fast Grab talent allows the attacker to seize an item out of an opponent's hand and move half his Combat Movement Rate away from the target. To make a Fast Grab, the attacker makes a Fast Grab Test against the target's Physical Defense. If the target is holding onto the item with two hands, increase the Difficulty Number by 5. If the item is strapped on (i.e., a shield), increase the Difficulty Number by 10. These modifiers are cumulative.

INSECT COMMUNICATION

Step Number: Rank + Perception
Action: No
Requires Karma: No
Discipline Talent Use: Wind-dancer
Skill Use: No
Strain: None
Race Restriction: Windlings only

The Insect Communication talent allows a character to communicate with insect life. Use of this talent does not ensure that the insects will be friendly, obedient, or cooperative, nor does this talent bestow intelligence on the insects.

The more complex and lengthy the communication, the more difficult it becomes to succeed at the Insect Communication Test.

Concept	Difficulty
Simple Greeting	3
Identifying Self	7
Request for Aid	9
Request for General Information	11
Request for Specific Information	14
Request for Exact Information	16
Giving a Precise Order	21

Identifying Self means the speaker can tell the insect who he is and declare his good intentions. A Request for Aid is a plea for help. General Information covers a broad range of questions such as, "What is the terrain like here? Is there any life nearby?" Specific Information answers such questions as, "What animal types live here? Are there any settlements nearby?" A request for Exact Information would reveal the answer to, "Is there an elven city nearby?"

A successful result means the character can communicate with the target and allows him to understand the answer to his question or request. Remember that insects do not share the Name-giver's level of intelligence, and the answers they give might be hard to understand.

MORPHISM

Step Number: Rank
Action: No
Requires Karma: No
Discipline Talent Use: None
Skill Use: No
Strain: No
Race Restriction: Humans only

The Morphism talent allows a journeyman to magically take on properties of the other Name-giver races. At each rank after the first, the Morphism talent increases the journeyman's Attribute Values. Rank 1 in this talent represents the journeyman learning to adapt his use of magic to alter his body and so does not grant Attribute bonuses.

For each rank higher than the first, the journeyman gains a specific bonus to one of his Attribute Values as shown on the Morphism Bonus Table. These bonuses are not cumulative; only the highest bonus is used. For example, Rank 4 of the Morphism talent adds +1 to the journeyman's Charisma Attribute Value. At Rank 10, he gains a +2 bonus to Charisma. When the journeyman reaches Rank 10, he gains only the +2 bonus, not both.

The race to which an attribute bonus is normally granted appears in parentheses next to each bonus. In some cases, more than one race receives the same bonus, which allows the player to choose from which race his bonus originates.

MORPHISM BONUS TABLE

Morphism Rank	Attribute Value Bonus
1	None
2	+1 Wil (elf/troll)
3	+1 Per (elf/windling)
4	+1 Cha (elf/t'skrang)
5	+1 Tou (ork/t'skrang)
6	+1 Dex (t'skrang/windling)
7	+2 Str (dwarf)
8	+2 Dex (elf)
9	+2 Tou (troll)
10	+2 Cha (windling)
11	+3 Tou (dwarf)
12	+3 Str (ork)
13	+4 Tou (obsidiman)
14	+4 Str (troll)
15	+6 Str (obsidiman)

In order to learn this rare talent, a journeyman must first discover its existence. Most adepts who hear of it learn of it as part of a myth or legend, and many dismiss the talent as mere rumor—and are encouraged in that belief by journeymen reluctant to share the knowledge of the Morphism talent.

Once a journeyman decides to believe in the Morphism talent and to learn it, his real task begins. He must find another journeyman who is at least Ninth Circle, who knows the talent, and who is willing to train him. This combination remains very rare. Training in this talent costs twice as much and takes twice as long for the adept as training in any other, standard talent. To gain this talent at Rank 1 costs a minimum of 5,000 silver pieces and requires 80 hours of training.

Interestingly enough, as a journeyman gains ranks in this talent, his appearance begins to take on aspects of the races whose Attribute bonuses he has "borrowed." The skin of a character with the Dexterity bonus of a t'skrang might begin to take on a greenish tint and appear somewhat scaly, for example, and a journeyman who gains the Strength and Toughness bonuses of an obsidiman might begin to look like he is made of stone.

Mike has decided to create a journeyman character. He begins by assigning the character two Versatility talents, giving each Rank 2. He then chooses the Animal Bond, Avoid Blow, Tracking, and Karma Ritual talents, each at Rank 1.

After several adventures, Mike wants to advance his journeyman character to Second Circle. To increase 4 talents, each costing 200 Legend Points, to Rank 2 costs 800 Legend Points. Now that his character is a Second Circle journeyman, Mike wants him to learn two new talents, Durability and Melee Weapons. First, he must increase each of his Versatility talents by 1 rank in order to learn 2 new talents. Then he must find adepts who can teach him these new talents. After finding appropriate teachers, Mike's character must pay 800 silver pieces in training

costs for these talents (200 sp per current Circle x 2 talents). He must also pay 100 Legend Points for Rank 1 in each of these talents. As soon as the character meets the requirements for the next Circle, he can attempt to learn more new talents, continuing in this manner as he progresses through the Circles of his Discipline.

After many, many adventures, Mike has reached the Ninth Circle in the journeyman Discipline, and wants to learn the Morphism talent. First, he must find a journeyman of at least Ninth Circle who knows the Morphism talent and will teach it to him. After a long search, Mike's character finds an Eleventh Circle journeyman with whom he can train. The character begins training, first paying his instructor 10,000 silver pieces—5,000 (based on the instructor's Circle) x 2—and working on this new talent for 80 hours over a period of four weeks. When his character's training is complete, Mike spends 300 Legend Points to acquire Rank 1 in the Morphism talent. As he increases his Morphism talent rank, Mike's character will take on the Attribute bonuses of other races.

PILOT BOAT

Step Number: Rank + Willpower	**Skill Use**: Yes
Action: Yes	**Strain**: None
Requires Karma: No	**Race Restriction**:
Discipline Talent Use: Boatman	T'skrang only

The Pilot Boat talent represents the art of maneuvering t'skrang riverboats all along the Serpent River. This talent allows the character to understand the workings of the riverboat and assist those piloting the vessel. The character piloting the riverboat must use Pilot Boat to guide the ship in combat or near port by making a Pilot Boat Test. The Difficulty Number of this test is determined by the maneuver being performed. When docking a riverboat, use a Difficulty Number of 5. Difficulty Numbers for maneuvering in combat vary from 5 to as high as 15. See **Ship Combat**, pp. 130–36, **Companion**, for ship combat rules and appropriate Difficulty Numbers.

If a character is supervising the fire engine, he may use the Pilot Boat talent to augment the speed of the vessel. A character must have at least Rank 5 in Pilot Boat before he may attempt this. The Difficulty Number for this use of the Pilot Boat talent equals the Speed of the vessel (usually 7). To increase the speed of the boat, the character makes a Pilot Boat Test. For each success level above Average, the character improves the Speed of the vesselby 1 for a number of rounds equal to his rank in Pilot Boat. See pp. 130–31 of the **Earthdawn Companion** for information about ship Attributes.

Piloting the riverboats appears to be part science, part magic. Though riverboat crews occasionally take on laborers without the Pilot Boat talent, these crew members end up performing all the nastiest chores. Riverboat crew officers usually possess Rank 4 in Pilot Boat, and captains, Rank 7.

READ RIVER

Step Number: Rank + Perception   **Skill Use**: Yes
Action: Yes   **Strain**: None
Requires Karma: No   **Race Restriction**:
Discipline Talent Use: Boatman   T'skrang

The Read River talent allows the boatman to help his crew guide the riverboat through the often treacherous waters of the Serpent River, which is filled with sandbars, deceptive currents, and hidden reefs. This skill can also be used to track another riverboat along the river, identify approaching ships, and anticipate features of the river such as towns, t'skrang villages, or good places to fish.

To track another riverboat or notice approaching ships, make a Read River Test against the Pilot Boat step of the pilot of the target riverboat. For all other uses of the Read River talent, use a Difficulty Number of 7. The success level of the Read River Test determines how accurately the character notices hazards or anticipates features along the river. See p. 245, **ED**, for using success levels.

SCENT IDENTIFIER

Step Number: Rank + Perception   **Skill Use**: No
Action: No   **Strain**: No
Requires Karma: No   **Race Restriction**:
Discipline Talent Use: Windscout   Windlings only

The Scent Identifier talent enables the character to identify a creature on the basis of scent alone. This talent does not give the character any special bonuses to track the creature, only to distinguish its species. To identify a creature, the character makes a Scent Identifier Test against the target's Spell Defense. Each level of success reveals something different about the target's identity.

An Average test result discloses the target's race or species. A Good or Excellent result reveals the target's gender and age. An Extraordinary result reveals the target's general health and emotional state at the time it passed the character's current position. If the target is someone the character knows, the Extraordinary result reveals the target's identity.

This talent must be used within 2 hours of the creature's passing. If the area experienced wind and/or rain since the creature passed, increase the Difficulty by 5 for each weather condition.

WIND DANCE

Step Number: Rank + Dexterity   **Skill Use**: Yes
Action: Yes   **Strain**: No
Requires Karma: No   **Race Restriction**:
Discipline Talent Use: Wind-dancer   Windlings only

The Wind Dance talent serves two purposes. First, it serves as a method of communication between windlings. By flying in certain patterns, windlings can reveal important information without saying a word, in much the same way as bees communicate the location of pollen. Two windlings with the Wind Dance talent can communicate in this fashion with no tests required.

Second, the windlings can use Wind Dance in place of their Physical Defense when attacked. To do so, the windling makes a Wind Dance Test and records the result. The result becomes the character's Physical Defense for the next round. If the attacker fails to hit the windling, the attacker becomes disoriented as a result of the rapid, intricate aerial maneuvers of the defending windling and suffers a –2 step penalty to all tests in the next round.

Skilled windlings can weave messages into their Wind Dance defense, enabling two or more windlings in combat to communicate silently while avoiding an enemy's blow.

QUESTORS

The members of each Name-giver race tend to become questors for a few, specific Passions. This does not indicate that some races only believe in select Passions. The more likely explanation is that certain Passions more often inspire members of a given race to become questors than do other Passions. For example, elf questors show an affinity for Jaspree and Astendar, reflecting their racial love of nature and beauty. In keeping with their racial desire for change and freedom, windlings most often quest for Lochost, the Passion of Rebellion, Change, and Freedom. Because health and the home carry great importance for all the races, they may all become questors of Garlen.

Some members of all Name-giver races quest for the Mad Passions, though these questors remain rare. Among those who devote their energies to the Mad Passions, members of each race tend toward one of the three. The following guidelines will help players choose an appropriate Passion for characters who become questors.

Elves: Commonly quest for Jaspree and Astendar, and sometimes quest for Mynbruje. Will quest for all Mad Passions, but most rarely for Raggok.

Humans: An equal number of humans quest for all the Passions, including the Mad Passions.

T'skrang: Commonly quest for Chorrolis, Thystonius, and Upandal. Will rarely quest for the Mad Passions, and of those most often for Vestrial.

Windlings: Commonly quest for Lochost and Floranuus. Of the Mad Passions, will only quest for Vestrial.

SPECIAL RULES

The races described in this book all possess unique characteristics, represented in game terms by the following special rules. These rules include the details of windling flight, the new skills of Gliding (t'skrang only) and Swimming (all races), guidelines for playing characters of human ethnic subgroups, and glossaries of the Elven and T'skrang languages. Unless otherwise noted, rules listed for each race apply only to characters of that race.

ELVES

The elves hold a unique spiritual belief they call The Journey and the Wheel, which states that as an elf ages, his spirit must Follow five Paths before ascending into the metaplanes. Most elves believe in the growth process represented by The Journey and Wheel, though since the Scourge, fewer observe all the traditions associated with these beliefs.

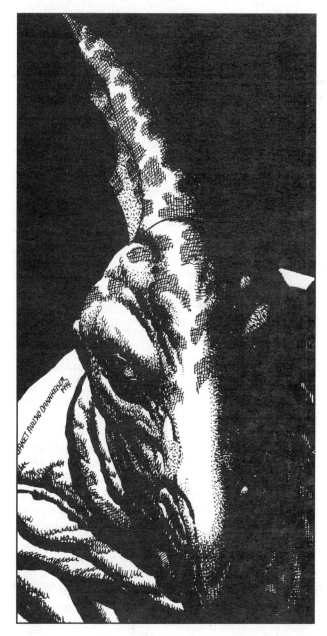

If a player chooses for his elven character to Follow the Paths, he must also choose the view he embraces, that of the Sa'mistishsa (strict Followers), or that of the Dae'mistishsa (loose Followers). This distinction makes an important difference in the growth and advancement of the character.

Sa'mistishsa

Those who embrace the view of the strict Followers believe that as an elf ages and travels along the Paths, he must follow a new Discipline on each Path.

When a character who follows this view chooses a new Discipline as he moves onto the next Path, he must abandon the talents and skills of his old Discipline and all the ranks and advantages it conveyed and begin again with the new Discipline. The experience of the old Discipline still exists as part of the character's knowledge and background, but until he reaches the Path of Lords, it remains unavailable to him.

Players may create First Circle elven characters and choose to place them on a Path further along the Wheel, such as the Paths of the Traveler or the Sage. In this case, the player may completely flesh out the Disciplines the character would have followed while journeying on earlier Paths so that all those talents and skills become available when the character reaches the Path of Lords.

When a character begins his journey on the Path of Lords, he may once again use the talents and skills of his previous Disciplines at the same Circle and rank as when he changed Paths and can now begin to increase the ranks of those talents and skills as normal.

Dae'mistishsa

Elves who embrace the spiritual view of the loose Followers suffer no game restrictions, but we do suggest a consideration for roleplaying the character. As the character travels on each new Path, his view of the world should change slightly to reflect the focus of his current Path. For example, an elven elementalist who follows the Path of Warriors would certainly act differently than one who follows the Path of Sages. In addition to allowing the player to stretch his roleplaying abilities, this adjustment in world view makes it plausible for the character to change the way he treats his fellow adventurers and alter his role in the group.

Sperethiel Glossary

The Elven language, called Sperethiel, is commonly used in most elven settlements and serves as the official language for all elven rituals. In Sperethiel, context and intonation give words a wide range of subtle meanings and implications. Conventions of speech and address allow further shadings of meaning that reflect the relative status of the speaker and the listener. A person speaking Sperethiel would not say the same thing to a social superior in the same way as he or she would speak to someone of equal or inferior status.

adj. = adjective
adv. = adverb
conj. = conjunction
(for) = formal

(inf) = informal
(ins) = insulting
interj. = interjection
mod. = modifier
n. = noun
prep. = preposition
v. = verb

a *conj.* Or.

belet *adj.* passionate

Beletre *n.* The Passionate.

carronasto *n.* Stillness; non-motion.

celé *n.* A non-elf.

celénit *n.* Insulting form of celé.

cirolle *v.* To travel.

co *prep.* To. Shifts to *con* before a vowel.

dae *adj.* Loose.

daron *v.* To die.

draesis *n.* Wheel.

Eoerin *n.* Wise; scholars of elven spiritualism.

faskit *n.* Legal code; law.

goro *n.* Outsider, one who is not a subject of the elven court; a stranger.

goronagee *n.* One apart, especially an elf not part of an elven group.

goronagit *n.* Insulting form of *goronagee*.

goronit *n.* (ins) Barbarian.

-ha *adj.* Suffix indicating emphatic repetition

heng *v.* To speak or understand a language.

heron *v.* To be alive; to exist.

im *v.* To be.

imiri *n.* Memory of something, memorial.

-it Derisive suffix, becomes *-nit* after a vowel.

ke "of the", changes to *k'* before a vowel

li (for) Interrogative affix.

li-ha "Isn't that so?"

llayah *adv.* Literally, "I agree with you" or "I will do it."

makkaherinit *n.* A young and foolish person.

makkalos *n.* Stupidity.

makkanagee *adj.* Willfully stupid.

medaron *n.* Death.

meleg *v.* To feel in a physical manner.

Mellakabal *n.* "Shining Ones"; used exclusively in the context of *Tesrae ke'Mellakabal* (Citadel of the Shining Ones)

meraerth *n.* Warrior.

mes *n.* Path.

milessaratish *n.* Servant-soldier.

mis *v.* To follow.

mistish *n.* Follower.

morel *n.* Life.

nagé *adj.* Willful.

-nagee *adv.* Willfully.

od *conj.* And.

ozidan *v.* To leave behind.

pechet *prep.* Except for.

perest *v.* To have.

perritaesa *n.* Scholar.

qua (inf) Interrogative affix.

raé *n.* (inf) An elf.

raegh *n.* Lord (non-specific).

raén *n.* (for) One who is of the people, an elf.

resp *v.* To listen.

reth *n.* Elf. Literally, "listener of harmony."

reth'im *n.* Elven culture. Literally, to be elven.

-ri Interrogative suffix, also used rhetorically. <"Is that not so?">

rillabothien *n.* An unresolved chord in music. Poetically, an unresolved situation in a relationship.

rinellé *n.* Rebel; deserter.

sa *adj.* Strict.

sallah *n.* Silence, non-speech.

samriel *n.* Discomfort, implying necessary discomfort as in medical treatment.

se Positive beneficial prefix.

serathilion *n.* Attraction that cannot be denied. Demanding desire.

serulos *n.* Machismo; childish masculinity.

se'seterin "Bright morning" <good morning>.

shay *n.* Forest.

sielle *adv.* Yes. Literally, "it is the way of things."

speren *n.* Harmony; peacefulness.

sperethiel *n.* 1. Speech. **2. Sperethiel.** Elvish; the elven language.

teheron *n.* Life; existence.

téch *interj.* Common curse word equivalent to "damn."

teleg *v.* Maintain a condition <*telego carronasto*, "keep still">.

telene *v.* To learn.

tesrae *n.* citadel or holding.

thelem *n.* Law of nature.

thiel *n.* Music. Poetically, a pleasant sound.

ti *prep.* Of. Shifts to *t'* before a vowel.

-tish *adj.* Suffix. One who, as in *one who* (verbs) *or one who is a* (noun). Often an *i* is inserted between a consonant and the suffix, as in *telegitish*, "keeper."

veresp *v.* To reply, to answer.

versakhan *n.* An enemy.

wineg *n.* An ork or troll. (Insulting, as *troglodyte*)

-ya *mod.* A negator suffix.

HUMANS

Though most players will choose to create human characters from the base human population, they may decide to play a character from one of the ethnic groups described in the **Essay on Humans** chapter of this book, p. 32. Game-related rules and information for each of these groups appears below.

Cathan

Roleplaying a Cathan character poses great challenges. This ethnic group appears to be naturally curious

about most things, but does not believe in taking risks. Because Cathans spend their lives in a dangerous environment that forces them to constantly look out for their own welfare, they simply never think to offer help to someone else unless asked. Living in the Servos Jungle makes them self-sufficient, and they assume others possess the skills necessary to survive without help.

The Cathan do believe in teamwork, however, and will lend their efforts to the common good until personal risk becomes too great. The Cathan may be roleplayed as child-like—they must be coaxed into doing dangerous deeds and then persuaded that the treasure or goal outweighs the risk involved.

Players may choose to add +1 to their Cathan's Dexterity Attribute at the cost of subtracting –1 from their Strength Attribute. Cathan characters begin with Rank 1 in the Climbing, Hunting, and Missile Weapons skills. Players may find several drawbacks to playing a Cathan. They rarely wear any armor heavier than leather, prefer spears and bows to heavy swords or axes, and most of Barsaive treats them as savages. Playing a Cathan requires the player to accept a fairly narrow scope of roleplaying, as that character's dominant (and perhaps only) traits should be curiosity and self-preservation.

Cathan characters may not follow the Disciplines of sky raider, swordmaster, warrior, or wizard. Cathans rarely follow the cavalryman Discipline, but they may.

Dinganni

A player may choose to have his human character originate with the Dinganni ethnic group. A Dinganni may follow any Discipline except illusionist, sky raider, thief, or wizard. Regardless of their sex, Dinganni characters may add +1 to either their Strength or Toughness Attribute.

A Dinganni will leave the tribe in only two circumstances. The character may leave the tribe to learn the ways of other races and then return to introduce different ideas and technology to the tribe. Otherwise, only exile could force a character to leave the tribe, and the reason for exile must be convincing.

The Dinganni use a unique melee weapon called a talon, whose design allows the wielder to tear a foe's bones from his body.

	Damage Step	Str Min	Weight	Size
Talon	3	10	2	2

Galeb-Klek

Characters with Galeb or Klek blood show obvious physical distinctions if compared to one another, but otherwise look much like other humans.

The children of the Galeb and Klek ethnic groups are called the Galeb-Klek, and their racial integration offers a few game bonuses. A Galeb-Klek may add +1 to his Strength Attribute if he favors his Galeb heritage, or +1 to his Dexterity Attribute for his mother's genetic legacy.

The upbringing of the Galeb-Klek is more enlightened than that provided by many other human groups. Their mothers and fathers, direct descendants of the original crossbreeding, are considered intelligent and sensitive, which makes them effective educators as well as good parents. Galeb-Klek try to uphold good and protect the innocent whenever possible. They need not endanger themselves unnecessarily to do so, but neither would they perpetrate a second wrong to make a right.

Players may choose to contradict the Galeb-Klek stereotype. A nonconformist Galeb-Klek implies a person who lacks honesty or scruples, and such a character would probably be disowned by his parents and friends. New acquaintances who discover his ethnicity will trust him more easily than might be expected, and will feel a greater need for revenge if betrayed.

Because the denizens of Barsaive are rediscovering their world and each other, each race has the opportunity to prove or disprove its reputation as set forth in the Book of Tomorrow. The Galeb-Klek currently enjoy a great deal of respect. The player-character's actions will determine if the Galeb-Klek's reputation continues to be deserved.

Riders of the Scorched Plain

The Riders of the Scorched Plain represent a closed, mostly despised subculture of humanity. They survived the Scourge at the cost of innocent lives, a circumstance that others find difficult, if not impossible, to forgive or forget. A Rider must be an exceptional person to break away from this group and make his way successfully among the rest of society, or to remain a part of the subculture and earn acceptance in the outside world.

The fact that individuals of other races belong to the Riders proves that there are as many stories to explain the Riders as there are Riders. A player who wishes to play a Rider of the Scorched Plain must justify her separation from her people.

Rider characters begin with the Animal Handling and Stealth skills at Rank 1. They may choose any Discipline normally available to humans.

Scavians

Scavian characters are pirates, sailors, and above all else, swashbucklers. They love the open seas, danger, and the glory of the fight. On the surface, Scavians and the t'skrang share many characteristics.

Scavian characters begin with Rank 1 in the Sailing, Swimming (see p. 123), and Missile Weapons (Crossbow) skills. They may follow any Discipline except cavalryman. They sometimes become sky raiders by earning the respect of troll sky raiders through exceptional displays of leadership during battle.

Vorst

A player may choose to play a human character descended from the Vorst. As such, he will have toughened his body and mind against the threats of supernatural creatures and gains a +1 bonus to his Toughness and Willpower Attributes.

Vorst characters pursue every action to the fullest extent possible. If the character builds a raft, he lashes the timbers twice as many times as needed, melts tree-gum between the timbers, and bakes it in the sun for several days before he even considers putting it in the water. In game terms, most actions performed by a Vorst (including karma rituals) usually take one and a half times longer than normally required. Certain, commonsense exceptions to this rule apply: they cast spells during combat as quickly as possible, for example, but many other opportunities for roleplaying this Vorst characteristic will arise. However, players and gamemasters should use Vorst zealousness as a roleplaying tool and not allow it to impede the flow of the game.

In combat, Vorst are merciless. They dismember and cremate fallen foes, and any weapons or armor they reject they bury or toss into a lake.

Vorst do not follow the Disciplines of cavalryman, illusionist (Horrors rarely succumb to illusion), or troubadour (they disdain such foolish merriment).

T'SKRANG

Special rules for the t'skrang describe the use of their tails and the Gliding Skill. This section also offers a glossary of the t'skrang language and describes the Swimming Skill, used mostly by the t'skrang but available to other Name-giver races.

Tail Attacks

T'skrang often use their tails as weapons when engaged in combat. T'skrang characters use the Unarmed Combat talent to make tail attacks, and use a Damage step of their Strength step plus 3 steps.

T'skrang characters may make tail attacks in one of two ways. During a Combat Round, a t'skrang can make a tail attack in addition to his other actions, but suffers a –2 step penalty to all actions in that round, including the Tail Attack Test. A t'skrang character may instead choose to make only the tail attack in a round, in this case avoiding the –2 penalty described above.

A t'skrang character who has the Second Attack talent can use his tail attack as his second attack without penalty.

Some t'skrang lash small weapons to the end of their tails to enhance the effectiveness of their tail attacks. This tactic can only be used with weapons of Size 1 or 2.

The Damage step for attacks made with weapons used in this fashion is equal to the character's Strength plus 3 steps plus the weapon's Damage step. For example, a dagger lashed to the tail of a t'skrang with a Strength step of 5 would have a Damage step of 10 (5 + 3 + 2 = 10).

A t'skrang character can also use a tail weapon to increase his Physical Defense Rating by using the weapon to parry or deflect blows. This increase can add up to +3 to the character's Physical Defense, but for each point added, reduce all his step numbers by 1. For example, a character who uses a tail weapon to increase his Physical Defense by +2 must reduce all his step numbers by –2 steps. A tail attack or parry must be declared at the same time as other Combat Options, as described in **Special Actions**, p. 193, **ED**.

Weapons lashed to a t'skrang tail cannot be used with talents such as Riposte or Disarm. They can only be used to attack or parry as described above.

T'skrang Glossary

The following commonly used t'skrang words and expressions are described or otherwise referenced in **A Brief Treatise on the T'skrang**, p. 52.

amotla shivoam ga'nai Down the river to the sea, the t'skrang euphemism for death. This also refers to their custom of sending the ashes of their dead down the Serpent River to Death's Sea.

aropagoi *n.* The five t'skrang trading foundations that control the bulk of trade on the Serpent River.

aropagoinya *n.* A member of the central foundation of an aropagoi.

Atlosh T'zdram *n.* The Great Game; the t'skrang version of chess, played on a brightly colored mandala board. Also, a popular epithet for the game of politics.

chaida *n.* A hatchling's egg-parent.

choth edo k'tan var Up tail, out of the mud; an admonishment similar in meaning to "chin up," and "stiff upper lip."

clingor *n.* A type of sticky rope.

d'janduin *n.* A potent spice that gives food "hotness."

g'doinya *n.* The secret foundation name of an aropagoinya.

Hai Jik'hai Acknowledgment of an extreme act of bravery.

haropas *n.* Communion with the Passions; enlightenment.

Houros *n.* The serpent that eats its own tail; the t'skrang symbol for the universe.

iyoshkira *n.* Subterranean creature from which the Pale Ones craft their boats.

jik'harra *n.* Fearlessness; literally, brave passion.

kaissa *n.* The phase in a t'skrang's life in which it changes from neuter to either male or female.

khamorro *n.* Literally, deck scrubber; an adolescent t'skrang apprentice aboard a riverboat.

k'harro *n.* Passion; heart.

kiatsu *n.* Preparation; one of the four pillars of *haropas*.

krohyin *n.* Trade covenant; aropagoi organization for producing and gaining specific trade goods.

k'soto ensherenk *n.* The Name-passing ritual, used to pass ancestral memories between foundation leaders.

k'stulaa *n.* A flap of skin that extends from a t'skrang's wrist to hip. A rare physical trait among this race.

k'stulaami *n.* Name for the winged t'skrang.

kuratai *n.* A popular t'skrang spice.

kyaapas *n.* Balance, especially referring to the balance between *jik'harra* and family.

lahala *n.* Honored One; usually the eldest female in a foundation.

niall *n.* Foundation; an extended family of 40 to 60 t'skrang.

p'skarrot *n.* Measure; destiny.

refselenika *n.* (Abbr. as refs) Barriers constructed of elemental water that protect the village.

shivarro *n.* The river passion; a word to describe a t'skrang's fundamental attraction to life on the river.

Shivoam *n.* T'skrang goddess of elemental water; also, the Serpent River.

shivalahala *n.* The lahala of an aropagoi central foundation.

Shivos *n.* T'skrang god of elemental earth.

shustal Exclamation meaning "No more need be said."

Syrtis *n.* T'skrang god of elemental air; also, the moon.

t'chai kondos *n.* Egg-bonding. A magical ritual that binds a male eggtender to a hatchling for life.

T'schlome *n.* T'skrang goddess of elemental fire; also, the sun.

t'slahyin *n.* Crew covenant.

t'slashina *n.* The village diamond, that part of the village enclosed by the refs and the towers.

t'sleetha-t'sleethi Slowly and more slowly; take it easy.

trisnari *n.* An inn that serves food but does not provide lodging; a restaurant.

GLIDING

Step Number: Rank + Dexterity

The Gliding skill allows winged t'skrang to glide through the air using their *k'stulaa*, or wings. To use this

skill, a *k'stulaami* must be able to jump from a sufficient height. For each 10 feet of elevation, a k'stulaami can glide a distance of 20 feet. To glide, the character makes a Gliding Test against a Difficulty Number of 5 adjusted at the gamemaster's discretion for adverse conditions (strong wind, lack of wind, and so on). If the test is successful, the character can glide a number of yards equal to the test result x 10, provided he has sufficient elevation. If the test fails, the character falls to the ground, unable to catch the wind in his wings.

The Gliding skill also reduces damage from falling. Whenever a *k'stulaami* character falls, he can subtract his Gliding step from the Damage step used for the Falling Damage Test.

SWIMMING

Step Number: Rank + Strength

Rank + (Strength + 3 steps) for t'skrang

All t'skrang, and many other races who live near water, learn to swim as a method of movement, but also as part of their basic survival skills. In **Earthdawn**, situations that require a character to swim can be resolved in the following manner.

Characters use the Swimming skill to move in the water. This skill is based on a character's Strength Attribute. Characters who do not have ranks in this skill may use it by defaulting to their Strength step.

In order to use the Swimming skill, a character makes a Swimming Test against a Difficulty Number determined by the condition of the water around him, as shown in the Water Condition Table.

Each successful Swimming Test allows the character to swim for 10 minutes. The distance a character can move as a result of a single, successful Swimming Test is a number of yards equal to 10 times his Swimming step.

Swimming is a strenuous activity. For every 10 minutes a character swims, he must make a Toughness Test against a Difficulty Number of 12. A character who fails the test takes 1 point of Strain damage. A character can carry a limited amount of weight while swimming, equal to one-tenth his normal Carrying Capacity. For every 10 pounds over this Carrying Capacity a character carries while swimming, reduce his Swimming step by 1.

Characters who achieve a Poor success on a Swimming Test move only a fourth of their normal swimming movement rate for 10 minutes. A character who gets a result worse than Poor or a result of 1 has completely failed the attempt and begins to sink into the water. In this situation, the character must immediately make another Swimming Test. If the test is successful with an

WATER CONDITION TABLE

Condition	Difficulty
Calm water	3
Small waves (cresting at 3–4 inches)	4
Slow river current	5
Moderate river current	7
Serpent River/open ocean	15

Average result or better, the character has recovered and can continue swimming. If the character fails this test, he must make another Swimming Test, this time with a Good result or better, to recover. If the character fails this test, he must make a third Swimming Test, with an Excellent result or better, in order to recover. If the character fails this test, he begins to drown.

Characters who cannot breath underwater will eventually drown if they become trapped beneath the surface of the water or if they fail to make a required successful Swimming Test. A character can hold his breath for a number of rounds equal to his Toughness step. As soon as he runs out of breath, he begins to take damage from drowning. At this point, the gamemaster begins to make a Damage Test, each round using a step number of 4 + the number of rounds the character has spent under water since running out of breath. (For example, for the first Damage Test use a step number of 5.) No type of armor protects against this damage. The gamemaster continues making Damage Tests for drowning until the character dies, is rescued, or somehow reaches the surface of the water.

Obsidimen cannot swim. If they fall into the water, they sink and must find a way to climb out. Windlings only swim if there is no other way to survive, because getting their wings wet effectively cripples these Namegivers.

WINDLINGS

The special rules for windlings include their natural flight ability, windling combat tactics, and windling equipment.

Flight

While windlings can fly, they do not use it as their primary method of movement. Windlings tire quickly when flying and so usually limit their flight to approximately 20 minutes. At 20 minutes, the character may suf-

Windling characters cannot carry more than up to half their normal Carrying Capacity while flying. A character who tries to carry more than this amount while flying is considered Encumbered (see p. 212, **ED**). In addition to reducing his Dexterity, reduce the Encumbered windling's Toughness Attribute in the same way.

Though windlings' wings are very durable, when they get wet the wings become heavy and fragile, and severely limit the windling's ability to fly. In game terms, this lowers the windling's Physical Defense by 2, and the player must make a Strength Test against a Difficulty Number of 13 to determine if the character can fly at all. If the windling is able to fly with wet wings, for each period of 5 minutes that he flies, he must make a Toughness Test against a Difficulty Number of 9. If he fails the test, the windling takes 2 points of Strain damage.

These rules only apply if the windling's wings become soaked with water, as would happen if he fell into a river or stream. Fortunately, windling wings dry very quickly, usually within 10 minutes. In warm weather, they may dry within 5 minutes.

Combat Tactics

Their lighter physical make-up and the impracticality of trying to fly in heavy armor makes it possible for attackers to bring down a healthy windling combatant with one solid blow.

Windlings generally attempt to offset this disadvantage by using a unique series of tactics and talents in combat situations, the most prominent of which is a rapid swooping attack. The windling takes advantage of his flight capability to plunge toward an enemy, hit his opponent with a single blow in an area of vulnerability, then race into the sky out of harm's way before his stunned opponent can react and retaliate. Use of this tactic is considered splitting movement (p. 201, **ED**).

In keeping with their preference for distance attacks, windlings usually use missile weapons such as bows, spears, and blowguns and often coat their weapons with poisons and other drugs to gain an additional advantage.

Windlings prefer to strike from concealed positions, waiting until they have the advantage to attack, much in the style of guerrilla warfare. However, windlings find more honor in neutralizing an opponent's fighting capability than in killing. A windling warrior who disarms and disables an opponent gains stature as a fighter of great skill, and if the warrior can add a humorous and/or embarrassing element to the disabling, so much the better.

fer Strain from flying. For each minute after 20 the character continues to fly, he must make a Toughness Test against a Difficulty Number of 7. If he fails the test, the character takes 1 point of Strain damage. Each period of 5 minutes beyond the initial 20 also adds +2 to the Difficulty Number of the Toughness Test.

A windling must rest for the same number of minutes he spent flying in order to resume flying without Strain. For example, if a windling character flies for 15 minutes, he must rest for 15 minutes before flying again to avoid Strain damage.

Against a Theran opponent, however, windlings violate their self-imposed rule of defeat over death, rewarding these despised slavers by asking and giving no quarter.

Equipment

Windlings use all manner of equipment, but it must be custom-made small enough for them to use or wield. Unfortunately, its small size does not reduce the cost of this equipment: even though it requires less raw material, it requires far more, and far more exacting, labor. Human-sized craftsmen find it difficult to make small items with their large fingers and hands, and so charge more for their efforts. Similar goods made by windling craftsmen cost approximately 25 percent less, but have an Availability of Rare.

Food and Provisions: Windling-sized portions of food and provisions cost one-half the prices listed in **Goods and Services**, p. 266, **ED**. The windlings produce and sell a unique wine called keesris for 10 silver pieces per bottle, 2 silver pieces per glass.

Armor and Weapons: Windlings use armor and weapons sized for the other Name-giver races as often as they use such equipment of their own size (see **Windling Equipment,** p. 254, **ED**). **A Tale of Windlings,** p. 79, described the following items unique to windlings.

Sadoor Nets

These tough windling nets have the same stats as standard nets, with a higher Difficulty for characters trying to break out. Windlings often soak sadoor nets in various drugs.
Cost: 30 sp

Keesra

The contact poison called keesra is made from the same berries as keesris wine, and affects its victims by putting them to sleep. Targets of this poison wake up with a splitting headache and stinking like overripe berries. Many sadoor nets are soaked in keesra.

Type of Poison	Spell Defense/Step Number
Sleep	7/10
Onset Time	**Duration**
Instant	Effect Test result in hours

Whadhyra

A contact poison that paralyzes its victims, whadhyra is derived from the venom of a poisonous insect. The windlings usually use this poison on blowgun needles.

Type of Poison	Spell Defense/Step Number
Paralysis	6/10
Onset Time	**Duration**
Instant	One hour

Padendra

Padendra is the only fatal windling poison and is used only in times of great danger. This poison can be injected or ingested. The secret of making padendra is handed down from generation to generation in dirges that describe the alchemical means used in its creation.

Type of Poison	Spell Defense/Step Number
Death	7/10
Onset Time	**Duration**
2 Combat Rounds	Permanent

INDEX

Must I impart yet again the importance of indexing?!!?

Merrox, Master of the Hall of Records, addressing his apprentice